CHASING TAZ

Charon MC
Book 3

KHLOE WREN

Books by Khloe Wren

Charon MC:
Inking Eagle
Fighting Mac
Chasing Taz

Fire and Snow:
Guardian's Heart
Noble Guardian
Guardian's Shadow
Fierce Guardian
Necessary Alpha
Protective Instincts

Dragon Warriors:
Enchanting Eilagh
Binding Becky
Claiming Carina
Seducing Skye
Believing Binda

Jaguar Secrets:
Jaguar Secrets
FireStarter

Other Titles:
Fireworks
Tigers Are Forever
Bad Alpha Anthology
Scarred Perfection
Scandals: Zeck
Mirror Image Seduction
Deception

ISBN: 978-0-9876275-6-8
Copyright © Khloe Wren 2017

Cover Credits:
Model: Stefan Northfield
Photographer: Jules Godfrey Photography
Digital Artist: Khloe Wren

Editing Credits:
Editor: Carolyn Depew of Write Right
Proofreader: Christine Halls

Acknowledgements

As always, I have to give a massive shout out to my wonderfully patient husband. Who continues to put up with his insane author wife. And to my girls, as once again this book saw me locked away in my writing cave more often than not.

I couldn't have written this book without several people who patiently answered all my many questions about Marine and MC life. Heath, Dawn, Erin, Diana and Shannon (I'm sure there were more and I'm sorry if I missed you by name) I can't thank you enough for all your help. Especially Heath. To Maggie and Liz, thank you for sharing all your nursing knowledge.

To the Night Writers Facebook group. Without you guys and our sprints, this book would still be half written I'm sure!

To my Facebook street team, Khloe's Kickass Bikers, Beasties and Babes, thank you for your support and help with the baby names! Jennifer Jaques suggested Raven and Miranda suggested Cleo, which I loved so much I changed Mac and Zara's baby from a boy to a girl so I could use it! And Lisa Williams suggested Cutler, which I ended up using for a town name. Thanks ladies!

To all my friends who helped me get back up each time I stumbled while writing this book. Liz Iavorschi, Christine Ashworth, Tracie Runge, Eden Bradley and Tamsin Baker, you ladies especially.

To my editor, Carolyn, no matter what I throw at you, you always come through with a marvelous edit. I appreciate everything you do and thank you for another job well done.

To Jules Godfrey, thank you for grabbing Stefan at that wedding and snapping some shots! He's perfect for Taz. And to Stefan Northfield, thank you for posing for Jules and agreeing to be on my cover.

Due to me rushing to make deadline once again, my poor beta team missed out with this one! Sorry, ladies!

xo

Khloe Wren

Biography

Khloe Wren grew up in the Adelaide Hills before her parents moved the family to country South Australia when she was a teen. A few years later, Khloe moved to Melbourne which was where she got her first taste of big city living.

After a few years living in the big city, she missed the fresh air and space of country living so returned to rural South Australia. Khloe currently lives in the Murraylands with her incredibly patient husband, two strong willed young daughters, an energetic dog and two curious cats.

As a child Khloe often had temporary tattoos all over her arms. When she got her first job at 19, she was at the local tattooist in the blink of an eye to get her first real tattoo. Khloe now has four, two taking up much of her back.

While Khloe doesn't ride a bike herself, she loves riding pillion behind her husband on the rare occasion they get to go out without their daughters.

Dedication

To Carolyn,

Thank you for all your support and encouragement.

Charon:

Char·on \\'sher-ən, 'ker-ən, -än\\

In Greek mythology, the Charon is the ferryman who takes the dead across either the river Styx or Acheron, depending on whether the soul's destination is the Elysian Fields or Hades.

Prologue

Flick

The day started out just like any other. I'd finished my last assignment yesterday and today I was due to receive my next one. Yep, everything was completely normal and boring, until I opened the folder in front of me and saw those names. A shiver ran down my spine as I re-read them.

Donovan 'Taz' Lee
Jacob 'Mac' Miller
Colt 'Eagle' Benally

It had been about three years since I'd first seen those names. Closing the file, I shifted my focus onto my supervisor, Greg Cave, who was sitting opposite me and watching me like he was waiting for me to explode or something. I was finding it hard to believe he was the one asking me to investigate these three men, considering he was the one who'd stopped me from chasing them down when I'd first joined the FBI.

"Greg, did you mix up this assignment with another one or something? Because you can't be serious."

With a raised eyebrow, my boss and the director of the FBI headquarters here in Dallas, dared me to continue.

"You do remember who these three men are to me, right?"

After a minute of silence that made me more than a little nervous, not that I showed it, he finally answered me.

"I haven't forgotten. I actually thought you'd be excited to be put on this assignment. Finally, you'll get your chance to talk with these men."

Since I'd only just been handed the file, I obviously hadn't had a chance to read it and didn't know what the assignment would require, as Greg was well aware. But it was rare that I actually got to talk to many people when I went out in the field. As a forensic accountant, I was normally part of a team and my job was in the background, working with computers or ledgers.

"Talk to? What exactly does this assignment entail?"

"Eighteen months ago Lee, Miller and Benally were approached to take on a job for us. They accepted, and joined the Charon MC in Bridgewater, Texas, where they were supposed to report back to us with information about what the club was doing. As far as motorcycle clubs go, the Charons are pretty clean. Well, they actually look a little too clean, which is why we wanted a man or two inside."

Nothing about that sounded out of the ordinary. Former military men were often recruited for specific assignments.

"So what's gone wrong?"

Greg screwed up his face, as though he'd eaten something rotten and couldn't get the taste out of his mouth. "They were given an unsuitable handler. As a result, we've lost Miller and Benally."

I tilted my head. Was I reading this right? "Their handler was dirty?"

Greg cleared his throat, which was basically an answer in itself. Unfortunately, it wasn't unheard of for agents to leak information, or take bribes. The Bureau did what it could to get rid of those they found, but there were always more. "Yes. They gave us something extremely valuable, which became useless, thanks to him. Once the three of them found out their information had been leaked, they began ignoring their handler's calls. It put a woman Benally cared for at risk, so he in particular became difficult after that incident. Then, he pushed Miller over another matter, and now both Miller and Benally have informed us they don't care what we do, they will never help us again."

"So I'm to go after Lee? And what, bring him in?"

That was the standard protocol, but clearly this situation wasn't normal.

Greg shook his head. "That wouldn't do us any good with the last man standing. We believe the best way to move forward with Lee is to send you in to be his partner."

I focused on keeping my face and voice neutral, to not show my confusion or shock. "Why?"

"We've received intel that the Charon MC have recently become closer with the Satan's Cowboys MC, and that the Cowboys intend to use that connection to expand their distribution channels. We need to know if, and how, that happens. We're following the theory it will be easier to catch them doing something new, that they haven't had time to set up fully and secure."

"Does he know I'm coming?"

"Nope. He has no clue at all."

Great, that was going to be just wonderful to deal with. "When do I leave, and where, exactly, am I going?"

"Tomorrow morning, and you're heading down to Bridgewater. Pack for a long stay. You'll find all the information you need in that folder. I know you prefer to stick with accounting work, but for this assignment you're going to go in as a bartender."

That part I could handle. I'd worked as one during college. In fact, I had a feeling that would be the easiest part of this assignment.

I stood up to leave and was halfway to the door when Greg called out. "Vaughn?"

"Yeah?"

"This assignment gets priority. Once you finish it, then you can ask Lee all the questions you want about your brother. But not until afterwards, understand?"

"Understood, sir."

With that, I turned and left. What the hell would I ask anyway? "Hey Taz, I was just wondering if you could tell me what happened with Andrew Vaughn in early

2014 that got him dishonorably discharged?" Yeah, that would go over as smooth as sandpaper, I was sure.

No, to find out what had caused my brother to become a completely different man, one who'd abandoned his entire family, I was going to have to be more subtle about it. And apparently, I had to wait until I finished this assignment to do it.

Chapter 1

Taz

I knew how this was going to end, but I couldn't stop it. No matter what I tried, this fucking nightmare always played out the same way. Just like it had in reality.

Looking down at my sneakers, I kicked a rock off the footpath. I didn't want to go home, so I was taking my time, just like I always did. But not too much time. We lived in a shitty part of the western suburbs of Melbourne, Australia, and if I walked too slowly, I'd become a victim to worse things than what I was going home to.

Ever since Gordon, my stepfather, lost his last job over a month ago, I never knew what I'd find when I got home after school. I wish Mum would kick his ass out. I was thirteen now, and old enough to help her out. I'd do more for her and my little sister, Grace, than that piece of shit currently did.

If only Gordon would just fuck off. I clenched my fists and released them a few times. I prayed for the day I was strong enough to successfully fight back. I'd tried. I would always at least try to keep him from hurting Mum, but so far it had only ended in me getting a beating. Still, it had saved Mum from his fists so it had been worth it. However, while I was at school I couldn't step in front of her. Little Gracie was only three years old, so she was stuck home with the monster all day too. So far, he hadn't laid a hand on her. If he ever did, I'd take a knife to him in his sleep. Little Gracie was an angel. So sweet, and despite the house of horrors she was living in, always had a big smile for me when I got home each day.

The faint scent of smoke made my nose itch. It was early April, which meant it was still fire ban season, but that didn't stop people burning off rubbish whenever they bloody well felt like it. I didn't pay much attention to it until a block later, when the smell got stronger and I looked up from the footpath to search for the origin of all the smoke. My heart stopped beating and my lungs froze for a horrible moment when I saw the pillar of dark smoke coming from our house, just over a block ahead of me.

"Fuck. MUM! GRACE!"

I was sprinting before I was aware I was moving, flying down the footpath, faster than I ever had before. I skidded as I turned onto our front lawn. The heat from the fire licking up the front wall of the house had me backpedaling.

"Donny! Stay back, son."

Mrs. Sticks from next door was rushing over to me, reaching for my arm but I couldn't let her get me. I had to try to get Mum and Grace out first. Shaking my head at her, I dropped my bag off my shoulders and bolted to the back of the house. Easily jumping the little fence at the side, I scrambled up the steps and wrenched open the back door. Thick smoke escaped, instantly surrounding me and making me cough and wheeze, but I wasn't going to let it stop me.

"Mum! Grace!"

I couldn't hear anything over the roar of the fire that had engulfed the front of the house. Mum and Gordon's bedroom was up there, but Grace and I had rooms here in the rear of the building. Lifting the neck of my shirt up over my nose to block at least some of the smoke, I went for Grace's room first, hoping she was in there. She was often napping at this time of day. Feeling my way through the smoke, I found my way to her bed. I could make out her body on the mattress, hoping she was just sleeping, I gave her a shake, but she wouldn't wake up. The smoke was getting thicker and I pressed my nose against my shoulder to try to block even more of the shit so I could take a breath. Knowing I didn't have much time, I didn't bother trying to wake her again, but gathered her limp body against my chest and ran for the back door. I tried not to think about Mum. She had to be in the front of the house. If she'd been in the back, she would have grabbed Grace and gotten out already.

Tears stung my eyes as I bolted out the back door and carried my sister around to the front yard, where I could hear sirens. I was coughing with every breath, my lungs burned and my body shook, but I refused to drop my sweet little Gracie. No way. It took a moment to open the side gate and then I was back in the front yard. Thankfully, the fire hadn't reached this side of the house yet, so I could still pass through. I needed to get Grace to the ambulance. They'd fix whatever was wrong. It was their job, so they had to. I refused to accept any other outcome.

Mrs. Sticks was running over to me when I looked up.

"Oh, Donny, here, let me take her—"

"No. She's mine."

The pain that flashed in her expression didn't affect me at all. My mind had focused solely on getting Grace to the ambulance. I couldn't even think about anything else.

"Okay, that's okay, lovie. You bring her over to the ambulance. You need to let them take you both to hospital, okay?"

She wrapped an arm around my shoulders and guided me over to the multiple vehicles with their flashing lights.

Panting, I sat up in bed, the blue and red flashing lights filling my vision for a few more seconds. Fuck. I hated that nightmare. Hated even more the fact it wasn't really a dream, but a memory. I scrubbed my palms over my face as my heart continued to thunder in my chest. No way would I be getting any more sleep tonight. I looked at the clock beside my bed and groaned. Two in the fucking morning. I'd only been asleep for an hour. With a growl, I laid back down. I needed to at least try to get some more shut-eye. I had shit to do today that required more than one fucking hour of sleep.

Ten minutes later, I growled and reached for the stereo remote. AC/DC *Thunderstruck* came on, filling the silence, helping to banish the memories as I rolled out of bed and strode over to my en suite bathroom.

I had no idea why I'd let my two best friends, Mac and Eagle, talk me into buying this place and moving out of the clubhouse. There was always noise and some chaos at the Charon MC clubhouse, and that was how I liked it. Silence was deafening and I hated it. When the world was quiet around you, it left your mind free to think, to roll back into your history and fuck you up. At least that's what mine did to me, which sucked. Because there was nothing you could do about the past. It was done and set in stone, leaving behind those that survived to try and deal with it. It was bad enough the shit invaded my sleep, I didn't need it messing up my days, too.

Rolling my neck, I stood under the spray of the shower, letting the warm water wash away the last traces of sleep and the memories of the nightmare that had sent my life on a downhill slide. Soaping up my palms, I began the task of washing myself by running my hands over all the various tattoos that covered my arms. The flowers and monsters I'd had etched into my skin over the years. I didn't look as I ran my palms over my chest. The webs and skulls, along with the names that I'd had inked across my pecs, were things I did my best never to look at. Some days I wondered why I'd ever been fucking stupid enough to get the names inked on me in the first place, but then I'd remember something good. A sweet moment between the three of us and I knew why. My mother and baby sister deserved to be remembered for who they were when they'd lived, not how their lives had been so brutally cut short.

With a growl that my mind had gone there again, I flipped off the taps and got out. Running a towel over myself as I walked, I headed back to my bedroom to get dressed. When Guns 'n' Roses *Knocking on Heaven's Door* came on as I pulled a shirt over my head, I stiffened.

"Fuck me."

The world was clearly against me this morning. I seriously did not need to start my day stuck inside my head like I was. I shut off the song, grabbed my cut and headed for my front door as I put the leather vest on. I'd head down to the gym and see if I could pound my demons back into their cage with a workout. If that didn't work, I'd have to wait till later today to find someone to fight with in the back room. Fuck, I was glad when Mac had renovated the place last year and he'd left that back room alone. Years ago it had been a full on fight club type thing, with most of the club involved, but now there were only a handful of us that used the space. Still, even with the low numbers, I loved being able to jump in the ring and fight. All the men who went in that back room to fight were like me—we all had demons riding us that needed to be beaten into submission on a regular basis.

I swung my leg over my bike and the moment it came to life beneath me, some of the tension left my body. Maybe I'd start with a nice, long ride, then I'd head into the gym.

Flick

Once I'd parked next to the surprisingly modern looking gym, I blew out a breath as I hopped out of my car. After reading the file on Donovan 'Taz' Lee, I wasn't sure what kind of man I was going to encounter. As a child and teen, he'd been through more trauma than anyone should have to suffer in their entire lifetime. I couldn't imagine how a thirteen-year-old boy would handle the deaths of his mother and young sister, let alone being shipped from Australia to America to live with an unknown relative right afterward.

The file hadn't given me many details of his life between coming to the USA and his enlistment in the USMC when he was eighteen. And the information for afterward was only about his military accomplishments. He was one of the best snipers the USMC ever had. I was sure they weren't happy when he'd decided to retire nearly three years ago.

Unfortunately, the file didn't include details of missions he'd been on. As unrealistic as it had been, I'd been hopeful it would have at least some basic information, because that could have potentially answered some of my questions about what had happened with my brother's discharge from the USMC.

As I walked to the front door, I ran my gaze down the line of bikes. Naturally, they were all Harleys. There were half a dozen all parked at the exact same angle, each machine was clean and sparkling in the early morning sun. Since arriving in town three days ago, I'd quietly done a little recon. I knew Taz rode the green Harley sitting at the front of the line-up. But I'd already known he would most likely be here, even before seeing his bike. He seemed to like to start his day with an early morning workout.

I pushed open the door to Acheron Gym and took a step inside. I wasn't sure what to expect from a biker gym, but this certainly wasn't it. All fresh paint and cleanliness. The equipment spread out around the space looked new too, aside from a few machines that had a well-worn appearance. What didn't surprise me was when, in under a minute, I felt the gazes of several of the men on me including the one I came for. Taz was in a loose tank and shorts, and I got to look my fill as he set the weights down he'd been lifting and swaggered toward me. And it was a swagger, no way could you label how he moved as simply walking. I clenched my jaw to make sure it didn't drop open in awe. Tingles of awareness shot through my system as he got closer to me and it took all the self-control I had to not shiver under his hot gaze.

"Well, hello there, luv. You need help with something?"

For the first time in a very long time, I found myself struck mute as I stared into his baby blues. His words had been drawled with a sexy-as-fuck Australian accent I hadn't been expecting. I mean, he'd been living in the US since he was a young teen, he had no right to still have such a devastating accent.

"Taz, go back to your workout already and quit tormenting the poor woman."

A deep voice broke the connection between us and with a shake of my head, I turned to the newcomer. I recognized Jacob 'Mac' Miller from the photo I was given of him. He was taller than Taz, and looked a little older. His head was cleanly shaven, while his jaw was not. He was handsome in a rough sort of way, but thankfully he didn't affect me like Taz had, which was a relief.

I cleared my throat. "Ah, hi. I wanted to inquire about joining?"

Mac gave me a smile before he responded. "Excellent. How about you take a seat for a second while I grab the paperwork?"

"Hey, Mac? I can start showing her around, while you're doing that."

Fuck me, but that accent was going to kill me. I swallowed past the lump in my throat as Mac raised a brow at me in question.

Shrugging a shoulder, I responded with a "Fine by me," even though it wasn't fine. Holy shit, how the fuck was I going to be able to work with this man when I couldn't even think straight in his presence?

Mac strolled away toward a door in the back of the large main room and Taz cleared his throat to grab my attention back to him.

"So, what's your name, luv?"

I cleared my throat. "Flick. You're Taz, yeah?"

He smirked and nodded. "Yep, that's me. Flick your real name?"

I shook my head. "Nickname, just like I'm guessing Taz isn't your real name."

No way was I making it easy on him to dig information out of me. I needed to play it at least a little cool. The best way to get this partnership to work was to do a little groundwork in front of his club first. A little flirting and fun, then when I told him the real reason I was here and what we needed to do, our cover would already be established and his club would think nothing of us spending time together on a regular basis.

At least that had been the plan. Now, I really wanted to know how his hands would feel running over my bare flesh. I couldn't hold back the shiver that thought gave me.

"You cold there, Flick?"

I gave him a glare because he knew full well I wasn't fucking cold. "I'm fine. So, you going to show me around this place or what?"

Chuckling he lifted a muscular shoulder in a half shrug. I barely held in my groan as his inked skin rippled with the movement. "Sure, luv. Follow me for the grand tour."

Chapter 2

Taz

The woman was a fucking knockout. Long, wavy, jet-black hair, steel blue eyes, tanned skin. And she had curves I wanted to get my hands on. She was wearing workout gear, skintight black pants and a loose shirt. Well, it hung loosely on her everywhere but where her lush tits pressed against the fabric, and if I wasn't mistaken, her nipples were hard. The twin little bumps in the material had my mouth fucking watering.

This was crazy. I'd never done the girlfriend thing, only ever one-night-stands and quick fucks to ease an itch. And since joining the Charon MC, I hadn't hooked up with a woman who wasn't a club whore. It was so much easier to go to the clubhouse where the pussy was wet and willing, than try to find a woman that was okay with me screwing her all night, then walking away in the morning. But even I had to admit it was starting to get old. The whores didn't require any chasing—there was no mystery at all to any of them. I'd gotten over the novelty of being able to walk into a room, snap my fingers, and having a woman on her knees in front of me a second later unzipping my pants, long ago. It didn't exactly offer any kind of challenge. This chick, though, she'd definitely be a challenge. Despite the fact she clearly liked how I looked, she was holding her chin high and the look in her eyes told me she was no pushover. Hell, she wouldn't even give me her full name. This could be fun.

I still wasn't interested in settling down with a woman. Just because my two best mates, Eagle and Mac, had both hooked up with women and knocked them up, didn't mean I wanted to follow in their footsteps. But the anniversary was coming up in a little over two weeks, and I was going to need to stay really busy if I was going to keep myself distracted from focusing on the fact it had been twenty years since I lost my mum and sister. With that in mind, maybe it was worth the risk to see if I could seduce this bombshell. Even if she did turn out to be a woman I wanted around for longer than a night, I was sure I could resist making it something truly permanent.

I started walking around the main room and she stayed beside me, her subtle perfume filling my lungs and making my cock twitch. Dammit. That was something I didn't need right now. Gym shorts didn't exactly make it easy to hide a raging hard-on.

"This is the main room, where all the equipment is. This is a mixed gym, there's no special ladies room, so I hope you don't mind working out in front of a few blokes?"

She chuckled, the sound not helping my fight to keep my dick from standing at attention. "I'm used to working out with men in the room. It doesn't bother me."

"That's good. There's always more than a few men in this place. The room in there is where we run classes. There's actually one on tonight."

"Do *you* run the classes?"

I smiled over at her when I heard the hint of hopefulness in her voice.

"Sorry, luv. Tonight's class is Mac's baby. He runs a women's self-defense class once a week. You're more than welcome to come along. All classes are included with your membership fee."

Her face was a mask of indifference, like she wasn't interested, which intrigued me. It wasn't the normal reaction I got when I told a woman about the class.

"What, you don't agree women should learn a few moves to protect themselves?"

"Oh, don't get me wrong. Every woman should learn at least a few moves. It's just I know how to take care of myself, so I don't need to take a class."

I stopped walking and turned to face her, running my gaze down her body. She didn't look like a fighter. She was clearly fit and toned, but she didn't have that roughness about her I'd seen in other female fighters who'd come by the gym. When my gaze returned to her face she had an eyebrow raised and was smirking.

"Like what you see?"

I gave her a wink. "You'll do."

That earned me another of her husky chuckles, along with a head shake.

"I was just thinking that you don't look like a fighter."

She crossed her arms over her chest, pushing her tits up and making it really hard for me to keep eye contact. "Really? And what does a fighter look like, exactly?"

"Not like you, luv."

She nodded her head and when her lips slowly spread into a smirk I started to worry. What was she up to? I didn't have to wait long to find out, because a moment later she dropped her bag and, in a flash, kicked a leg out aimed at my knee. I spun to avoid the kick and before she could do anything else, I body slammed her up against the wall to the sound of my brothers wolf whistling us. I wrapped a hand in her hair, holding her head back so she didn't hurt her face against the drywall.

"What the fuck was that?"

"Me proving I could defend myself. Clearly, not very well."

I had my body pressed tight against hers, so she couldn't move her arms or legs to reach to hit or kick me. The only thing she could have done was to head butt me, but the hand I still had wrapped in her hair prevented her from that move, too.

"You gotta have better moves than that to take down a Marine, baby."

"Taz! What the fuck? Get off her."

Mac came thundering across the room, I knew I only had a few more seconds to enjoy being pressed up against this lush woman. I leaned in and brushed my lips over her cheekbone, enjoying the fuck out of the way she shuddered beneath me. As Mac wrapped his palm around my shoulder I moved my mouth to her ear to whisper to her.

"Maybe I will make that class tonight, if you're gonna be there. Wouldn't mind seeing your moves when we've got a mat I can throw you down on."

I let Mac pull me back and when he spun me to face him, his gaze was pure fury. With reason, generally speaking, manhandling potential customers wasn't a good move.

"Relax, brother. Little Flick here was trying to catch me off-guard with a move to prove she didn't need your class. But don't worry, I think I've got her convinced she does, in fact, need it."

The fury drained from his expression and turned to disbelief when Flick scoffed. "I sure as hell wasn't expecting you to react by bulldozing me into the damn wall. If you hadn't done that, I'm sure I could have held my own."

I smirked at Mac before I winked and turned to focus back on Flick.

"The whole point of self-defense is to be ready for the unexpected. And, luv, that sounded like a challenge. I'd take you out back right now to prove you wrong, but the boys out there get their knickers in a twist whenever a woman tries to go back there."

Flick frowned and flicked her gaze to the rear door. "Knickers? And what's *out back* that's so macho girls can't go?"

"Don't mind Taz, he likes to throw in Aussie words to keep us Yanks on our toes. Knickers are panties and out *the* back is an old school boxing ring for the ol' boys. When we renovated this place a few months back, they wanted their own space, so we gave it to them."

I let Mac finish before I cut back in. "So I guess you'll have to come tonight if you want to try and show me more of your moves."

Mac sighed loudly beside me, but I ignored him as Flick lifted that stubborn chin of hers and glared me straight in the eye.

"You're on."

My cock jerked at her show of strength. I'd lost the fight to keep from cracking a boner when I'd been pressed up against her very fine body. Now the bastard was throbbing against my gym shorts and I knew if she glanced down she'd see exactly the effect she had on me. I needed to get my ass away from her before she did.

"Excellent. I'll see you tonight, then."

With that, I turned and strolled over to the changing rooms, winking at a couple of the boys when they snickered at me as I passed. I didn't even try to adjust myself, I knew there was no hiding the pole in my fucking shorts. Hopefully a nice, cold shower would help ease things, so I could fucking function for the rest of the day until I saw her again tonight.

Flick

Mac had told me I didn't have to come to the class if I didn't want to. Taz would get over it. But I found myself wanting to go. My body had been humming all fucking day after this morning. Having Taz pressed up against my back had been distracting. Especially since I hadn't missed the fact his rather large dick had been hard, or the way it had throbbed against my ass, where he'd had it pressed. That had been the real reason I hadn't gotten out of his hold. Damn man distracted me with lust. Bastard.

I put my hair into a braid, then wrapped it around into a knot that I tucked under, so it would be harder to grab onto. When Taz had tugged my hair this morning, arousal had shot straight to my core. My panties had been damp by the time Mac pulled Taz off me, so I didn't want him to pull that shit again tonight. No way would I be able to keep my wits about me if he did.

Pulling into the parking lot of the gym for the second time today, I turned off my car and jumped out. I was more excited now than I had been this morning. Fuck, I needed to be careful around that man. He could break a girl's heart without even trying, I was sure.

I was about to push through the door when a large palm slid around my waist and pulled me back. On reflex I slammed my elbow back, but before it could connect, another large hand wrapped around my bicep, holding my arm still.

"Whoa, hellcat. I was going to ask if you were ready for tonight, but clearly you are."

I growled as I spun out of Taz's grip. "What the fuck? You make a habit of waiting in the shadows to grab women without their permission?"

Fury heated my blood. Well, fury and lust, but I was refusing to acknowledge the fact that the way this man could manhandle me turned me on.

"Easy, luv. We just happened to arrive at the same time, and I thought it might be fun to tease you a little before class."

"Don't bullshit me, Taz. I hate it. If you'd just arrived, I'd have heard your bike." I glanced over at the row of bikes and saw his was third from the end—further proof he hadn't just arrived. But I caught myself before I pointed that out. I wasn't supposed to know which bike was his. "Which one is yours, anyhow?"

"Green one is my beast. You like bikes?"

I raised a brow at him. "There's two bikes after yours, I doubt they both pulled up just now. Especially since their riders aren't out here. And yeah, I like bikes. I like pretty much anything that can go fast."

For a moment an expression of wariness flashed over his face, but it was gone before I could be sure. Did I say something I shouldn't have? Something to give away I knew more about him that what I'd learned this morning? I wasn't ready to sit down and tell him the real reason I was here. I needed to reel him in a little more first, enough that he wouldn't get mad and kick me to the curb when I told him the truth. At least, that's what I was telling myself.

"There's a lot of things that go fast around here, luv. And not all of them have wheels. C'mon, or Mac will start without us."

Without another word I followed him inside, taking some calming breaths as I purposely didn't focus on his ass. Mac was standing at the front of the room when we walked in and he glared at Taz before his expression softened when he looked at me.

"Glad you could make it, Flick. Hopefully you didn't have to fight your way in through the door." He glared at Taz again.

I chuckled. "I got in with no problems. Thanks."

As Taz went over to stand near his friend, I looked around the class. It was a good mix of young and middle-aged women. A couple of the younger ones clearly had stars in their eyes as they didn't look away from Mac, and now Taz. I nearly gagged at the desperation radiating off them. MC groupies were apparently a thing. At least, if they paid attention, these groupies would learn something from their crushes.

"All right, ladies, because Taz has joined me tonight, we can do things a little differently. We'll demonstrate some moves, then we'll divide you up into two groups. I'll take one group, while Taz will take the other. That way, we'll have time at the end, if you ladies want, for me and Taz to do a little sparring match for you."

The younger girls whistled and clapped, calling out that they'd only agree if they sparred first. My eyes rolled on their own accord. Yep, those two were full-on groupies. Mind you, watching two Marines spar was a sight to see, and no red-blooded woman would turn that shit down. I moved to stand toward the back of the group, not wanting to attract attention as Mac explained, then demonstrated several moves with Taz. It was nothing I hadn't already learned at various courses I'd done, but a refresher never hurt. Not to mention it was good exercise, and the eye candy didn't hurt, either.

Half an hour later we'd finished practicing. Mac had put me in his group so I could actually concentrate, which was a relief. I'd already made an ass of myself earlier in front of both him and Taz, so it was nice to be able to redeem myself, at least in Mac's eyes.

"Right, ladies. That's the work over with, let's have a little fun. What do you say, Taz? Up for a little sparring match to entertain the class?"

Taz laughed and rolled his head on his neck. "Any excuse to put you on your ass, brother."

Mac rolled his eyes. "Shut up and get over here. Ladies, stand back off the mat, please. I'd hate to see one of you hurt while we're focused on throwing each other around."

This time I didn't hang back. Nope, I wanted to see this, so I moved to stand alongside the others. Within seconds, Taz had the bigger man on the mat and in a choke hold. Damn, that man was fast. Mac flipped them over and they grappled for a few moments.

My face was heating up and I had my thighs clenched as they threw each other around while they tossed friendly insults back and forth. They'd both pulled their shirts off before they started and now their skin was slick with sweat. They were both covered in heavy muscle but Taz was bulkier and shorter than Mac. Fuck, but I really could watch Taz move around all damn day with the way his ink stretched and shifted over all those bulging muscles. I was so lost in the fog of a daydream, I didn't realize they'd stopped until Taz spoke.

"You waiting for something, luv?"

I shook my head to clear my vision and glanced around to see the rest of the class had left. Shit. I winced as heat flared over my cheeks. I was so busted and I couldn't think of a single lie to get me out from under Taz's scrutiny.

"Ah, I just zoned out there for a second. The class is finished, then?"

Taz used his discarded shirt for a towel and wiped off his torso, face and neck. Unable to look away, my gaze followed each swipe.

"Like what you see?"

"You'll do."

If he was gonna throw my words back at me, I'd return the favor. He barked out a laugh as he stepped up closer to me.

"You wanna have a sparring session, or do you want to go clean up and change so I can take you out for a drink? Either way, the night'll end the same way."

I raised an eyebrow at him. "You're pretty confident of yourself, aren't you?"

He took another step, and I backed up, straight into the wall. Dammit. He came in close and put a hand on the wall over each of my shoulders, caging me in. He smelled of sweat and leather and it was like catnip to my libido.

"In the Marines we're taught to be really observant. And when I notice a woman who can't keep her eyes off me, who is so lost in a sexy daydream after watching me spar with my brother, she misses the class being dismissed, who's nipples are so fucking hard they're poking through her shirt...yeah, I get pretty confident she wants me and that the night will end with her under me. I can guarantee you'll enjoy it, babe."

I closed my eyes as my body shuddered at his words. Clearly, my plan had worked a little too well. So well, in fact, it had backfired, and now I feared it was he who had hooked me, not the other way around. I needed to get away from him so I could breathe for a few minutes.

Chapter 3

Taz

When Flick pressed her palms against my stomach, a groan tore from my throat. Her fingers were soft, yet firm, as she smoothed them up my front, over the bumps of my ribs and pecs. My cock thickened and throbbed for her hands to go south, rather than north. I couldn't speak at how good it felt to have her touching me like she was.

Next thing I knew, I was on my back.

"Fuck, woman! What was that shit?"

She'd thrust her thumb into a pressure point near my collarbone, then with a leg wrapped around mine, got me down on the ground in seconds. Now I had her on top of me, holding me down. It took a few seconds for the lust to clear from my mind enough for me to think, and when it did, I saw her grinning down at me like she'd won. I smirked up at her for a split second before I quickly had her flipped over, and under me. Moving quickly, I had my legs over hers in a way she couldn't move, and her hands were locked together above her head with one of my palms wrapped around them. I dropped my face into her throat and inhaled against her neck. Damn, but she smelled so fucking sweet. When I felt her muscles tense, I quickly moved to press the side of my face against hers, giving her no room to move.

"Don't you dare try 'n head butt me, hellcat."

She growled and bucked beneath me, but got nowhere. Damn, but I was loving the fire in this woman.

"Get off me, then and I won't have to."

Her voice was husky and considering my rock-hard dick was pressed up against her mound, I could feel exactly how hot she was for me. I nipped at her earlobe before kissing my way along her jaw. When I got to the edge of her lips, I swiveled my hips against hers, loving how her breath caught in her throat. She closed her eyes for a moment and when she reopened them, they held a different kind of fire. In my attempt at seducing her, I'd moved my lower half, releasing her legs a degree. She made use of that before I could recapture them. For the second time tonight, I found myself on my back with her perched above me. But this time she didn't stay there to gloat. Nope, she jumped back and up to her feet, before moving away. I held her gaze as I slowly rose to my feet.

"Nice move, luv. Guessing the fact you're all the way over there means this little game of ours is over?"

I wasn't sure what the fuck she was playing at. She'd been teasing me, hot for me, now she was acting cold and calculated. There was no doubt she was up to something, but what it was, had me stumped. She wasn't the usual type of woman who went all crazy for a club brother because he was in an MC. But she'd definitely known which bike was mine before she asked me earlier.

For every step I took, she took one away, but this time she was aiming at the door. I wasn't going to be able to trap her as easily as I had the last time. Mac stepped inside the room, his gaze flicking between us, taking in the body language, before he crossed his arms over his chest.

"You two done playing? Because I'd like to get home to my woman before daybreak, if you feel me?"

The words cracked through the sexual tension in the room and Flick gave a little shake of her head before she spun and bolted from the room. I heard the door chime a few moments later as the little chicken ran away.

Mac held my gaze as I walked toward him.

"What's with you and this chick? She ain't a club whore, brother."

I shrugged. "I'm fully aware of who she isn't. But I'm not entirely sure who she is, either. She's up to something, I can feel it."

"So you're just playing her, then? Seeing what she wants?"

I broke away from his gaze and looked around the room, at the large mat on the floor, the mirrors along one wall.

"I like her. She's got some bite and fire in her. I don't know where it'll all go, because I'm not fucking joking. She's up to something but I will figure it out."

"Best get Keys to look into her then. I've got her name and address on her gym application. It's not strictly ethical, but she doesn't ever have to know."

I looked back to Mac. Along with Eagle, he'd been my friend for over a decade, through the Marines, and now in the Charon MC. When our former CO approached the three of us about coming into the Charon MC about a year and a half ago, we'd agreed and stepped up. To begin with, it was with the intention of being undercover agents for the FBI. But they'd screwed us over hard last year after Eagle's old lady, Silk, had been taken by the L.A. mob. We'd given the feds information on the mob, and the dirty fuckers handed it straight over to the bastards. Since then, all three of us had stepped back from anything to do with our original purpose. Our handler came after Mac a while ago over his old lady, but that shit ended just as badly as the first round. So, Eagle and Mac had told them to fuck off. And I'd stayed silent. The fact the feds seem to be letting my silent treatment of them slide didn't sit real well with me. Something had to be brewing.

"Not yet. I'll see what I can get out of her myself, first. What if she's with the feds? I ask Keys and he finds that out, it could blow wide all three of our covers. Then, what? We both know what the club did to Eagle."

Silk was the VP's niece, and Eagle had gone after her before he'd finished prospecting. Of course, Scout, the club president, tried to tell us it was because she'd been taken by the mob while Eagle was guarding her, but that was on them, not him. They'd not told Eagle that anyone specific was after Silk, so he was guarding her from a distance. Either way, it all ended with Eagle getting a beat down from the club that had him laid up for weeks. If they found out the three of us were supposed to be spying on the club for the feds? Yeah, I didn't think that shit was gonna go over well. Even if we could prove that none of us had handed over a damn thing about the Charon MC to the FBI.

Mac's expression turned ice cold. "You keep me in the loop on this shit, you understand? We won't bring the club in yet, but don't you forget for a fucking second that you, me and Eagle are in this shit together. We'll have your back and make sure you don't get stabbed in it because you let your little head do the thinking."

I rolled my eyes. "When have I ever let my little head do the thinking?"

He just raised an eyebrow at me, and I laughed. "Yeah, yeah. Okay, I hear you. I'll keep you posted. But right now, I'm going to go take a cold shower. Then maybe head out to the clubhouse for a bit. Get some relief since Flick's run off like a bloody rabbit."

Mac growled at me. "You're not allowed to use that phrase about a chick. Not anymore."

I punched Mac in the arm. "I'm not gonna start calling her bunny like you do your old lady, so settle down."

It still cracked me up that Mac called Zara bunny because she'd kept running from him like a scared little bunny. Even fucking funnier that Silk had convinced her to get a Playboy bunny tattooed on her hip. I'm pretty sure that only happened because Zara got drunk as fuck and the girls ganged up on her. By the time she'd sobered up, no way would Silk have let her back out of it, so now she had a little pink and white Playboy bunny on her hip.

After a quick shower and change of clothes, we walked out together. I watched Mac's back as he locked up, we both jumped on our bikes and with a quick goodbye, went our separate ways. Mac was, no doubt, going home to climb into bed with his pregnant old lady. As I headed toward the clubhouse, I couldn't help but wonder what it would be like, having someone waiting on me like that.

Flick

After going home for a quick shower and change of clothes, I was ready for my next task. If I was going to stay in town for any length of time, I needed to find a job. Conveniently, the club owned the local bar, Styxx, which was looking for staff. Handy, that. I was pretty sure the FBI was somehow responsible for the vacancy, but I was choosing to not think about it.

It had been about an hour since I fled the gym like a coward and I'd had time to rebuild my walls. Taz slammed through them without even trying, which was extremely disturbing. I hoped he stayed at the clubhouse tonight, and didn't decide to go to the bar. I wasn't sure I could handle another dose of him today.

It thankfully didn't take long to drive over there. Bridgewater wasn't a huge city, so conveniently, the pay-per-the-week hotel room I'd found was close to the bar, and also not too far from the street where Taz lived. I could have probably found something closer to either site, but I didn't want to be too obvious about my interests.

Making fast work of parking my car, I headed toward the front door. A large man stood beside it, arms folded over his leather vest. He eyed me head to toe and silently nodded me in. Guess I'd dressed slutty enough to be granted access. Go, me.

Once inside, I took a moment to get my bearings. The bar was an older one, and what I'd expect of a biker bar. The furniture was solid and sturdy looking, basically like it could, and had, withstood a beating or two. Most of the men in the place looked the same way, actually. The women were mostly dressed in less clothing than me and were draped over a man. There was a small group of younger looking girls at the bar. At a guess, they were college girls who'd dared each other to see how the wild side lived. Hopefully, they got through the night in one piece. More than a couple of the men were watching them with heated looks, but it didn't look like any of them were in any hurry to make a move on the coeds.

With a deep breath, I moved over to the bar and waited for the man behind the counter to notice me. I was wearing a short skirt and a white halter top. It showcased my girls nicely and if I leaned over, I knew those behind me would get a peek at the bottom of my ass cheeks. I smirked at the thought of what Taz would do if he saw me like this. The fact he seemed to be as affected by me, as I was by him made me feel better about this situation.

"Hey there, sugar, what can I get you?"

I ordered a local beer and waited until he came back with my order before I got chatty.

"I hear you've got a job opening?"

He ran his gaze over me with a smirk. "You think you can handle working in a biker bar, babe? Because it ain't as easy as it looks. These boys can get rough, especially after they've had a few."

I held his gaze with a cool look. "Guess you won't know until you give me a go."

A look of admiration flashed in his gaze as I stood up to him. "You worked a bar before?"

"Yeah, it's how I got through college."

That had him frowning. "Since you don't look young enough to be a dropout, why are you here looking to work in a bar instead of whatever you studied?"

I smiled brightly and got ready to lie my ass off. My fake history wasn't actually too different from my real one. It was always easier to go with what you know.

"I did finish. I'm an accountant by trade, but I had some trouble at my last job and decided I needed a fresh start. So, here I am in Bridgewater, applying for a job in a bar."

"Why not another accountant job?"

I shrugged. "I need a break from numbers and if I apply for another accountant job, they'll contact my past employer for a reference. Let's just say I'd prefer him not knowing where I'm now living."

That made the man's frown deepen. Shit, maybe I shouldn't have gone so far with my story.

"You'll need to talk to Scout before I can take you on."

I knew Scout was their president, but I didn't want this guy knowing that I knew that.

"He the owner of the bar?"

The guy laughed. "You could say that. Scout's the president of the Charon MC, the club that owns this bar. He likes to have a chat with anyone new to town. We've had a few women come into town recently that had some serious trouble on their tails. So now we like to know what might be coming at us before it gets here. Let me give him a call and see if he can come over here. Because I really do need to get someone working sooner, rather than later. Last chick I had just up and left, no fucking warning."

While he served a few others, I turned my back to the bar and took in what was happening in the rest of the place as I sipped my beer. While there were a lot of leather vests with the Charon skull and wings on the back, there were even more non-club members. All the men had that same rough look to them, though. I guess the wannabes had to catch the club's attention somehow.

I guessed, logically, a bar owned by the club would be a good start.

"Sugar?"

I spun back to face the guy behind the bar—I really needed to get his name.

"Yeah?"

"Scout's busy tonight but he'll be in tomorrow night. You able to be here at seven? That way if he clears you, you can start straight away. This place doesn't get too busy until around nine most nights."

I nodded, "I can be here then. How many nights will you want me working?"

He gave me a broad smile. "However many you'll do, sugar. We're closed Mondays, and trust me, whatever nights you work will be my new busiest, once word gets out you'll be serving the drinks."

That had me rolling my eyes. Ultimately, all men were the same. Show them a nice rack and a tight ass, and they all got real thirsty. I'd figured that out working in that bar back in college, too. "I look forward to the tips, then. At this point I can work every night, but I'm sure that'll change at some point. How casual are you with the hours?"

He chuckled at me. "If you're happy to work every night most weeks, when you need a night off, just give me forty-eight hours' notice and we'll be sweet."

"Great. Um, what was your name?"

He pointed to the patch on his vest. "I'm Nitro. I run this place, among other things. So, once Scout gives you the nod of approval, I'll be your boss." He frowned. "We started the conversation off all wrong didn't we? I don't have your name either."

I held out my hand. "Felicity, but everyone calls me Flick."

He shook my hand with a firm grip. "Nice to meet you, Flick. You relax and enjoy yourself tonight, then tomorrow night we'll see how you go keeping this bunch liquored up."

I tilted my beer at him before I went back to people watching. I'd gained a few curious watchers, but I ignored them all. Taz was the only male attention I wanted. I was here to work, not screw around.

Chapter 4

Taz

Nothing was fucking working today.

I'd woken early from another fucking nightmare, then when I'd tried to get back to sleep, thoughts of that chick, Flick, had me feeling more than a little uncomfortable. Damn woman was invading my thoughts all the bloody time. I didn't like it. Not one bit. And she had my dick perma-hard. Seriously, nothing calmed the bastard down. Rubbing one out in the shower certainly hadn't helped. Neither had flipping the water over to freezing cold.

Earlier in the week, I'd booked in with Silky Ink to get a new tattoo done this morning. I'd figured the nightmares weren't gonna ease up until after the anniversary, at least that's what normally happened, and I'd hoped the pain of getting some new ink might block out the memories for a while.

So, I'd spent most of my morning at Silky Ink, getting a piece added over my ribs. Hurt like a motherfucker and had worked at dulling the thoughts churning in my brain for a little while. But the moment that needle left my skin, I was right back where I started. It was like my brain only had two channels now, history and XXX-rated Flick.

Once I was through getting my new ink, I figured I'd get some club business done and headed out to see Old Gus at his gun shop and range. I'd started going out there soon after I arrived in Bridgewater, Texas about a year and half ago. It was run by an older bloke who was more than a little rough around the edges. Old Gus didn't think too much of the Charon MC that I was now a part of, but he loved the USMC. So, when I'd first headed out there, I'd mentioned I'd been a sniper for the Marines and proceeded to prove how good I was with a few shots, I was instantly Gus's new best friend. He loved it when I went out there. I suspected the old bugger sold tickets to his mates to come watch me shoot when he knew I was coming. Of course, since I'd been working on softening him up over the last five or so months, I just smiled and joked with whoever he brought around to observe me shoot at shit. Scout, the president of the Charon MC asked me to get in good with the old bloke so we could buy the place. Scout wanted the place under Charon control, and since I'd already been going out there, he gave me the job. It was no hardship for me, I actually liked spending time with the man. He didn't talk much, but seemed to understand I had some demons chasing me without needing to ask about them.

And on a normal day, firing off a few dozen shots out there would keep me level. But not today. Even with the twinge of pain in my ribs with each shot, it still didn't level me out like it normally did.

So that left me here at the clubhouse. It was late afternoon and my club brothers were starting to roll in for the night. The whores were already here and, as always, ready to go.

That had been one of the things that I'd loved about joining the Charon MC. There was always a stack of women hanging around that were wet and willing, and weren't looking for any strings attached to their fucking. It had been nearly a year and half since Mac, Eagle and I had prospected into the Charon MC, and since then, all three of us had found our place here. Eagle with Silk, now Mac had settled down with Zara, and I'd discovered that burying myself in nameless, faceless pussy was a great way to switch my brain off.

It had all worked out nicely. At least until I'd met Flick yesterday. Damn woman. Even now my cock was hard for her.

Speaking of which, I needed to focus on getting that particular need satisfied. I strolled through the clubhouse, nodding and greeting a few of my brothers as I passed to the back hallway where the whore room was. This early on, there were still old ladies and kids running around, so all the sexual shit needed to stay contained to this one room. Later on, once it was just club brothers, the fun and games spread out throughout the whole place. It was a system that worked and everyone respected the boundaries in place. Because if a whore was out of that room doing shit while kids were still roaming around, she was gone and banned from ever returning.

"Hey, ladies. How we doing today?"

I thickened my Aussie accent, knowing how much they all swooned for it. I'd lived in the US since I was thirteen, but I'd managed to maintain my Aussie drawl. And man, was I fucking glad, because that shit worked wonders with the ladies. I grinned. Not that it mattered with these particular women. They were here for one thing: fucking a biker. The very definition of a sure thing. I could stroll in here and grunt and still have several of them on their knees, begging for my cock. But my mother raised me better than that, and I'd never disrespect her memory by being cruel or hurtful to a woman.

And because I gave the club whores a little flirting action, they fucking loved me and I got preferential treatment. Well, I flirt and I'm in here often enough they all know I've got the goods. My piercing seems to go over well, too.

"Hey there, sugar. You look tense. Need some help with that?"

I grinned as Tiffany plastered herself against me. As she mashed her tits against my chest they popped out the top of her corset, revealing how hard her nipples were around the metal through each one. I tweaked one roughly, knowing what she liked, and chuckled when her pupils dilated.

"I need it rough, Tiff. You up for that?"

She groaned, undulated against me. Then cupped my cock through my jeans, rubbing the heel of her palm firmly up and down my length.

"You know I love you rough, sugar."

I wrapped my hand in her hair, tugging her head back until her neck was exposed to me. Leaning in, I nipped at her soft skin. She didn't smell sweet like Flick. I shook that thought from my mind. Flick had run off like a little coward, so she had no right to ruin this moment. I focused back on Tiff, who was fucking perfect for what I needed tonight. She loved it rough. I'd taken her many times and knew exactly what buttons to push to get her motor purring.

I gripped the zip-tab at the front of her corset and pulled it all the way down. The thing popped open and fell to the floor, leaving her big—fake—tits out in the air for me. I spent a few moments twisting and tugging her nipples while I nipped along her jaw. Once she was squirming and whimpering, I tugged her hair, guiding her down.

"On your knees, luv."

She slid gracefully down in front of me and didn't need to be told what I wanted from her. My cock was throbbing for some attention, and thankfully, unlike my big head, my little one didn't care who took care of it.

Flick

After a long, boring day of not doing much, I was more than ready to head over to the bar. I was more than a touch curious about what kind of man would be the president of a motorcycle club. Was he older or a younger guy? I got dressed in a similar outfit to last night—same short denim skirt, but tonight I'd gone with a tight black tank. It would hide any spills I might make serving drinks. I had on a red satin bra underneath and it peaked out if I over-reached. That should get me some good tips, assuming Scout let me work. I had no fucking idea what I was going to do if he said no.

Minutes later I was back in the parking lot of Styxx. The same big guy was at the door and he nodded me through again. Clearly a man of many words, that one. The place was nearly empty this early and I went directly over to the bar, where Nitro was watching me with a grin as I came toward him.

"Here she is, prez."

An older man sitting at the bar turned to face me and I was struck mute for a moment. This guy was seriously everything you think of when you think stereotypical biker. Long beard, which was more gray than dark brown, long hair in a low pony tail. A blue bandana was folded and wrapped around his head, and his face was that of a man who'd spent a lot of time outdoors. No wonder he was the president. He'd get the job on looks alone.

"Well, so she is. Evenin' Miss Felicity Abbott. Care to come back to the office for a little chat?"

I stiffened and narrowed my gaze at the man. "I don't mean any offense, but sorry, I don't know you well enough to be going into an enclosed room with you."

He chuffed out a laugh before turning back to Nitro. "Give the girl a drink, and we'll be over in the corner. Tell anyone who comes in to leave us the fuck alone."

With a nod and a smirk, Nitro got me a beer, the same brand I'd had last night, and set it in front of me.

"Follow me, Flick. We'll sit in the back corner, that good enough for you?"

I lifted my drink and turned to follow him. "Sure."

Sipping my beer, I took my time following him across to a table set against the side wall, toward the back. Naturally, Scout took the seat facing the door. Dammit. I hated not being able to see what was coming at me, but I'd have to suck it up for the next little while. Hopefully this whole interview thing didn't take too long.

Scout cocked his head to the side and watched me as he took a deep drink from his own brew.

"You look tense. Don't like having your back to the doorway, huh? What training have you had that gives you that particular instinct?"

Ah, fuck. Okay, so Scout might be old, but he was clearly as sharp as a tack. Dammit.

"My father was Army, and he brought his work home enough I learned some things. Apparently they stuck. I didn't realize I'd given away I was uncomfortable."

He gave me a smirk. "I was looking for it. I doubt most people would have noticed anything. I heard about the fun you had at the gym yesterday."

Heat flashed across my cheeks and I cleared my throat. "Ah, what exactly did you hear?"

He chuckled at my embarrassment, but not in a mean way. It felt more like he was poking fun at me and seeing how I reacted.

"Mac tells me you got some moves on you. You handled his class like someone who's done it all before. That's a point in your favor for working here. It's not often someone'll step over the line with the staff, but it happens on occasion, and as much as I can guarantee you they will be dealt with if it does happen, that won't change the fact you could get hurt. So, you knowing how to handle yourself is a good thing. Now, tell me about this old boss you're running from. He gonna come looking for you loaded for bear?"

I blinked at him, my shock real. "Um, I sure as fuck hope not. Who would do that?"

He gave me a head tilt before he drank another mouthful. "You'd be surprised what some people will do to get back what they consider is theirs."

"Well, so long as I don't try to work in accounting, he won't come looking for me. He'll be happy thinking he's ruined my career. He's the kind of man who likes to ruin someone from sitting behind a desk. He'd never get his hands dirty."

"So he'd hire someone else to come after you?"

I shook my head. "No, he's not about physical damage. He believes true damage is done financially and to a person's reputation."

"Which I guess is why I have an accountant sitting before me trying to get a bartending job."

I gave him a shoulder lift and took a drink. "Basically. So, have I passed this test? Or do I need to go look elsewhere?"

Scout's gaze lifted over my shoulder a moment before he grinned at me, and stood. I followed his lead, standing from my seat. I desperately wanted to look behind me but didn't want Scout to question me again about why I was so focused on my surroundings.

"You passed the test, Flick. And if you hear anything at all from that old boss of yours, you come straight to me understand? I'll get him dealt with for you in no time flat. You're working for the Charon MC now, that makes you club property and we always take care of what's ours."

I frowned. Property? I wasn't so sure I liked that idea but I could deal with anything for a short period of time. And this was just like every other undercover assignment I'd been on, it would be over at some point and I'd return to my normal life up north.

"Um, sure. Okay, if I do hear from him, you'll be the first to know."

"Good girl." He leaned in and kissed my cheek. His beard was surprisingly quite soft and tickled my neck and face. "This is gonna be fun."

He'd barely finished whispering the words when I was pulled backward with a growl.

Instinct took over and in fast, smooth moves, I braced my feet, then grabbed the upper part of the arm that was now like a steel band across my upper chest. Using a judo move I'd practiced many times, I threw my attacker over my shoulder, onto his back on the floor in front of me.

"What the fuck, Flick!"

The hoots and hollers from the dozen or so men in the bar had my face heating. Shit. I hadn't realized it was Taz who'd grabbed me. At least he'd missed the tables and chairs. Dammit. I needed to dial back my instincts or I'd blow things majorly here.

"You really shouldn't grab people from behind like that."

I moved to offer him a hand up but Scout beat me to it. He was laughing his ass off, but somehow managed to get a grip on Taz's arm and haul him up onto his feet. Taz shook his head and stretched out his spine.

"I guess I should be grateful you didn't drop me on my head and knock me out." He turned to glare at the still-laughing Scout. "Shut it, brother. If you hadn't had your mouth on her, I wouldn't have grabbed her in the first place!"

"Why do you think I kissed her? The boys told me she had you in knots at the gym yesterday. Guess they were telling the truth." He turned to scan the dozen or so men gathered around them. "Anyone get that on video? Because that was something I'd love to be able to watch over and over again. Marine gets handed his ass by a civilian woman. Love it."

He walked over to the bar and most of the men followed him over there, leaving me relatively alone with Taz.

"I really am sorry. I didn't realize it was you and my instincts sort of took over."

He rubbed the back of his neck as he glared at me. "Those are some bloody strong instincts. Who the fuck are you?"

Shit. I didn't want to lie outright to him, but I couldn't exactly spill the beans here in the bar owned by the Charon MC. I moved to press myself up against his front, making sure my girls were pushing up, nearly out of my top. His gaze dropped down and I felt the bulge in his jeans grow bigger against me.

"How about you let me do my first shift here at the bar, then afterward we can go someplace quiet and I'll explain exactly who I am and what I can do for you?"

His palms slid down my back until he was gripping my ass. His fingertips grazed the skin just beneath the skirt hem, making me shiver.

"You only got the drop on me because I was focused on Scout, not you. Don't think you'll be able to do that shit again and get away with it, luv."

Clearly, I'd done all sorts of damage to his ego and pride tonight. I had a feeling his club brothers weren't going to let him forget this for a long time. I leaned up and pressed a kiss to the corner of his mouth. At six feet,

I was only a couple inches shorter than Taz, so I didn't have to stretch much to reach him. He stilled as I feathered a couple of small kisses to the corner of his mouth. A moment later, my back was against the wall and he had his mouth over mine, thrusting his tongue between my lips when I gasped. He pulled one of my legs up around his waist. My skirt rode up so when he ground his denim covered dick against me, it was over my rapidly dampening thong.

"Yo! Taz, she's supposed to be working the bar tonight, not you. You can play with her after."

Nitro's booming voice cut through the lust and once again, heat bloomed over my face. Taz was like my own personal catnip. I completely lost my mind and wanted to play whenever he was near. Fuck. I pulled my leg free and he moved back half a step. It was enough room I could pull down my skirt and straighten my tank and bra to make sure all the goods were covered.

"You're mine tonight, Flick. Don't try to run again, because I'm done playing fucking games. I will come after you this time."

I swallowed past the sudden lump in my throat. I had no doubt he would chase me down. And part of me wanted him to. Fuck, I was in so much trouble with this man.

Chapter 5

Taz

I sat towards the back of the bar for the rest of the night, watching Flick. Who the fuck was she? I was a solid six feet two, and not so easy to move. Yet, she'd pulled some bloody stunt that had me flying over her shoulder before I knew what the fuck was going on. It was bloody rare for those kinds of instincts to come from civilian training.

Didn't help she pulled it in front of Scout and enough of the others that word had spread and now most of the damn club was at the bar to see the woman who'd put me on my ass. I was gonna be copping shit for this for fucking months. At least no one was fast enough with their phone to catch it on video. Scout would have had way too much fun with that.

Speaking of the devil, the Charon president was heading my way with two bottles of beer. He handed one to me as he took the seat beside me.

"That's one hell of a woman you caught yourself, brother."

"I ain't caught shit yet. But that changes tonight. No way is she gonna pull shit like that and then run off at the end of the night like she did last night."

He scoffed. "Mac mentioned how she ran out of the gym like her ass was on fire last night. The way she was draping herself all over you earlier makes me think she's a pretty sure thing." He paused to take a long drink. "She ain't no club whore though, brother. And we need good bar staff more than you need to get your cock wet, feel me?"

I shrugged, taking a swig of my own brew. "I'm aware she ain't a club whore, but what tells you she's a good worker after a couple hours of watching her work?"

"After she dropped you on your ass the way she did, ain't no one dumb enough to try to grab her. If they do, it'll provide great entertainment to watch her throw their ass out all by herself. And thanks to word spreading about her moves, the bar is about as busy as it gets tonight and she's not faltered once. Nitro's impressed and wants to make sure she's happy enough to stick around."

I turned to hold Scout's gaze. "So basically you're telling me not to fuck her?"

He barked out a laugh. "Hell no, brother. I'm telling you if you want to fuck her, you better be ready to fuck only her for the foreseeable future. You ready to settle down?"

That had me frowning. "I'll do just about anything for the club, you know that. But I ain't marrying some chick

I just met so Nitro's got a good worker. Sorry mate. I ain't going there."

He rolled his eyes. "Don't be such a bitch. I'm not saying to make her your old lady, I'm saying if you want to fuck her, it's not gonna be your usual bang 'em and leave 'em shit. Make her your girlfriend or some shit. I don't care, so long as you don't fucking piss her off. Okay?"

I shook my head. "You're fucking nuts, you know that? I'll see what me and my dick can do for you later tonight, 'k?"

"Bastard. Fine. And we got church in the morning at ten. Be there."

I nodded. "Of course. Anything serious?"

He looked around the bar. "Nothing too serious, but we need that damn gun range and shop under our ownership sooner rather than later."

"I've been dropping hints whenever I've been down there. I'll report in at church about the time frame I'm thinking it'll be before we can move in."

Scout nodded, finished his beer then left me alone. I had no clue if Scout was going to go for my idea, but there was no way Old Gus was gonna sell to the club direct. However, he hadn't tossed me out on my ass when I'd suggested I personally take over his baby. I'd been researching the rules and shit to owning a gun range and shop, and I was pretty sure it would be easier to do as an individual rather than as an MC.

The rest of the night dragged on as it looked like every single fucking Charon had heard about me and had come down to laugh at me and check out Flick. Thankfully, Scout had been right and everyone kept their hands to themselves, so at least I wasn't fighting the urge to beat the shit out of any of my brothers. But every time she walked past me twitching that ass of hers, I checked the clock. I couldn't wait for the bar to close so I could get her out of here. I wondered where she lived. Was it closer than my place? She had me so fucking riled up, I didn't want to wait. Although, I still didn't know what the fuck she was playing at, or who she really was, so maybe my place would be better. I knew there were no nasty surprises waiting for me there.

As I watched her finish out her shift, my mind wandered to all the different ways I wanted to fuck her. Once I had her completely worn out, then I'd start the interrogation. Hopefully she'd be so worn out and content from all of her orgasms, she'd have her guard down and would spill all her pretty little secrets to me.

Flick

Midnight rolled around and Nitro told me to head out.

"You did great tonight. Be here tomorrow at five and you can fill out all the paperwork and shit before you start. As we go, I'll get you to do more, but for now I don't need you opening or closing for me." He looked over my shoulder with a laugh. "Not that Taz would let you stay that long tonight, even if I did. Have fun, babe."

This time I knew it was him when he came and stood so close to my back I could feel his heat. His lips brushed against my ear.

"You ready to come home with me?"

A shiver ran down my spine at his rough voice.

"I'm not riding your bike wearing this."

"Hmm. Why not? I ain't gonna wreck and I rather like the idea of your pussy pressed up against me while we ride."

Heat bloomed between my legs. Damn this man. I shook my head, half to clear it, half to say no. "I'll follow you in my car. I want to be able to leave when I want to, not when you feel like letting me go."

His palms came around me, sliding over my ribs and across my stomach before he lowered them until he could trace his fingertips over the skin of my thighs under my skirt hem.

"You like being in control, don't ya luv? I'll give in and let you follow in your car, but once we get through my front door, I'm in control. I promise you'll like it, but I ain't playing no fucking games about it. Understand?"

All I could do was nod. I was standing against the bar, so when he slowly lifted the front of my skirt to rub the backs of his fingers over my damp thong, no one could see what he was doing. I shuddered as he pressed down over my clit.

"Hmm, you wet for me luv? You want it bad don't ya? I'll take real good care of you tonight, don't you worry about that. You sure you wanna drive? Not sure it's safe in the state you're in."

Arousal was pinging around my system, short-circuiting my brain. It's the only reason I had for the fact I was nodding and saying okay to him.

"Good girl. And don't worry, your car will be perfectly safe here in the bar's parking lot."

After one last swipe over my clit, he pulled his hand free and turned me to face him. He wrapped both hands in my hair and took my mouth. Fuck, but the man could kiss. He seduced my mouth, his lips gliding over mine while his tongue danced with my own. I slipped my hands under his vest and shirt to feel his smooth skin and hard muscles. I squirmed against him, completely forgetting where I was until Nitro laughed darkly behind us.

"Taz, take her home already. No fucking on the bar. At least not here, that shit's for the clubhouse, not Styxx."

Taz growled as he ended the kiss and I dropped my head onto his shoulder. I was certain I'd made all the wrong first impressions tonight in this bar. I wasn't sure what any of these men though of me at this point. I'd started the night putting Taz on his ass, now I was all but fucking him on the damn the bar!

"C'mon, luv. Let's get somewhere more private."

Taz took my hand and I followed him out to his bike. There had been a long row of shiny Harleys earlier in the night but now it was only his and Nitro's left in the line-up. They were several feet apart, which made sense because Nitro got here a lot earlier that Taz had.

"You ever ridden before?"

"Yeah. The father of one of my college friends had a Ducati that he took me for a spin on once."

The scowl on his face would have made me laugh if I wasn't so bloody turned on. "What? You a 'it's a Harley or it's not a real bike' man?"

He scoffed in response and grabbed his helmet before coming to stand in front of me. With gentle movements he strapped the skull cap on my head.

"My place isn't far. Stay in close to my back, lean when I lean, and we'll be fine. I've never come off my bike yet, and I don't intend to start tonight."

With that, he slid his long leg over the bike and settled onto the seat, then with a feral looking grin he turned and patted the leather seat behind him. "C'mon, hellcat, hop on."

I blew out a breath, unable to believe I was actually doing this. I glanced over at my car.

"C'mon now, don't go coward on me and run off like you did last night. Get that sweet butt of yours up here."

My anger spiked, I might not know a lot about biker culture, but I'd heard enough talk tonight to know what some of them referred to as a sweet butt.

"I ain't a sweet butt, and if you think I am, this is over right now."

That had him laughing. "Oh, babe, you're too easy to tease. I wasn't calling you a sweet butt, I was calling your butt sweet. Now, get up here. If I have to come get you, you'll end up face down over the seat with my cock fucking you hard for all that pass by to see."

For a moment the thought of being bent over his bike and fucked hard from behind was all I could think about, then he made a move to get off the bike, and with a squeak I was over by his side, swinging my leg over the seat. As much as I liked the idea of being bent over Taz's bike by him, I didn't want to do it with an audience in a damn parking lot.

"You hesitated like you liked that idea. Interesting."

"Just shut up and ride, before I change my mind."

"Yes, ma'am."

He gunned the engine and I groaned as the vibration from the machine ran through me. I hit my head against his back a couple times and his shoulders began shaking. Guess he found my discomfort funny. Bastard. He reached back and ran his palm up my thigh. I shoved at it before he got under my skirt, which had shifted up more than what was decent already. He shook his head, grabbed my hand then put my palm against his stomach. Following his lead, I wrapped both arms around his middle and rested my cheek against his back. The cloth patches scratchy against my skin. The smell of leather and man surrounded me for a moment before he took off and the wind blew it all away.

True to his word, it was less than ten minutes later that we pulled up to his house. As much as I knew where his home was located, I hadn't risked driving past it yet, so hadn't really known what it looked like. The image of it in the file I'd been given on him wasn't the best quality. It was a nice looking, two story place, freshly painted by the looks of things. He pulled up to the garage before slipping a remote from his pocket to lift the door. As the door rumbled up, he revved the engine and I squirmed against his back as the vibrations had my arousal spiking even higher.

Once the door was up, he took us inside before hitting the button once again. He didn't turn off the bike right away and I was about ready to start rubbing my clit to finish myself off, I was that on edge. Finally, he cut the motor, chuckling as he looked back at me.

"You need to get off first, luv. Or would you like me to turn it back on till it gets the job done this first time?"

Embarrassed that he'd caught me in my sexy daydream, I glared at him while I gripped his shoulders as I stood on the pegs, and swung my leg over the seat. Just because the sexy bastard was right, didn't mean I was going to confirm it for him. Once I had both feet on the ground, I took off my helmet and sat it on the bench.

"We going inside or have you changed your mind?"

His gaze darkened a moment before he easily slid off his bike and prowled over to me.

"I ain't gonna change my mind, hellcat. But I sure do enjoy watching you squirm. You were fucking wet for me before we left the bar, I wonder how much wetter you are now... Because you sure seemed to enjoy that ride."

Before I could catch a breath, he had one hand wrapped in my hair, tilting my head up, while the other one slipped up under my skirt. He rubbed his fingertips over the now wet material of the front of my thong with a chuckle. "Oh, yeah, you *really* liked that ride didn't ya? And let me guess, now you're all ready for a different kind of ride?"

Catching the edge of the material, he shoved it aside and slid two of his big, rough fingers inside me with one deep thrust. With a gasp I arched and I flung my hands out to grip his arms to steady myself. With a growl, he took my mouth with his, nipping and licking at my lips before he thrust his tongue inside. His tongue was in perfect sync with his fingers down below and my brain shut down all function but trying to get closer to him.

Fuck, I couldn't remember a time where I'd been this hot for a man.

When I was about to come, he pulled his fingers free. Whimpering at the loss, I watched him lick the digits clean. My knees wobbled but before I fell, he slung me over his shoulder and began walking. Draped like I was, I couldn't see much other than his very fine ass, so I slipped my palms into his back pockets and squeezed with each step he took. Had to say, the way he tensed beneath me with every squeeze did something for me too.

Chapter 6

Taz

This woman was going to be the death of me. She may have been playing hard to get last night, but it seemed like tonight she'd decided to roll with it and wasn't holding back. That fast turnaround was another thing I intended to question her about later. But first I needed to make her come until she couldn't see straight, then fuck her hard. Only then, I'd start asking my questions, when she was all sex-soft and half asleep. And I'd had some fucking relief.

I walked directly to my room, trying to ignore the way she was grabbing at my ass with every step I took. When I stood in front of my bed, I gave her ass a firm slap before I tossed her onto the mattress. Her gaze bounced around the room, but I didn't give her time to take much in, or to start talking. We'd do plenty of that later. For now, I had other plans.

"Get over here, babe."

She rose up onto her elbows. "But you were the one who put me over here."

I crossed my arms over my chest and stared her down.

"Forgot to strip you first, so I need you over here, little kitty."

She raised her eyebrow at me as she rolled over and crawled to me looking like the damn cat I'd just called her.

"Kitty? Not hellcat?"

"Don't want your hellcat right now, Flick. And you're curious as hell, like a cat. So, kitty it is."

The second she was standing I took her mouth again. I wasn't ready to talk. I wanted action first. Wanted my hands on her body. Well, to be honest, I wanted my hands, my tongue and then my cock inside her body. Would her pussy taste as sweet as she smelled?

Gripping the bottom of her tank, I lifted it up, only breaking the kiss long enough to get it over her head. When she started to shove at my cut, I pulled back. But not before I flicked open the clasp on the back of her bra. She gave a cute little squeak when it fell from her.

"How in the hell did you do that so fast? I can't even do it that fast!"

"Practice makes perfect, kitty. Take your skirt and knickers off, let me see you."

She stiffened for a moment, like she was gonna sass me for giving her orders, but when I slipped off my cut, laying it over the back of a chair, then peeled my shirt off over my head, she seemed to forget all about sassing me. Something to remember, that. I flexed my biceps as I wadded up the shirt and tossed it into the corner of the room with my other dirty clothes. Feeling the heat of her gaze on my chest, I ran a palm over my ribbed stomach and pecs. I let my gaze run over her as she was getting her fill of me. Fuck, she was perfect. Her hair was long enough the ends curled around her tits, and her pink nipples were playing peekaboo amongst the black curls. My mouth watered for a taste of them.

I took a step closer to her as I dropped my gaze. As I'd expected after seeing her at the gym and how she'd taken me down today, her stomach was flat with sleek muscle. Her hips flared out nicely and her pussy was covered with neatly trimmed curls.

This woman was like a bloody fertility goddess or some shit. She was all natural too. Her tits looked soft and they hung in a way fake ones didn't. The fact she hadn't waxed every hair from her body was a nice change too. I couldn't wait to get my mouth on her.

Leaving my jeans on, I prowled to stand in front of her before taking her mouth again. She opened her lips to me immediately and wrapped her arms around my shoulders. With my palms on her ass, I lifted her up against me before stepping up to the edge of the bed. Breaking the kiss, I laid her down on the mattress, gently this time. Not giving her a chance to think, I dropped to my knees on the floor, and threw her legs over my shoulders as I pulled her toward me. Running my palms up the insides of her thighs, I got my first good up-close look at her pussy. Licking my lips, I ran my thumbs down either side of her opening before pulling her lips apart so I could lean in and get my tongue in deep for a taste. My eyes slid shut on a moan at my first swallow. She tasted as sweet as she smelled.

Licking up her center I flicked her clit before returning for another stroke within her channel. She groaned and I looked up her body to see she'd grabbed fistfuls of the sheets as she looked down at me with wide eyes.

"You taste so fucking good, babe. Gonna need a lot more of you down my throat before I'm done."

With that, I put my mouth back on her and began really working her over. She dropped her head back against the bed and arched her back, thrusting those tits of hers up in the air. The tips were tight with her arousal and I wished like fuck I could reach them without taking my mouth off her pussy, but it just wasn't possible in this position so I focused back on getting her to come for me. Moving to suckle on her clit, I thrust two fingers in deep and toyed with her until I found the magic spot deep within her that made her shudder and cry out for me. Once I had that nailed, I rubbed over it continuously as I alternated between tonguing her clit and nipping at the little bud.

"Taz! Fuck..."

With a growl, I kept at her until she screamed and her channel clenched down on my fingers. Fuck, I couldn't wait to have my cock in there, feeling her clench and ripple around me. I moved my mouth from her clit to her opening to lap up all the cream she'd given me. Some women tasted fucking terrible and I hated going down on them, but Flick was like some kind of nectar I'd never tasted before and couldn't get enough off. Before she began to come down from her high, I had three fingers inside her, stretching her for my cock, with my teeth back worrying her needy little clit. I also got my other hand involved this round. Gathering up some of her cream on my finger, I moved it back to rub over her asshole. Predictably, she tensed, but instead of telling me to fuck off, she shuddered then relaxed against me as I kept making small circles over her back hole. It didn't take long until she was panting for breath as she started thrashing her head on the bed. Fucking perfect.

Now she was primed and ready to blow, I went on the attack. At the same time, I thrust my fingers in her pussy deep, nipped her clit and slipped my finger up her tight little asshole to the first knuckle. Her upper body lifted off the bed as she screamed out and her inner muscles clamped down on me, holding me inside her as she came fucking hard.

My cock was throbbing for attention and if I didn't get these jeans off soon, I was gonna have a permanent zipper mark up the underside of it. As she started to come down, I gentled my strokes before easing free of her body. Slipping her legs off my shoulders, I stood and looked down at her. She was perfect, all sex rumpled, half asleep and spread over my fucking bed. Yeah, whatever games she was playing, I didn't give a fuck about right now. We'd sort whatever that shit was out, because she belonged right here. With me, in my bed.

Flick

Naturally, Taz would be freaking orally fixated. My core vibrated in the aftermath of having two massive climaxes. Hell, I could curl up and go to sleep a happy woman right now. But Taz hadn't gotten any relief, and I still hadn't seen the man naked. His chest and torso were a work of fucking art—and not just because of the tattoos, including a new piece on his ribs. The ink was raised and looked fresh, and I was sure I hadn't seen it when he'd taken off his shirt at the gym last night.

"Be right back, kitty."

Through hooded eyes, I watched him head to what I assumed was a bathroom. Once he was out of sight, I forced my body to move. Rolling over, I then crawled further up the bed until my head was on the pillow. I kicked the sheet and blankets down, but didn't bother pulling them back up over me. I was pretty sure Taz wasn't ready for sleep just yet. A yawn struck me just as he walked back in, naked. I may have whimpered.

"Don't go getting sleepy on me. I'm far from being done with you tonight."

Did I mention he was now gloriously naked? I had no clue what he'd just said because all I could focus on was the fact he had a pierced dick. I licked my lips and couldn't tear my gaze away from it. A small metal ball sat at the tip and another under the head. He stroked himself, flicking the piercing as I watched him.

"Like what you see, my curious little kitty? Because just you wait till I get this inside you and this ball is running over your sweet spot with every stroke."

I nodded, because I knew there was no way I could speak at the moment. With a chuckle, he strode toward me, and pulling the drawer beside the bed open, he pulled out a strip of condoms that he set on the nightstand after tearing one off. I was still staring at his dick when he palmed the length again, stroking twice before he put one knee up on the bed and moved toward me.

"Stop looking so scared, babe. It ain't gonna bite."

Humor laced his voice and heat flashed over my cheeks.

"I've never seen a pierced dick before."

"That's because it hurts like a motherfucker to get one, and takes for-fucking-ever to heal. I did it when I was young and dumb, so it's all healed up now and trust me, I know exactly how to use it to the best of its ability."

That made me scoff. I just bet he did. I reached for him and he took my hand in his and wrapped it around his length as he laid beside me. The metal was warm as it slid over my palm. I really wanted to know what it would feel like both against my tongue and in my pussy. He released my hand and moved to grab my breast. Using both hands, he kneaded the girls until I was arching into his touch, then he gripped my nipples, giving them a tug before he twisted them just enough to get my attention.

"C'mon, cowgirl, want you riding my cock."

Letting his dick go, I slapped lightly at his chest. "Just because we're in Texas, doesn't automatically make me a damn cowgirl."

He chuckled. "What? You don't want to ride me?"

I gave him a sly grin. "Never said that."

While he grabbed the condom, I moved up to my knees and straddled his thighs. He really was a beautiful male. Not in a pretty way, but in a rough, masculine way. His body and face showed he'd lived a hard life, he'd survived it all, and was here on the other side, living life. He rolled the latex down his hard length, then before I could move myself, he gripped my hips and lifted me. With a squeak, I pressed one hand to his chest then shifted my other to grip his dick to line it up with my opening.

He didn't shove me down like I half expected him to, but held me up so I slowly slid down his thick erection this first time. Damn, he was big. When my pelvis met his, he held still and I took a couple of deep breaths while my body adjusted to having him inside me. He didn't say a word, just stroked his palms up my thighs and arms, then onto my breasts until I relaxed. I swiveled my hips and he groaned, then tightened his hands on my shoulders, holding me down hard against him as he thrust up.

"Lean back and hold onto my legs."

He released my shoulders, and while holding his gaze, I did as he instructed. His eyes flicked down to my breasts and with a snarl, he sat up and wrapped his mouth around one nipple as he gripped the other between a thumb and finger. Arousal shot through my body and I flexed my hips in an attempt to get enough friction against my clit to come. He gave the first nipple a light bite, before he switched to the other one. By the time he'd finished toying with both buds, they were so sensitive I was ready to scream at the lightest touch. My clit was throbbing with need, and I clenched down on his cock, milking his length in an attempt to get him to fucking move already.

He laid back, a feral grin on his face and a hard, hot look in his eyes. He gripped my hips and started thrusting up into me hard and fast.

"Oh, fuck!"

I dug my fingers into his legs and my head dropped back as my body shook. Just as he'd told me it would, the top ball of his piercing had hit my g-spot directly from the first thrust. It didn't take long before I started to climax again. He tweaked my clit and I nearly passed out as my orgasm built higher and kept going. My mind shut down and I rolled with the intense pleasure that was taking over every cell of my being.

Chapter 7

Taz

Holy fucking shit! This woman was beyond sexy and watching her shudder through multiple orgasms was making it hard to hold off my own, but I was determined. I wasn't done with her yet and although she seemed pretty soft and compliant after this round, she'd be even more so after a couple more. At least, that's what I was telling myself. Honestly, it was more about wanting to see her whole body flush pink as she shuddered and clenched down on me like a fucking vise before she screamed my name. The fact she'd dug her fingernails deep enough into my thighs that she'd drawn blood didn't hurt either. I loved that she'd marked me, because I sure as shit had marked her up. Her nipples were red from all the attention I'd given them and she had a few little hickies over her chest too.

With the last shudder of her orgasm, her body went limp and I quickly grabbed her and rolled us over so she was on her back. Caging her under my body, I started kissing her mouth, bringing her back to life with licks and nips. With a moan she came back to me, stroking her palms up my arms until she had them wrapped around my neck. I moved to nibble along her jaw line.

"Don't go getting sleepy on me yet, I'm still not done with you, kitty."

She moaned and undulated beneath me. "You're still hard?"

"Yeah, babe. I've got the stamina to keep going all fucking night, if the mood strikes me."

I might not be able to hold off from coming for much longer, but with the way she had me so riled up, I was sure my recovery time wouldn't be long. My statement got me a raised eyebrow in disbelief. I kissed her nose lightly, then started to stroke in and out of her again.

"Don't worry, curious little kitty, I'll prove it to you so you don't ever doubt me again."

She arched up under me and I couldn't resist the offering she presented. Sucking deep on one of her nipples had her shuddering and crying out. She gripped my head but I wasn't sure if she was holding me to her, or pushing me away. Releasing her with a pop, I moved so I was kneeling between her legs. Palming her hips, I pulled her toward me with each of my thrusts up. Her channel rippled around me and I closed my eyes at how fucking good it felt to be buried inside this woman.

Suddenly, I understood what Mac and Eagle had been on about when they said their women were their home. Because that's what this felt like. Being inside Flick, felt like I'd fucking come home. When she started thrashing her head on the pillow I couldn't hold off. I needed to pound into her, to give her everything I had.

I pulled free, flipped her over, then pulling her up on all fours, I slammed back into her core, loving how she cried out and tightened around me. She dropped her shoulders down the bed as she trembled beneath me and I reached under her to toy with her clit while I kept thrusting into her. I knew the bottom ball of my Prince Albert would be rubbing over her g-spot with every stroke in this position, and between that and my playing with her clit she was trembling beneath me on the edge of another climax within moments. Feeling like stepping things up, I swiped the thumb of my hand not busy tormenting her clit, around my cock, getting it nice and wet with her cream. Then, I ran my finger down the crack of her ass, before pressing my thumb over her little hole. Like earlier, she tensed and muttered something under her breath I didn't catch. But she didn't pull away, or tell me to fuck off, so on my next thrust into her slick pussy, I pressed the tip of my thumb in, while I pinched her clit with my other hand. She blew apart, clenching hard down on me and I couldn't fight it. I came hard, filling the condom as fucking stars burst across my vision.

"Fuck me."

Slipping my thumb free, I dropped over her back, resting my forehead on her shoulder as she shook and whimpered beneath me. After a few deep breaths, I pulled back and eased my cock from her core. She tensed as I pulled the head free and stumbled over to the bathroom to clean up, lose the condom and grab a cloth to wipe her down.

When I got back to her she was out cold. Guess I wore her out a little too much. Ah, well, I'd let her nap for a bit, then I'd wake her for question time. I gently wiped between her legs and her ass before tossing the cloth in the direction of the bathroom. I'd deal with it later. Then, unable to resist her soft body, I slid in behind her, pulled the covers up over us and curled myself around her. She snuggled back against me so when I wrapped my arm around her, she was caged in tight against me.

Felt good. Actually, it felt way too fucking good. Fuck, I hoped whatever she was playing at, I could sort out so I could keep her. Because suddenly, the idea of settling down with just one woman didn't seem like such a bad idea at all.

Flick

Never in my life had I been so thoroughly fucked. I woke to a pleasant ache in my pussy and a twinge in my ass. That one was new. Twice last night, Taz had put his finger or thumb in my butt and I wasn't sure how to feel about it. I'd never let a man fuck me there, and I wasn't sure I wanted Taz's monster back there, either. But the finger thing felt good.

I could feel his warmth beside me, so I went to roll toward him. When I couldn't move, my lungs froze. I yanked on my arms as my eyes flew open to see why I couldn't move them. I was fucking cuffed to the rails of his headboard.

"What the fuck?"

He moved and I turned my face toward him and glared fire his way as he moved to cover my body with his. Accurately predicting my reaction, he blocked my legs from being able to kick out at him.

"Time to answer some questions for me, Felicity."

My body stilled. This was not how I wanted to tell him about the real reason I was here.

"Uncuff me and let me get dressed and I'll tell you whatever you want to know."

He rolled off me and stood beside the bed. He pulled his jeans on, then crossed his arms over his chest and stood staring at me.

"The sheet's covering everything important, and I ain't uncuffing you until I'm convinced you're not a threat to me, or mine. Now, why are you really in Bridgewater? Because I'm going to take a wild guess and say it's got nothing to do with an old boss."

I pulled on the cuffs again, seeing if I could twist free, but he'd put them on nice and tight. With a huff I looked over at him, trying to figure out how to tell him. Where to start that he wouldn't go off the deep end before I finished.

"We're on the same side. At least, we're supposed to be."

His body stiffened and his gaze turned cold, like ice cold.

"You're FBI?"

I nodded slowly, trying to work out what he was going to do about it.

"Figured they wouldn't let us just disappear when we stopped talking to them. So, you're our new handler, are you? Figured you'd get in nice and close to keep tabs on us?"

He didn't sound angry. Nope, he sounded furious. I needed to calm him down a notch or two. Somehow. I shook my head. "No, not your handler. They know Mac and Eagle are out. I'm here to be your new partner. My boss wants me to partner up with you to deal with—" I huffed again. "Can I please sit up for this conversation? Without being cuffed to the bed? I'm not here to hurt you, or arrest you."

He didn't move an inch. "If that's the case, why didn't you come straight to me and tell me up front? Why all this sneaky bullshit and fucking me first?"

Giving up trying to get free, I relaxed back against the bed. "Because your club needs to believe we met and hooked up naturally. If it looked manufactured, they'd have picked up on it and this wouldn't work."

"Starting out by lying to me won't work out well for you either, luv."

"I never intended for it to go this far before I told you who I was. But things got heated last night and—dammit—you make me lose my damn mind, Taz!

Would you please release the cuffs? I hate having my freedom to move restricted."

His gaze narrowed for a minute before he grabbed a little key off the table, climbed back on the bed and straddled my waist. He leaned up and unlocked me before leaning back. I slowly pulled my arms down and with a wince, I rubbed at the red marks around my wrists to ease the burn. He took one in his palm and held it out so he could examine the damage he'd caused me.

"Dammit. Why'd you fight it so fucking much? I didn't make them tight enough to hurt if you hadn't tugged on them so damn much."

Anger spiked through my blood. "How would you fucking react to waking up cuffed to a damn bed?"

Wrapping a large palm around each of my wrists, he pinned them on either side of my head before he leaned down over me until our faces were only separated by an inch.

"I hate being played or manipulated. You did both. I should just hand you over to Scout, tell him you're a fucking fed and forget all about you."

Oh, I wanted to kick him so bad, but he was sitting too high up. I could maybe knee him in the back, but all that would do is knock him forward into me.

"You do that, I drag you, Mac and Eagle under the bus with me. What do you think your precious president will think of the fact you three were sent in to spy on them?"

"We've never given any information on the club—"

I smiled in a falsely sweet way. "You and I both know that, but I'm guessing Scout'll wanna chat with you three before he believes you over the stories I'll spin. I heard about what happened to Eagle a few months back. Bad business, that. I can only imagine what they'd do to someone they thought was a rat."

His body vibrated above me and his grip tightened on my wrists while his face went red. He stayed silent and I watched him with a lump of fear in my throat as he processed what I'd said. I hadn't wanted to get nasty with him, but he'd pushed me into a corner. I wasn't ever going to take that shit lying down. Even if, technically speaking, I was physically lying down.

"What do you want?"

His voice was harsh and cracked like a whip through the air. I let myself relax beneath him, hoping he'd respond by calming down at least a little.

"It's not about what I want, Taz. You know—"

"Fine. What do *they* want? And stop fucking around, Flick. You know what I mean."

I sighed. "Fine. Be like that, then. Word has spread that the Satan's Cowboys MC has recently taken an increased interest in the Charon MC. The Bureau believes it's because the Cowboys want to start using your club to help them distribute product—guns and drugs. They realize that, like Mac and Eagle, you're now loyal to the Charons, but the Cowboys are a different matter. I'm to come in as your girlfriend and help you work out what the Cowboys are up to so we can stop them and break their distribution network apart. I believe the hope is it will be easier to stop something new that the Cowboys haven't had time to fully secure, than their more established networks."

"We? As in you and me take down one of the biggest MCs in Texas? Or, as in, we hand the information over the FBI, who if their track record is to be followed, will hand it straight over the Cowboys, who'll come after the both of us and not only blow our cover, but probably our heads off as well."

For a few moments I just stared into his baby blues, trying to think of how best to respond. "Your last handler, the one who leaked shit to the L.A. mob, went missing after what happened with the Iron Hammers. No one's seen or heard from him in three months."

He cut me off again. "Do *not* try to tell me he was the only leak in the FBI. I know better. We were naive when we took this job on, to think we could help make America safer. The silver lining is we found a place that does just that. The Charon MC don't do drugs, never have, and there's no way Scout will ever agree to traffic it for the Cowboys, or for anyone else. If anyone in this town needs help, we provide it. There's no red tape to fuck around with, no concerns of filling out fucking paperwork or ticking boxes. We see a need, we fucking fill it. Simple. Just like Mac and Eagle, I like my life here in Bridgewater. I fucking love being a part of this club. And I won't be risking it for anyone. Understand?"

I nodded, because it wasn't like I had a whole lot of options left. "What are you going to do about me, then?"

"I have no fucking clue, babe. Because if it wasn't for all this bullshit, I'd want to see if you could handle being my old lady down the road. But now? I'm not sure I can trust you to not fucking sell me out. What happens if I send you packing?"

I winced. "Not sure, but I'm guessing you'll be arrested and brought in to be reprimanded. How they choose to do that is anyone's guess."

With no fucking clue what he was going to do, I shut up and waited for him to do whatever it was. He had me pinned down and I was naked so I didn't have a whole lot of options open to me just at the moment.

An alarm sounded and I jerked in his grip as the loud sound shocked me out of our little staring match.

"Fuckin' hell. I gotta get to the clubhouse for church. Fuck!"

He huffed and closed his eyes a minute before he opened them and I saw clearly the heat and lust in them. He slammed his mouth over mine and took my breath with his intensity. This wasn't a gentle kiss, but an all-out assault on my mouth.

And I was twisted as fuck, because I loved every second of it.

Chapter 8

Taz

By the time I'd dropped Flick back at her car and made it to church, I was cutting it fine. Tossing my phone and keys into a locker, I rushed into the meeting room.

"Sorry, prez."

Everyone was in their places and it looked like they'd been waiting on me. Dammit. Scout gave me a knowing smirk.

"Figured you might be late in, considering who you got to take home with you. Tell me, she drop you on your ass again after you fucked her?"

That had me smiling. I knew I'd be copping shit over that stunt of Flick's for a while yet.

"Nah, I just lowered the risk of her tossing me again by making sure I fucked her till she couldn't walk."

Everyone laughed as I found my seat next to Eagle and Mac. Mac gave me a raised brow and I gave him a look I hoped he understood meant we had shit to discuss privately. Fuck, what a mess. Why couldn't Flick just be a nice chick? Well, a nice, tough, chick who refused to take my shit and would literally put me on my ass if I stepped out of line. Yeah, okay. So my woman wasn't ever going to be some freakin' hothouse flower that needed pampering twenty-four/seven. But still, a girl like Silk, who'd been raised in the club would have done the job. Why'd she have to be a fucking fed?

No matter how I tried to look at the situation, I couldn't see a way of fucking keeping her. I'd known her two fucking days, only started screwing her last night and I already didn't want to let her go. This was bad, so fucking bad.

A jab to my ribs from Eagle had me nearly crashing off my chair.

"What the fuck?"

"You done daydreaming, Taz? Because this shit's serious and I need your full fucking attention on it."

Shit. "Sorry, prez."

Pushing all thoughts of Flick aside, I locked that shit down and focused on club business.

"Right. Now we're all here, and paying fucking attention, we got shit to discuss. As most of you know, we've always fallen under the Satan's Cowboys jurisdiction. Basically, we exist because they allow us to. In the past, they've let us do our own thing and haven't bothered with us. We've been friendly, hosted their members when needed and paid our dues. Unfortunately, the down side to dealing with that fucking mess down in Galveston last year was that we've come to their attention. Especially the fact that we ain't running anything for them."

I bit back my groan. How had Flick known? Or rather, how had the FBI brass known this shit was coming? I rubbed the back of my neck as Scout turned his gaze on me.

"How's it coming along with Old Gus? He ready to retire yet?"

"I've mentioned that I wouldn't mind running a place like his one day, and he didn't shut me down. I'll be honest, he'll never sell to the club. But I think I can get him to sell to me. Especially if I tell him he's welcome to come in with his mates for free whenever he wants to use the range. Why the sudden urgency? What do the Cowboys want us to run for them that we need the range and shop to do it?"

It had to be guns or drugs—the shit-storm that went down with the Iron Hammers proved that the Cowboys weren't involved with human trafficking. So other than guns or drugs, there wasn't much left. And it was a fucking gun range and shop, so I guessed it was firearms, but I wanted to be sure.

"They know we're a drug-free club, and for the moment Viper is willing to let us continue that way, but only if we step up and help with the weapons." Scout paused to look around the room. "Basically, if Gus won't sell out to us legally and soon, they'll arrange an accident for him."

Viper was their president and wasn't known for taking his time with shit like this. The fact he'd all but ordered a hit on Old Gus left me cursing, along with several others. Gus wasn't a bad bloke, just old school and anti-gang. He refused to see the MC as anything but a bunch of thugs. But he'd served in Nam and was a decent guy. He sure as fuck didn't deserve to end up in a pine box because he happened to own shit the Cowboys wanted under their control.

"I'll head over there this afternoon, see if I can push him into something. I'm guessing they're more interested in the gun shop than the range? Just in case I have to compromise to get something out of Gus."

The range didn't take a whole heap of upkeep, just a lot of time to hang around and watch those shooting. The shop, on the other hand, had to be a pain in the ass to run for an old man. I could see it would be easier to convince him to let go of the shop if he could keep the range.

"I came to the same conclusion. We let him keep the range if it means we can have the shop. I've had our lawyers draw up all the paperwork required already. I'll just get them to change it from the club to you personally." Scout held my gaze steadily. "I need to have some kind of news to report back to Viper by the end of the weekend, feel me? If not, shit's gonna go south in a bad way for Gus real soon."

Considering it was currently Friday morning, that didn't leave me a whole heap of fucking time.

After that, we moved onto other business and I only half listened as I tried to work out what the fuck I'd say to Gus, without coming straight out and telling the man his life depended on him signing over his damn shop to me.

Flick

Having decided it would do me good to get to know Mac and Eagle's women, I headed into Marie's Cafe for a late lunch. I'd left it late in an attempt to avoid the bulk of the lunch rush. I didn't want to catch Zara when she was so run off her feet, she wouldn't have the time to be friendly.

The moment I entered, I knew I was in for it. Scout was there, with another man wearing a club vest, along with two women. I recognized the younger one as Eagle's woman, Silk, and she looked very pregnant. The little bell on the door had chimed as I'd entered, and naturally Scout looked up and caught my gaze.

"Hey, Flick! Go order, then come over here and let me introduce you around."

With a nervous smile, I headed over toward the back counter where an older woman was watching me a little too closely.

"So you're Flick, huh?"

I winced and rolled my lips in for a moment. "Yeah, but I have to say I'm a little worried what you've heard about me."

The woman waved me off. "Oh, sugar, don't be worried. You'll learn soon enough, nothing spreads quite as fast as gossip does inside an MC, let me tell you. And you putting Taz on his ass over at Styxx last night is the talk of the town today."

I buried my face in my palms. He was going to be so pissed off at me for that stunt.

"Shit. I didn't even mean to do it! He surprised me and I just reacted, you know?"

The lady shook her head on a laugh. "I sure as hell don't react like that when a handsome young man grabs me, but your generation is a different beast than mine, that's for sure. Now, what can I get you?"

"Um, just a coffee with cream, thanks. And maybe one of those muffins." I pointed to the covered plate of what looked like homemade apple and cinnamon muffins sitting on the counter.

"Sure thing, sugar. You go on and sit with Scout and the others and I'll bring it over to you in a bit."

"Um, what do I owe you for it?"

She gave me a cheeky smile. "Oh, you paid for it when you put Taz in his place. I've been waiting for a woman strong enough to tame that one. You've got one hell of a task ahead of you if you want to claim that man. You'll need more than a coffee and muffin, but it's a start. Now, off you go."

In a daze, I headed over to the table where an extra chair had been added between Silk and Scout.

"Here she is, the woman of the hour. So, Flick, tell me. How'd your night end?"

My cheeks heated and I kind of just sputtered a little when I tried to respond. I mean, really, what the fuck was I going to say to that?

"Oh, quit it, Scout, you'll frighten the poor girl off. Hi, Flick, I'm Rose and this is my old man, Bulldog, and this one is our niece, Silk. She's with Eagle and they live right next door to Taz so you'll no doubt be seeing each other around."

I'd read in my search for information about MCs that bikers called their spouses either their old man or old lady. I really wasn't sure how I felt about those labels. But like Scout had told me, I was club property now I worked at their bar. I was me. Owned by me. I wasn't a pet or a piece of furniture. However, I needed to push aside my issues and deal with it while working this assignment.

Unsure what to say, or how much they all knew about me, I focused on Silk and the fact she was pregnant.

"Hi, everyone." I nodded to her tummy. "How long have you got to go?"

She caressed a palm over her swollen belly as her face lit up with a grin of pure joy. "Still have three months to go. Some days that feels like forever, and other days it can't come fast enough."

I sat down and a younger woman, who I guessed was Zara, brought over my order and set it in front of me.

"Here you go. Have to say, it's nice to actually meet you, after all we've heard."

Glancing around the table with a raised eyebrow, I knew I had to handle this head on.

"And what exactly have y'all heard about me? I haven't been in town that long to create too much drama."

That had the whole table laughing, before Scout spoke up.

"Honey, you caused quite the stir at the gym the other day, then again last night when you put Taz on his ass—literally. It's not every day that shit happens, especially considering he's a bloody Marine. That shit'll spread like wildfire and you'll be the talk of the club, and town, for a while yet."

Bulldog cut in. "Even more so because you went home with him, and he was late to church this morning because of it. He won't be living this one down for a good, long while."

My face heated again as I felt Silk and Zara's gazes zero in on me. "You stayed the night with him? Like in his bed, at his house?"

I frowned at Silk. "Um, yeah. Why is that a surprise?"

"Because in the eighteen or so months I've known that man, he's never spent an entire night with any woman. I've actually never known him to do more than mild flirting with women outside of the clubhouse."

Zara laughed. "And the flirting is generally with one of us that's spoken for and he only does it because he knows it'll rile up his brothers. He doesn't mean it at all. But you, you he not only flirted with, but he took you home with him. Interesting."

I picked up my coffee to take a drink, unsure what they wanted me to say. The whole girlfriend/boyfriend plan had sounded great on paper, but if Taz was a man-whore who never did relationships, it wouldn't work. No way would he remain faithful to a pretend girlfriend, if he'd never had a real one. Our chemistry was off the fucking charts and we were a great match in bed, but could I be enough to keep him satisfied if he was used to such variety? Would he feel too tied down by having to stick with the one woman if we continued this ruse? And what would he do if he did grow to feel that way?

I needed to get away from these people and do some serious thinking. Maybe try to pull together a backup plan. Although, I wasn't sure what that would be. Fuck. I needed more time with Taz to ask him how he really felt about going into this mission as lovers. He was a man of his word, and if he said he was in, he would honor his commitment.

Wouldn't he?

And so what if I wanted the ruse to be real. It wasn't an option so I had to keep my heart out of this whole thing.

Chapter 9

Taz

Frustration rode me as I pulled up outside Styxx. I hadn't been able to get Mac and Eagle alone yet to tell them what the fuck was going on. Instead, I spent the afternoon out with Gus, telling him all about how I needed to find some work I could really sink my teeth into. It was the best angle I could think of to convince him to retire early, but he didn't seem to get with what I was aiming at. I really didn't want to see the man get killed over this shit, but if I couldn't work out how to get him to sell to me, that's what was going to happen.

After backing my bike into the lineup of Charon bikes out front, I slid off and headed to the door, giving the prospect guarding the door a nod on my way past. Naturally, the first person I saw as I entered was Flick, twitching her ass as she walked across the room to deliver drinks. What the fuck was I gonna do about her? Rubbing a hand over the back of my neck, I headed to the bar to grab a stool and wait to get a drink.

"Hey, Taz, brother. What can I get ya?"

"Just a beer tonight, mate. Can't stay long."

Nitro chuckled. "Just dropped in to check up on your girl, then?"

With a nod, I glanced over at her to see she was making her way back to the bar. "Yeah, something like that."

When she saw me, her face lit up, like she was truly happy to see me. But it was all a lie. Wasn't it? She was just pretending so she could get, and stay, close to me. And I was a fucking moron because I was still trying to work out how we could be something more. Apparently watching Eagle, then Mac, settle down had, in fact, affected me, because here I was dreaming up fucking white picket fences after only a couple days with this chick. Even though I knew she was just fucking me as a cover.

A cloud passed over her expression as she started to come toward me, swinging those damn hips of hers with every step. Taking a swig of my beer, I spread my legs to give her room to come in close to me. Taking the hint, she moved between my thighs, until she was up against my front. She was wearing another tight little tank and the way she was pressed up against me had her tits nearly coming out of the thing. I slid a palm down her back until I reached the bottom of her little skirt, then moved up under the material, palming her bare fucking ass cheek because the little tease was wearing a fucking g-string.

When she leaned in, clearly angling for a kiss, I gripped a handful of her ass and gave it a good squeeze before I took her mouth. Without looking, I reached over to set my beer on the bar before wrapping that palm around the back of her neck. A shudder ran through her when my cold skin touched her warm neck.

Nitro chuckling had me pulling back from the kiss. Dammit, I lost my fucking head every time I touched this woman.

"I'd say you two need to get a room, but I kinda need Flick to get back to work, so do you think you two can keep it in your pants for another few hours?"

"I'll do my best, but you know me."

Nitro laughed again. "Yeah, you fucking man-whore. Flick, get away from him while you can, sugar. Or you'll be bent over the damn bar."

The damn woman's eyes dilated and I couldn't help but smirk. "Like that idea, kitty? You want me to be so fucking hard for you that I don't care who sees me fuck you?"

Her breath caught and made my cock throb. I glanced over at Nitro with a raised brow. He'd been watching us with his arms crossed. He shook his head at me with a roll of his eyes.

"Now you've gone and turned her mind to mush, you might as well take her back to the office and deal with it. I need her working, not fucking daydreaming about your cock, brother. Go on, but make it quick."

I didn't bother listening to the rest of his rant. He'd get over it. Slipping off the stool, I easily tossed Flick over my shoulder and headed out the side door, down the hallway toward the toilets and the office. We were about halfway down the hall when she came out of her stupor and started thumping at my back.

"Cut the shit, Taz and put me down! You can't just haul me around whenever you feel like it! You'll get me fired."

I shrugged the shoulder she wasn't over. "Nah, Nitro gave me his blessing. Your job's safe." I entered the office and once inside, flicked the lock and strode over to the desk. Conveniently, Nitro kept the place neat as a pin. Everything was locked away in filing cabinets, so the desk was clear of everything except a landline phone and a small pot of pens. I also knew he swept the room for bugs daily so it was safe to speak somewhat freely in here.

Leaning down, I set her gently on the edge before I moved to stand between her thighs. She tried to push me away but she wasn't trying real hard. When I leaned forward, she laid back on the desk. When you knew for a fact a woman could put you on your ass, it was hard to take her seriously when she was barely shoving at me. But I wouldn't have her accusing me of rape, so I stopped with a hand on the desk on either side of her head, caging her in beneath me, just how I liked her to be.

"How far you willing to go for this little farce of yours? You've already got the club thinking you're leading me around by my cock. You intend to keep using it? Or was that just to get your lovely foot in the door?"

Hurt flashed in her eyes before she glared up at me.

"Seriously? I am not leading you around by your dick. It's not my fault you choose to think with the wrong head. Not like I forced you to go all caveman and drag me back here."

I shook my head. "Don't even try to put this all on me. I saw your pupils dilate when Nitro mentioned I might just throw you over the bar and fuck you if we kept up kissing like we were. Tell me, my curious little Kitty, if I felt your knickers right now, what would I find? Would I find them dry because you're just playing a game here? Or are they soaked through?"

"Dammit, Taz! You know I'm into you. If I wasn't, last night would have played out a lot differently."

That had me chuckling. "Oh, yeah? How do think it would have gone?"

"I would have talked to you the moment we entered your house. Explained then what was going on. Actually, if I wasn't attracted to you, I wouldn't have gone home with you at all last night. I would have met you for coffee at a quiet cafe someplace and explained the situation. Sleeping with you isn't part of the job—"

I cut her off. "Fucking me is just a perk, right?"

As she lay there blinking up at me. I couldn't get my fucking thoughts straight. This was ridiculous. I should walk away, go over to the clubhouse and fuck a few of the whores till I was sated. No drama that way. Maybe I could scare her off and she'd leave on her own accord. Although, if she did do that, I had no fucking clue what the FBI would do with me. Or Eagle and Mac. Fuck, this whole thing was such a bloody, fucking mess.

Yet despite all that, my cock was still hard and throbbing for attention from the woman laying beneath me.

Flick

"I don't do relationships. Ever. Never have, and I didn't plan to ever start. Now, you want to pretend like we're in one. Several problems with that, luv. Most pressing at this moment is my need for sex. I like it, like to have it real regular. As in, a few times a day. Up to now, I haven't been real fussy about who provided it. You want to be all exclusive and shit? Then you need to agree to keep my beast fed well. Are we clear?"

I blinked up at the mountain of man who had me caged against this hard desk. What was he playing at? I needed to figure out what was really going on here, because from all I'd learned, Taz was a man-whore. He was telling the truth that he liked sex, but him suddenly demanding it a few times a day, every day? What the fuck was up with that? Surely he didn't normally spend all day, every day at the clubhouse working over the whores there. And honestly, this whole spiel felt more like a wounded pride speech. I'd seen him when he'd come storming in earlier, he hadn't been a happy man. I pretended to not see him until he'd had a chance to drink at least half his beer, hoping that would have settled him down some. Then when I did approach, I'd almost convinced myself he'd reject me then and there, publicly ending things before they really began. And that had cut deep. Deeper than it should have. So I'd slid up to him and tried to prevent it.

And now, for my efforts, I was flat on my back with a horny caveman looming over me.

I frowned up at him, trying to work out how in the hell to defuse this situation.

"I like you Taz. Well, I like you when you're not busy trying to be a dick. You know you're fantastic in bed, it's not like it's a hardship to be fucked by you." I tried to sound casual, like I wasn't really more than a little interested in this man. "And maybe when this assignment is all done and dusted, we can stay together and see where this thing between us goes."

A sparkle lit his eyes for a moment. "So, that's a yes to you keeping my beast fed, then? Good."

Such a fucking man, he was choosing to ignore most of what I said, but then his mouth was on mine and I suddenly didn't give a damn. Tearing his mouth away, he stood up and opened his belt and his jeans. Slipping his wallet out, he grabbed a condom and suited up in record time.

"You wet for me, kitty?"

Since I couldn't talk as I watched him stroke that big, pierced cock of his, I nodded. My thong was more than damp. In fact, I could actually smell the musk of my arousal in the air around us. I probably should be embarrassed, but before I could think that one through, he was pushing the material of my thong aside and sliding that big cock of his in deep.

His groan echoed around the room, while, with a gasp, I arched my back up off the desk. He gripped my hips and pulled me toward him, so he slid balls deep on the first stroke.

"Fuuuck, you feel so good."

"Uh huh."

With that he started pounding into me, pulling me down on each stroke. Needing something to hang onto, I reached over my head to grip the edge of the desk. The movement pushed my breasts up and his gaze locked onto them. A moment later, he released my hips to shove up my tank and flick open the front clasp of my bra. A feral smile flashed over his face as he took hold of my hips again and went back to his deep thrusts. Now unbound, my breasts bounced with every stroke and his gaze stayed glued on them.

"Put your feet up on the edge of the desk and keep hanging on. Gotta get my hands on your tits but don't want to stop fucking you deep to do it."

With a nod, I shifted my feet up, using the edge of the desk to knock my shoes to the floor, before I rested my heels on the desktop. It opened me up further and his next thrust was the deepest yet and had me moaning. Loudly. Pretty sure they would have heard that one out in the bar.

"Good girl. Now, scream for me. Let every fucker out there know you're mine and I'm doing you right."

He reached up and gripped both nipples and gave them each a twist at the same time. The pain shot through my system, straight down to my pussy where he was still thrusting in deep, hitting all sorts of nerves with that piercing of his. After several more strokes, and the second vicious twist of my nipples, I did as he'd requested. I came hard, screaming out his name as my entire back lifted up off the timber desk top. Vaguely, I felt his palm run up under my back and lift me up. My feet slipped from the desk as his second hand cupped my ass and pulled me tight against him as he continued to fuck me. I tilted my pelvis into each thrust while he took my mouth with his. He now had a hand wrapped in my hair and he used it to keep my face tilted so he could kiss me deeply.

By the time he shuddered and came I was a limp mess. Lifting me against him, he moved to sit on the couch, keeping his cock inside me.

"Fuck, babe. I lose my head whenever I get near you."

"Uh huh."

It was all I could say, he'd worn me out so completely. I snuggled in against his chest, pushing the leather of his vest aside to get closer to his skin. His t-shirt was thin and I could feel his heat through it easily. I rubbed my cheek with a small sigh as his hands trailed up and down my body.

After a while he cleared his throat, but didn't stop stroking my skin.

"Guess, we should get you cleaned up and back to work. If you're serious about doing this thing, you need to move in with me. I'm not gonna spend half my bloody time trying to track you down when I need you. Understand?"

His words were like pouring cold water down my spine. Shifting my hips so his dick slid free of my body, I moved off his lap and stood. I didn't turn away as I readjusted my thong. Which was now wet enough to be uncomfortable, but there was fuck all I could do about it right now. Then I refastened my bra, pulled down my shirt, then straightened my skirt. All the while I held his gaze, glaring fire at him.

"I'm not some whore who's only here for you to fuck, Taz. I take my job here at the bar seriously, and I will be doing other work when I'm not here. No way will I *ever* be the kind of woman who'll sit at home, just waiting for her man to come fuck her to give her a purpose. So, don't ever let that fucking thought even enter your mind again. Am I clear?"

He raised an eyebrow at me, before he silently and calmly reached over to the side table to grab a tissue, then dealt with the condom. After he'd tossed the tissue into the trashcan near the couch, he zipped himself up. I tried to not think about the placement of those two items and how many couples had fucked on that couch just like we had and needed the trashcan and box of tissues so close. I went over to him, and mimicking his pose from earlier, I put a hand on the couch on either side of his head and leaned in close. I had no fucking idea if this room was bugged so I whispered in a low voice.

"I'm here as your equal. As a fully trained agent. As a female, I can't get into the MC like you can, so you're taking lead, but don't forget for even a minute, that I am not beneath you."

He gave her a panty-melting smirk.

"I don't know, kitty, you seem to do pretty damn well being beneath me."

With a growl, I thumped him lightly on the shoulder before turning to stalk out of the room. I was so over his attitude. However, I didn't make it out of the office. I didn't even make it to the door before I had his arms—his thick, strong, masculine arms—wrapping around me to pull me back against him.

"Don't you dare throw me again."

I shook my head with a laugh. "I won't. I didn't mean to last time. Scout had forced me to have my back to the room, so I was on edge already, then you surprised me. I really did just follow my instincts. I truly am sorry about it."

He chuffed. "Yeah, sure you are. Anyhow, I'm serious about you moving in, and not just so I can fuck you whenever I feel like it. It'll be easier to keep up with each other's intel, and other stuff too. Also, I live between Mac and Eagle. Neither of their old ladies know about our connection to the feds, so you need to keep quiet around them with it. But it won't raise any eyebrows if Mac and Eagle are hanging out at my place."

Some of my anger lifted and I softened against him. He started rubbing his palms up and down my arms and more of my anger dissipated at his gentle touch.

"You could have led with that explanation, you know?"

He nibbled up my ear. "Nah, than I would have missed out on you throwing your little snit. You're fucking adorable when you're riled up, babe."

I stiffened, ready to give him another mouthful when he chuckled low near my ear.

"As cute as it is, I wouldn't recommend you throw another snit right now, kitty. Or I'll have you bent over that couch with my cock back inside you. Then Nitro will be shitty with us both."

"If you get me fired, I will revoke the 'no throwing you again' thing."

With a laugh he reached past me, unlocked the door and opened it. Then he gave my ass a tap as I walked out.

Infuriating man.

I finger combed my hair down as we walked down the hallway. When we came out, the place was a lot busier and I rushed to help out at the bar. Nitro gave me a smirk.

"Feeling refreshed, sugar?"

"Something like that."

My cheeks burned hot when he started laughing, along with several others around him. Guess Taz got his wish and they all knew he'd done me right. Bastard.

Chapter 10

Taz

After sending a quick message off to Mac and Eagle, I left the bar and headed home. If I stayed, I knew I'd be dragging Flick back to the office every chance I got and then Nitro might really fire her, or kick me out on my ass. It was better for all if I just left now. Plus, it gave me a chance to chat with my brothers.

The ride home helped clear my head from Flick, because damn that woman was like some kind of super-addictive drug that knocked down my brain function to only cover the bare basics. By the time I parked my bike in the garage and headed into the house, Eagle and Mac were waiting on my back deck for me. I grabbed a few bottles of beer on my way out there to join them.

"Your women coming over too?"

They both shook their heads. "Pregnancy makes for early nights. Apparently growing a tiny human sucks the life out of the mother."

With that comment, Mac swallowed half his bottle in one go.

Eagle chuckled. "It gets better, slightly. But yeah, this late is well past bed time for my girl too. We're free to talk about whatever you want, brother."

While the first part of that comment was directed to Mac, Eagle had held my gaze for the last part. Following Mac's lead, I downed half my beer in one go.

"We all knew we couldn't get away with just ignoring them, right?"

Mac cursed low before speaking. "Spill it, brother. What are we looking at?"

"Flick's one of them. Says they know you two are lost to them, but apparently they still have hope for me. They sent her in to be my partner. And being my girlfriend is the way they recommended she go, so she set up a couple of *meetings* where the club would see us together to give it some weight."

"So she played you."

"Yeah, Eagle. She fucking played me like a damn fiddle."

I scrubbed my palm over my head, then with a sigh, drained the rest of my beer.

"What do they want from you? Do they still want info on the Charons?"

Before I answered Mac, I went and grabbed us another round of beers from the kitchen fridge. I honestly had no fucking clue what to do with this situation. Because every time I got near Flick, I lost my fucking head. After handing the cold bottles around, I sat back down.

"Keep in mind she told me this shit this morning. Before we had church." I paused again to take a mouthful of beer. "Seems the feds have worked out that all three of us have settled in here and won't rat on our club, but they also know that the Satan's Cowboys have taken an interest in the Charons lately, and the feds want the Cowboys."

Eagle blew out a breath. "Fuck, man."

Mac's gaze narrowed. "What did she threaten if you refuse?"

"We'll all get arrested, our covers will be blown, and the club will be told we were here to report on them. Basically, reading between the lines, they'll lie through their teeth to someone who'll get word to Scout or Bulldog that we ratted on the Charons, and all three of us will end up in the ground."

Mac's fingers went white with how hard he gripped the bottle in his hand. "This is all total bullshit. So much for the FBI being the fucking good guys. They'd throw us under the bus like that?"

Eagle shifted in his seat. "Honestly? After that shit they pulled with the mob? Then again with Zara? I'm sadly not surprised they would. Just because we're Marines who risked our asses to keep America safe, doesn't give us any kind of special treatment from the Bureau."

I scoffed as I remembered something else Flick had told me. "Flick said our old handler was dirty, that he was the leak. And that he's been missing since all that shit went down with the Iron Hammers. Seems the bloke's been missing for three months now."

Mac laughed and took another drink. "Yeah, and the feds had just the one leak. Load of bullshit. But seriously, what the fuck are we gonna do here?"

I shrugged. "Not much to decide, really. We need to keep our ears to the ground and if we hear something we can pass on that won't come back and bite us in the ass, I'll pass it on. But if this gun shit goes through, I'm gonna be in the fucking firing line. No pun intended. If I buy out Gus, and we start handling guns for the Cowboys through the back of the shop, it's my neck on the fucking block if the feds bust it wide open." I took another swig of my beer. "Oh, and I've told Flick she needs to move in with me if she's serious about this partner thing."

That final statement was greeted with silence. I glanced at my two best friends and they were both staring at me with their mouths wide open.

"What the fuck, you two?"

Eagle winced, then ran a hand through his long black hair that declared his Native American heritage loud and clear. "We all know she doesn't have to move in to make this shit work. You forget how long we've known you, brother. You don't do live-in lovers, and I can't see you taking one on willingly just because Uncle Sam suggested it. What's really going on between the two of you?"

When I stayed silent because I couldn't fucking work out how to answer, the pair of them started chuckling, so I growled at the bastards.

"Quit fucking laughing. It's all your bloody fault, anyway."

I continued to sip my beer as my two mates laughed their asses off at me. Just as I was contemplating turning the hose on them, Mac settled down enough to speak again.

"Wait. So it's our fault you want to settle down? Like it's contagious or some shit? And you just grabbed the first available female once the feeling hit? Because, if that were the case, you'd have shacked up with one of the club whores already. You've got all of them addicted to your cock at this point. Crook your finger and you'd have them falling over themselves to be your old lady."

Eagle slapped his thigh. "I know what it is! He's into her because she put him on his ass. You're such a masochist. It got you all up in knots when you finally met a woman who didn't trip over your shit to suck your dick, but instead—literally—put you on your ass."

That set them both off again and I sighed. What was the saying? Something about with friends like this, who needs enemies?

"Fuck off, the pair of ya."

With that I stood and went to the hose hanging neatly near the tap at the edge of my porch. Turning it on, I sprayed my supposed buddies.

"Pick on me in my own fucking house, while drinking my beer, will ya?"

Now I was the one laughing as I watched the pair of them jump up and run for their own homes, screeching like a pair of bloody galahs. Storing the hose, I headed for the door. A check of my watch told me it was still hours from Flick finishing her shift at the bar. Once I had the empties in the bin and the back door locked up, I decided to head to bed. I'd gotten very little sleep the past two nights and with all the alarms I had rigged up around my house, I'd get woken the moment Flick came anywhere near me. That, and if she did turn up, I was going to need some energy to deal with her.

And fuck her again. I shook my head. I really needed to quit thinking about that woman's pussy. It was dangerous and it could get both me and my cock in some deep trouble.

Taz

As I woke to the sound of my phone ringing and an empty bed, my mood went south because Flick hadn't made it. Damn woman. After a glance at the screen, I answered the call.

"Yeah, Scout, what's up?"

"Looks like you're in for a busy day, brother."

At Scout's gruff voice, I forgot all about Flick and where she wasn't.

"Why? What's going on?"

"Gus got rushed to hospital last night. One of the doctors down there is a friend of the club, and he's just called me to give me the head's up."

That had me sitting up straighter. "What's he in for? I thought we had more time than this?"

"It was a heart attack, could have been natural. Either way, I need you to get down here to the clubhouse asap. Doc told me his next of kin is a niece who lives up in Dallas. She's already at the hospital. Now, what's the bet, the last thing she'll want to deal with is a gun range and shop for the next few weeks while he recovers? So, I've had the lawyers do up some forms for her to sign. We don't want you to go pissing off the authorities, so you can run things for Gus until he's back on his feet. You go in as though you're just helping the man out, because that's what friends do, right?"

"Ah, yeah. Sure. I'll be over to the clubhouse in a bit. Just let me get cleaned up, since you want me out in public and all."

I hung up and headed to the bathroom, all the while wondering how the fuck the Cowboys could have caused a man to have a fucking heart attack. Coincidences were rarely just that, and this was a fucking huge one.

Once dressed, I rode over to the clubhouse. Clearly, Scout didn't want me to take my time as he basically handed me the folder with the documents in it and shoved me back out the door. Not that I minded, I wanted to go see Gus and if he was able to speak, I wanted to have a chat with him. I wasn't overly looking forward to dealing with the niece. In all the chats I'd had with Old Gus, he'd never once mentioned any family. Mind you, neither had I, so I guess it's not that surprising I didn't know anything about his.

Imaginary smoke tickled my nose as I pulled up to the hospital. Happened every damn time I had to go into one. Memories of the ER in Melbourne where the doctors had had to sedate me, because when they'd announced that Grace was dead I'd completely lost my shit. I'd destroyed several machines by the time the nurses and docs had contained me that day.

Storing my helmet, I scrubbed a palm over the back of my neck. There were just fourteen days until the twentieth anniversary. Two short weeks until the nightmares and flashbacks would, hopefully, ease for another year. Fuck. I totally understood why Silk chose to disappear off the grid for a few weeks each year around 9/11. Since she'd been orphaned in the attacks, she didn't want to see any media or sympathetic faces for that time, which I could respect. Because if I could, I'd do the same damn thing each April. Find some cabin in the woods, just like Silk's, drink myself into a coma and not come out in public again until well past the anniversary. But my situation wasn't the same as Silk's. It wasn't the public I needed to avoid to make it all go away, it was the shit inside my fucking head that did me in each year. And if I did manage to drink myself into a coma, what's the bet I'd then be stuck in some kind of flashback hell I'd be too drunk to get out of?

With a growl and a shake of my head, I forced those thoughts aside, and strode into the hospital. With a strong leash on my emotions, I took a step toward the admissions desk, but stopped short. Who the fuck was I supposed to ask for? Gus, or his niece? Who I didn't have a fucking name for. Scout had said Keys could have found the name, but it would take time and that was something he didn't think they had. With a huff, I decided I'd just have to hope wearing my Charon MC colors got me past the red tape I shouldn't be allowed to bypass.

With my most charming grin, I strolled up to the counter and waited until the pretty young nurse turned toward me.

"Hey, luv, a good friend of mine, Gus Shell, got brought in last night with a heart attack. I was wondering if you could tell me if he's out of ICU yet?"

For a few seconds she just stood there in a daze. Maybe I shouldn't have thickened my accent quite so much. Normally, the whole Aussie drawl thing worked like a charm, but sometimes people would pretend like they couldn't understand what I was saying. I cleared my throat and tried not to laugh as she snapped out of her trance and typed into her computer.

"Ah, let's see. Um, are you family? Sorry, I didn't catch your name."

I gave her another big smile. "Name's Taz. So, is he going to be okay?"

She shook her head, not missing the fact I'd not answered the family question.

"Sorry, I can't tell you that if you're not family."

Clearly she wasn't going to bend the rules for me easily.

"Listen, I'm not family by blood, but Gus and I are good mates. His niece is with him, right? I've got some paperwork that I need to pass on to her, for Gus's business. Hate to see him lose everything while he's in here."

The woman's gaze trailed over me again, catching on the patches on my cut.

"C'mon, luv. Give me five minutes to see how Gus is doing, get either him or his niece to sign this stuff. Then I'll be out of your hair because I'll need to go open his shop for him."

A doctor came up behind the woman, looked me over briefly before turning toward the woman.

"What's going on here?"

"Ah, this gentleman wants to have a quick visit with Mr. Shell, to speak with Ms. Vaughn..."

She blushed and cut herself off. Clearly she shouldn't have said the niece's name out loud in front of a stranger, and it was also obvious this doctor made the girl nervous. I put out my hand to the doctor, shaking his hand briefly.

"Hey there, doc, name's Taz. I'm good mates with Old Gus, and I've arranged to have his shop and range looked after while he's recovering. I just need a signature or two from him, or his niece, if he isn't up to it. Also, wouldn't mind laying eyes on the man, to see how he's doing. If that's okay, I won't take long."

I held up the folder of papers to prove my point. The doc focused on my cut with a frown for a few moments.

"Gus is a good man, and he doesn't deserve to lose his livelihood while he's receiving treatment. I'll take you back to him and give you ten minutes, then you're out. Don't make me regret it."

Relief had my shoulders relaxing. "Thanks, mate."

With that, I followed the doc through a pair of doors. While trying to figure out why the name Vaughn seemed so familiar, I shot Scout a text as we walked, to let him know I'd gotten through and was on my way in to see Gus. We stopped outside a room with a large window, the blinds were half drawn so I couldn't make out who was inside.

"Wait here, please."

"Sure thing, doc."

I moved to look around his body as he opened the door and stepped inside. Who I saw had me cursing under my breath.

"Oh fuckin' hell, you've got to be kidding me."

This shit just got a whole helluva lot more complicated.

Chapter 11

Flick

I winced as I glanced past the doctor through the doorway. Not that I doubted whose voice I'd heard.

"I don't have to let him in, Felicity."

I waved him off. "No, it's no problem. I know Taz, um, quite well. I just wasn't expecting him here, that's all."

With a nod the doctor left the room and Taz prowled in, closing the door behind him.

"What the ever loving fuck, Flick?"

Yeah, I felt like asking him the same thing.

"Hey, Taz. Um, how did you know I'd be here?"

His gaze flicked to the bed where my Uncle Gus lay sleeping after his bypass surgery.

"I spend a lot of time out at the range with Gus. When I heard he'd been brought in last night I came to see how he was doing. Scout told me his niece was here, but he didn't know her name. Won't take him long to find out though, and when he sees it's you, shit's gonna hit the fan. The hospital has you as Felicity Vaughn, while your

ID says you're Felicity Abbott. Not good, babe. That shit'll come bite you on the ass sooner rather than later."

Blowing out a breath, I ran my fingers through my hair. I needed to call Greg, to somehow get them to change my name on the records here at the hospital. Fuck it all to hell. I hadn't even known Gus was here in town!

"I know. I need to make some phone calls. I didn't know he was here in Bridgewater, nor did I know he had me listed as his next of kin. None of this was something I could have planned for."

"You need to stay here now? Or can you come back to my place with me? Be better to talk there. Safer."

I glanced over at my sleeping uncle. "Yeah, I can go. I'll tell them to call me on our way out. C'mon, it's damage control time."

After giving my uncle a kiss on the cheek and whispering to him that I'd be back, I turned and followed Taz out of the room. I found the nurse in charge and told her I needed to go deal with some stuff but would be back later. She promised to call me if anything changed, and then I found myself being guided from the hospital by Taz, out toward his bike.

"I'll follow you in my car." I could see in his face he was about to start arguing, so I held up my palm. "No. I need to be able to leave if something happens with my uncle."

He frowned, then sighed. "Fine, but if you're not right behind me the whole way, I will come after you. Understand?"

"Yeah, I hear you."

I went to step away, but his hand snapped out and caught my wrist. He dragged me in against him before I could twist free. Then his lips were on mine, and I forgot all about trying to escape. By the time he ended the kiss, I was leaning against him and trying to chase his lips as he pulled back.

"Dammit, you make me lose my head, woman. We'll work this shit out. Probably best if you quit the bar and pull out of this assignment while you can, though. Keys will find out your real name, and there'll be hell to pay."

Taking a step back, I straightened my shirt and pushed my hair back behind my ears. "Which is why I need to get to your place soon, so I can make some phone calls about altering my name in the hospital records."

With a nod, Taz released me and I made a beeline for my car. The sooner I could ring Greg, hopefully, the sooner this could all be sorted out and I wouldn't have to leave. So far Taz hadn't mentioned anything about my real last name, so I was still hopeful he hadn't worked out I had anything to do with my brother. Vaughn wasn't that common of a name, but maybe Taz hadn't known my brother's real name, just his handle. Because as much as I wanted to quiz him about my brother, now wasn't the time. Nope, what I needed to do now was deal with my name being changed, then figure out why the hell the club was so interested in my uncle. Because Taz had said Scout had told him about Uncle Gus being in hospital, which meant it was club business.

Bridgewater was small enough of a town it didn't take long to get anywhere and within fifteen minutes I was pulling up behind Taz's bike at his house. Pushing aside all my worries, I hopped out and silently followed the man inside. The moment the door was shut I had my phone out and was dialing my boss.

"Cave."

"Vaughn here, boss. I have a situation."

"Let me have it."

"I've hit something unexpected. My uncle, who I didn't realize lives in Bridgewater, had a heart attack last night and had me listed as his emergency contact. So, I'm currently listed at the hospital here as Vaughn, not Abbott. And my uncle has the interest of the Charons. Taz came to the hospital to check on him, not expecting to find me there. Is there any way to have my name changed in the system over there?"

"Dammit. I'll get on it and have it changed. I didn't know you had an uncle?"

"Long story, he's technically a half-uncle. I won't bore you with the family drama behind it."

"So, I'm guessing you have no idea why the club is interested in him?"

"Not yet. I'll report in when I do know."

"Right. Well, go find that out and I'll deal with fixing your cover before it blows wide open. Watch your back down there, Vaughn."

"Yes, sir."

Hanging up, I pocketed the phone and with a groan, scrubbed my face with my palms. What a fucking mess.

"Wanna bore me with the family drama behind you having a half-uncle?"

With a sigh, I turned to face Taz. Taking in his stance, I didn't think *no* was really an option.

"Only if you'll tell me what the club's interest in him is, and only if we can do it with beer." I frowned. "Just one, since I'll probably need to be driving later. But a nice, cold beer would go down real well right about now."

With a chuckle he gave me a nod. "Follow me, babe."

I followed him through to his kitchen where he retrieved two bottles of beer from the fridge, before leading me over to a table.

"Ladies first. Then I'll tell you why the Charons are interested in Old Gus."

Taz popped the lids off the bottles and I took a long drink before I started to speak.

"My mother's father cheated on his wife. The result of the affair was Gus. Grandpa Vaughn was a bastard. I never liked him, even as a child I avoided him. According to my mother, she'd had no clue she wasn't an only child until Gus turned up on their doorstep one day. His mother had died in a car wreck and while going through her things, he found his father's identity. Poor kid was sick with grief and simply looking for some family connection, and instead got a door slammed in his face. He'd just turned eighteen the month before, so at least he didn't have to deal with foster care or anything like that. Anyhow, my Mom had been eavesdropping on the conversation and when she realized her dad was going to shut him out, she took off. Got a wad of cash from somewhere and was out the back door before anyone could stop her. She chased Gus down and gave him the money, told him she'd help him however she could. He thanked her and told her he'd write, then he was gone."

Pausing to take another drink, I watched Taz's reaction. His jaw had gone tight and his eyes glazed over with ice. Had that happened to him as a teen? When he'd been shipped to the US from Australia after losing his parents. Had he been shut out of his new family?

"It was a while before he wrote. He'd signed up for the Army, just in time to go to Vietnam. They corresponded while he served. Then after he got back, he disappeared for the most part. He'd turn up on our doorstep every now and then, but we never knew where to find him. I honestly had no idea he was here in Bridgewater, or what he was doing here. I've also got no clue as to why he's listed me as his emergency contact."

Taz

I'd never realized how much I had in common with Old Gus. I knew why he'd listed Flick. No doubt, on one of those random visits, Flick had sat down with him and gave him some fucking affection and care. Because I'd been in Gus's position myself. But I hadn't been eighteen and able to walk away. Nope, I'd been forced to push through that fucking slammed door.

I could vaguely hear Flick's voice, but I wasn't tracking her words, not now the memories were bubbling up. My chest tightened like it had on that day when child services had picked me up from the airport and taken me to my new home. Fuck, I'd been a scared, fucking thirteen year old kid, one that had just buried my mum and sister. The thought of sweet little Gracie dead and cold in the ground still made my eyes sting. It wasn't fair. That Mum and Grace were dead while that fucking bastard was alive. He was still in jail doing hard time for setting that fucking fire after strangling my mother, but he was fucking above ground. And that shit wasn't right.

"Children are to be seen, not heard. And I'd prefer it if I didn't see you either."

I shook my head, trying to dislodge the memory of the words my Aunt Pam had said so often. She'd first lost her parents to illness, then her baby brother, my father, died while off at war. By the time I was dumped on her doorstep, she'd had no love left to give. She'd been cut too deep to heal. As an adult I understood that, but as that thirteen-year-old boy who'd just lost everything, all I'd seen was a door slammed in my face. I'd needed some fucking compassion, some comfort, but all I'd gotten was cold hard reality. Aunt Pam had taken on the family ranch and worked hard to keep things running. From day one, I was put to work too. Only good thing I could remember about those years was working with those horses.

"Taz? Come back, babe."

Another shake of my head and I found Flick standing in front of me, between my spread thighs. Her palms reached forward and cupped my face, the warmth of her skin seeping into all the cold dark places deep within me. I closed my eyes on a shudder and she moved even closer. I widened my legs as I wrapped my arms around her to bring her in flush against me. I needed more of her, needed her to thaw me out inside. I rested my head against her chest, and she leaned down to press a kiss to the top of my head.

Fuck, this was such bullshit. I wasn't that lost kid, any more than Gus was that young man. I needed to grow a set and toughen the fuck up. I was a Marine, dammit. Not some pansy-ass, metro-sexual, bullshit man. With a growl I pushed to stand, breaking her hold on me. On a gasp she stumbled backward. Feeling like a bastard, I caught her before she could trip and hauled her back in close. Her sweet scent filled my head and I slammed my mouth down on hers, losing myself in the kiss. Yes, this is what I needed. To sate my body with hers. Then, maybe, I'd be able to think straight.

Reaching down, I attacked her pants, ripping them open before shoving them down her thighs. I didn't take my lips off hers until I was forced to so I could get her shirt off over her head. Lifting her onto the table, I moved to tear off her shoes and jeans. Her knickers went the same way. Taking her mouth again, I reached to flick open the front clasp on her bra. I palmed her tits, squeezing them, before tugging on her tight little nipples. The scent of her arousal rose up between us, and with a growl, I pushed back from her and dropped to my knees so my face was at the perfect height to make a meal out of her.

With one of her legs over each of my shoulders, I pulled her forward so her ass just hung off the edge before I set my mouth over her pussy. She was slick with cream already and I lapped it up before demanding more from her. Rubbing a thumb over her needy little clit, I drank down everything she gave me.

I rode her hard, using my fingers, tongue and teeth to send her higher and higher. She thrashed around on the table, moaning and whimpering as I pushed her body even harder. Thrusting my tongue deep, I pinched her clit and slipped a finger, slick from her juices, into her ass and was rewarded with her climax. She screamed out my name, shuddered and gushed more cream straight into my mouth. I swallowed it all down, needing her taste to fill me up.

But it wasn't enough. I needed more of her, all of her.

Rising to stand, I ripped my shirt off and shoved down my jeans, lining my cock up with her entrance. Desperate to feel her, I thrust in balls deep on the first slide, groaning as her soft channel rippled around me. Fuck, that felt good. *Too good.* Pulling out, I thrust back in.

She wrapped her legs around me, digging her heels into my ass as she moved with me. Planting one hand on the table near her head, I leaned over to take a nipple into my mouth, I suckled, then tugged on one, then the other. I kept at her until she was thrashing her head on the table. Lifting my upper body back up, I gripped her hips and thrust in deeper, but with her legs around me, I couldn't get in deep enough.

With a growl, I tugged her legs off my ass, and slipped my cock out of the warm haven of her pussy. Before she could utter a protest, I flipped her over onto her stomach and pulled her back until her feet were on the ground. Then, I lined up my cock and slammed back in. She tensed and squealed when I bottomed out, getting much deeper than earlier.

"Fuck, babe, that feels so fucking good."

With a tight grip on her hips, I began thrusting into her, hard and fast, making sure to line up my piercing over her g-spot with each stroke. Within minutes my balls were drawing up and sweat slicked her back. Her smooth ink-free skin lay before me like a blank canvas. In that moment I decided she needed some color. I'd take her down to Silky Ink and get her something kickass to break in her virgin skin. The thought of her wearing ink because I'd suggested it had my cock kicking within her, my come bursting free and filling her up.

Fuck! No condom. No fucking wonder it felt so good. I'd never taken a woman without gloving up first. Damage was done now, though, so I didn't slow down or stop. Nope, I kept sliding in and out of her hot, slick pussy, making sure I ground her clit in against the edge of the table with each stroke. As my cock twitched with the last of my orgasm, she started hers. Slipping over the edge with a scream, she gripped down on my cock like a vise. The sensitive flesh jumped back to life at the stimulation so I continued to pump gently into her as she came down from her climax. Once she went limp, I pulled free and rolled her back over. Her face was flushed with her arousal, her eyes hooded as she smiled up at me lazily.

"You're too fucking sexy for your own good, kitty."

Lifting her legs so they rested up my torso and chest, I lined my cock back up with her dripping entrance and easily slid back in. With a groan she arched her back and slapped her palms against the table.

"Tell me if this is okay, babe. If you're too sore, I'll stop. I'm not trying to hurt you here."

She shook her head. "No. Feels good. That fucking piercing is insane without a condom. I'm on the pill by the way. And I'm clean."

Holding my pelvis against hers, I let her legs slip down my arms, so her knees were hooked over my elbows, before I leaned forward and took her mouth in a deep kiss.

"I'm clean too, babe. Never forgotten to glove up before today."

Keeping her legs over my arms, I held her open and watched as my cock slid in and out of her pussy. So fucking hot. Wanting to send her over the edge again, I moved her legs back up so her heels rested on my shoulders. With a firm grip on her hips, I slid her so her ass was off the edge enough for me to reach what I was after.

Keeping one hand on her hip, I moved the other down under her. And after running my fingers around my cock to wet them, I slid my hand between her cheeks and started to play with her asshole. Fuck, I wanted to take her there.

"Ever had a man take you back here, kitty?"

She shook her head, and a grin spread over my face. "You'll take me here. Not yet, gotta work you up to that. But you'll fucking love it. You like my fingers up there, dontcha?"

I slid a finger inside her tight little hole, thrusting in as I pulled my cock out of her pussy. Keeping the rhythm up, I added a second finger in her ass.

She groaned in answer to my question, clenching down on my cock and my fingers. Damn, this woman was so fucking perfect for me.

Chapter 12

Flick

This man melted my brain. Every time he touched me, all thoughts vanished and I found myself with his dick inside me. Catnip—the man was pure Flick catnip. Not that I'm complaining. He had a very nice dick. Pierced and oh, so talented.

"Play with your tits, kitty. Tug those tight little nipples for me."

As though he controlled my body, my hands slid up over my chest to follow his instructions. The tips were so tight they ached and a whimper slipped free as I began to roll each one between a thumb and finger.

He slipped his fingers free from my ass and swiped more liquid from around his cock before pressing back in. I swear he was using three fingers now, and the stretch burned and had my arousal coiling higher. Fuck, I'd already come hard twice. But this third one that was building now was gonna knock me on my ass, I was sure of it.

I had sensation going on everywhere, so I couldn't focus on any of it. His beautiful dick was thrusting into my pussy, strong and steady, while his fingers were doing the same in my ass. My nipples were tingling and pulsing as I tugged and rolled them. Then there was his gaze. His baby blue irises held mine captive. I couldn't look away as he played my body like a fucking pro.

Then he switched things up. Instead of alternating, he thrust both his cock and his fingers in at the same time. He swiveled his hips and ground down against my clit and that was it. My climax crashed over me, blackening my vision and leaving me screaming.

When I came back to consciousness, I was flat on my back on Taz's bed, with his palms stroking me from shoulder to hip. With a shudder, I turned to look into his face.

"Hey, my little kitty, you're back."

"What about you?"

I reached up and cupped his cheek with my palm. "You went somewhere earlier, want to talk about it?"

He squeezed his eyes shut a moment before he reopened them and shook his head. "No. It's the past. It needs to stay there. You still want to know why the club's interested in your uncle?"

I knew he was trying to distract me, and I let him. Because it was clear he didn't want to go for a trip down memory lane right now. Besides, I didn't think my body could handle bringing him back again if he did. Taz was one hell of a lover, but it was hard on a woman's pussy. And ass.

"Of course I do."

"He owns a gun range and shop here in town. When we—Eagle, Mac and I—first came to town, I started hanging out down there. I find it relaxing to shoot at shit. It's like another world when I'm in the zone, shooting. The familiarity of it is calming to me." He paused and shook his head. "Anyhow, the club's been wanting to take over the facility for a while but Gus won't budge. He doesn't like the club for some reason. When Scout realized I was friendly with Gus, he asked me to see if I could get him to sell me the business. It was something I was doing slowly, you know? I really do like the man and didn't want to take his baby out from under him. But now the Cowboys have put the pressure on for us to own the place sooner rather than later."

Taz's expression went hard and I was pretty sure I knew why.

"You think they caused his heart attack somehow? I highly doubt it. His doctor has already started telling me all about the dietary changes I need to help him make. It may have worked into the Cowboys' plans, but it really is a coincidence. As far as I know, you can't create a blockage in someone's heart on purpose."

I'd started running my fingers over his chest as I'd spoken. Tracing the webs and skulls, then when I started on the name "Lola," he stiffened and grabbed my hand.

"Don't."

"Don't what? Touch you? Tough shit, Marine. I like touching you, so get used to it."

"Only the names. You're more than welcome to touch me anywhere else."

I frowned at him in confusion. "Why get the names tattooed if the mere thought of them causes you pain?"

"I'm sure you've read a file on me. You know who they are."

"Yeah, I read your file. But it was factual information, no emotion, no clues as to how you dealt with any of it. I want to know the real you, Taz. Not what some report says."

Fire flashed in his eyes as a tick started in his jaw. Maybe I'd pushed him too far, but before I could tell him to not worry about it, he started speaking.

"Lola was my mother's name. Grace was my baby sister. I was thirteen years old when I came home from school to find our house alight with them both inside. Neither made it, even though I managed to get Gracie out of the house. It was too late. So I have their names inked on my chest, near my heart. Most days I wonder why the fuck I did it, because I've barely been able to look at myself in the mirror ever since."

My heart cracked wide open for him. He might be a big, tough Marine now, but deep inside, he was still that little boy who'd lost everything in one horrific day. Taking a deep breath, I placed my palms over the names and leaned up to press my lips against his. I didn't have words to ease his pain, but maybe I could soothe him with a kiss and caress.

A phone ringing in the distance had me pulling back.

"Dammit, where did my pants end up?"

I went to roll out of bed but Taz stilled me. "I'll get it, babe."

He strolled out of the room buck-ass naked and I wasn't ashamed to say that my gaze stayed glued to the man's very fine ass the entire time. Once he was out of sight, I rolled over and screamed into the pillow. This entire situation was such bullshit. I wanted to be here, not because it was a job, but because deep down I knew the truth. I was falling in love with Taz. Who wouldn't? And now it looked like my long-lost uncle was in the mix with all this shit too. The last thing Uncle Gus needed was a fucking MC like the Satan's Cowboys after him! Or the FBI using him to set up the Cowboys. Which I knew is what would happen if I reported what Taz had just told me back to Greg. It's what I should do. Report all the facts, but for the first time in my career, I didn't fucking want to.

And really, it wasn't like I had firm information at this point anyway. Just some random gossip really. I needed to wait until I had provable facts. Yep, that's what I'd tell Greg when I next reported in, that I didn't have enough information yet. That I needed more time.

I yelped when pain flared in my ass, and I rolled over to glare at Taz, who stood there with my phone in his hand and a big smirk on his face.

"What the fuck?"

He shrugged. "You had it in the air, so I tapped it." His gaze focused in on the juncture of my thighs and heated. "Although, I can think of other things I could tap."

His cock was hard and ready to go again. Damn, did the man never wear out? He crawled onto the mattress, moving up until I was caged beneath him. Again, all my thoughts fled as he lowered and pressed his lips to mine. Then the sound of my phone ringing again had him growling and jerking away from me.

"Dammit, you make me forget myself, woman."

He handed me the phone then moved to lie beside me, resting his large palm over my belly. Seeing the hospital's number on the screen, I hit answer.

"Felicity, here."

"Ms. Vau- sorry, Ms. Abbott, this is Dr. Shaw from Bridgewater hospital. I'm just calling to update you on your uncle's condition. He continues to be stable, but we'll continue to keep him sedated through the night. I'll call again if his condition deteriorates, but I would recommend you make the most of things and get some sleep tonight. When you come in tomorrow, we'll go over what we need to do next. Of course, if you'd prefer, you are more than welcome to come in again today, but he won't know you're here."

As the doctor had spoken, Taz had begun to move his hand. Teasing little touches of his fingertips up my torso and over my breasts. It was extremely distracting. And arousing. Should I go into the hospital? Like the doctor said, there wasn't much point until they eased him off the pain meds.

"Thanks for the call, Dr. Shaw. Um, I think I will follow your advice and come in tomorrow morning. I have to work tonight, but please call me if anything changes and I'll head straight over. I'm working over at Styxx, so I'm not far away."

By the time I finished speaking, Taz had wrapped his lips around one nipple while his hand had gone south. His fingers were now swirling over my lower lips, and dipping between them, while his suckled on my left breast. It was way more distraction than I could concentrate through. I had no idea what Dr Shaw said next but I uttered a goodbye and hung up. Dropping the phone onto the bed, I closed my eyes on a moan. Any soreness I felt earlier vanished as Taz used his very skilled fingers and mouth to bring my arousal up toward another peak.

I tilted my pelvis up toward him, trying to get him to slip those talented fingers of his in deeper. He didn't take the hint, and growled at me when I did it again.

Taz

I knew I should leave her be. I'd been rough with her in the kitchen and she had to be at least a little sore, but I simply couldn't resist her. When I'd come in earlier and seen her on her front with her bare ass up in the air, it was a temptation that I couldn't turn away from. Then while she'd talked on the phone, I'd made myself comfortable and begun to pet her. Naturally, that had led to me having my mouth full of her flesh and my hand between her legs. I did my best to keep my touch light. I didn't want her so distracted, she couldn't hold onto her conversation, but I did want to have some fun with her. Learn her body, where all her sensitive spots were.

She hung up the phone and spread her legs as she thrust her hips up toward me again. I gave her a growl at her obvious attempt to get me to push my fingers deep inside her. Fuck, I'd like nothing more than to bury myself deep within her again. But I didn't want to hurt her.

"Stop teasing, Taz!"

I released her breast from my mouth and gave it a small bite.

"Stop demanding what you can't handle. I was rough on you downstairs, no way can you take me again without hurting from it. So, I'm just gonna lay here and play while we chat a little."

She made this cute little growling noise. Kinda sounded like an angry kitten.

"What the fuck do you want to discuss?"

I smirked as I gave her nipple another lick. My poor baby was all wound up.

"I think you need an attitude adjustment first."

Before she could snap at me again, I sucked the tip of her breast deep into my mouth and moved my hand so I could torment the fuck out of her clit. With a gasp, her whole body tensed then she blew apart, shattering for me and filling the air with the scent of her musk.

"Hmmm. You smell so fucking good, kitty."

Shifting so I was propped up on one arm, I licked my fingers clean as she watched me with her sexy as fuck, half-closed eyes. My cock was as hard as a rock again, wanting in her. The thing didn't give a fuck that she was sore.

"Right. Time to talk. The verdict on your uncle?"

After blowing out a breath, she rolled to her side and mimicked my pose. She reached her hand for mine, linking our fingers together.

"Doc says he's holding stable but will be under heavy sedation until at least tomorrow. He suggested I not come back in until the morning. Catching up on sleep was his recommendation for my night tonight."

She was smirking at me and I shrugged a shoulder. "Yeah, doubt that's what you'll be doing tonight. So, you're still planning on going into work?"

"Well, since the doctor made a point to call me Ms. Abbott just now, I think my cover is safe."

For a few moments I stared into her eyes. How much could I trust her? How loyal to the FBI was she? Fuck, but I wished she wasn't anything to do with law enforcement. If she were just a chick I picked up and liked, this would be so much fucking simpler.

"We need to be careful what we pass onto the FBI, Flick. Gus being your uncle is probably going to expose you to extra information you shouldn't know and if you turn it all over to the feds, and they leak it?" A shudder ran through me. "The Cowboys won't give a fuck you're female, Flick. They'll snatch you off the fucking street and torture you for ratting on them."

Taking a deep breath, I tried to rid my mind of the images of her body laying broken and used, which is what they'd do to her. They'd use her until she died from the abuse.

Her soft, warm palm on my cheek had my eyes opening.

"Taz, babe, it's not like I'm defenseless. I won't be easy to take down."

I scoffed. "No, kitty. Nothing about it would be easy. They'll be so fucking hard on you."

My voice cracked on the last word. This situation was getting so fucking messy. If I didn't care for her, it would be simple. I could send her away, if only it didn't hurt to breathe when she wasn't fucking near me.

I was so screwed.

"What was the paperwork you brought to the hospital about?"

"There's two agreements. One is to give me the legal rights to run his shop and range while he recovers—basically, it's making me his manager so the authorities won't come after me or him. The other is for him to sell me the shop and range. The price is left blank, because we'd never discussed that. When we heard he was in hospital with a heart attack, we weren't sure how out of it he'd be when I got to him. The lawyers already had the sale forms drawn up at Scout's request, but added the employment ones this morning."

That had her frowning at me. "I'm not comfortable signing over his business to you, Taz. But I guess you running things for him would be okay. Can it wait till tomorrow, when he's hopefully going to wake up enough for me to chat with him?"

I gave her another one shoulder shrug. "I guess so. It's never good to have a business shut for any length of time, but he is the only gun shop and range anywhere near here so it's not like he'll lose too many customers. Just piss them off." Releasing her hand, I moved to hold her chin so her gaze held mine. "The Cowboys aren't going to try anything in the next couple of days. At this point, I'm doing this to help out a friend, not trying to get into a position that will help the MC. Understand?"

She nodded as much as she could in my grip. "Yeah. I hear you. It's just this whole thing with my uncle is more responsibility than I was anticipating I'd have on this assignment."

With a wince, I dropped her face and rolled over to get up. Dammit, I kept forgetting she was here on an assignment—that I was nothing but part of that. She spoke like she gave a fuck about me, but I couldn't allow myself to be fooled. Somehow, I needed to keep my heart separate from her.

"Right, well, we'd better get cleaned up and moving. You jump in the shower, I'll go make some coffee. I need to get to the clubhouse, and you need to get to the bar."

I kept my back to her as I pulled up my jeans, and before I could button the fly, she had her palm on my bicep. With a deep breath, I let her turn me around.

"What did I say to shut you down just now?"

I gave her a broad smile, it was fake, but hopefully she wouldn't see it that way.

"Not a bloody thing, luv. I'm good. Just got lots of shit to get done today."

She shook her head and didn't release me.

"Don't *luv* me. That's what you call women that mean nothing to you. Or when you're pissed off at me, so it's also proof I just fucked up and said something wrong. What was it?"

I shook my head. Damn woman wasn't going to let this go.

"Look, it's nothing. You just reminded me this is all nothing but an assignment to you. Like I keep proving, I lose my fucking head around you and keep forgetting that fact."

Pain flashed over her expression before she moved in until her naked body was pressed up against mine.

"You're not the job, Taz. This chemistry we have between us is insane, and it scares the fuck out of me half the time, but it's not work. I'm not here with you because of the assignment. I'm here with you because I want to be."

I caught her face between my palms, staring hard into her eyes.

"Don't fucking bullshit me about this, Flick. I've never, and I mean never, had a relationship with a woman before. I've never wanted that deep of a connection. You threw all my good intentions in the bin the second you came storming into my world. If you're serious about me not being the job, you're gonna have to fucking prove it."

A cute little frown wrinkled her forehead. "And how, exactly, would I do that?"

"When you researched for this assignment, you discover what an old lady is?"

Now she looked nervous. Good. If she agreed to this too quickly, I'd know she didn't fucking mean it.

"Yeah. A biker's old lady is like his wife."

I gave her a nod, then turned my whole world on its head by saying words I never expected to say to any woman.

"Then say yes to being my old lady, let me own you. That'll prove it."

I wasn't telling her how, as my old lady, she'd be under the protection of the entire Charon MC. Even if her cover was blown, she'd be safe.

At least I hoped she would be.

She watched me for a few moments, until my heart was racing with the thought that she wasn't going to agree. Then she twisted her face to the side, pressed a kiss to my palm and whispered the sweetest word I'd ever heard.

"Yes."

Then she shocked the shit out of me by dropping to her knees, pulling down my jeans as she did.

"Fuck, kitty."

I wrapped a hand in her hair as she wrapped her mouth around the head of my cock and sucked. Contentment at her accepting my claim on her mixed and swirled with the arousal she was now creating. There was nothing quite like having the woman you'd fallen head over heels for kneeling in front of you, buck ass naked, sucking your cock like her life depended on it.

Chapter 13

Flick

When I arrived at the clubhouse in the early evening, one full day after agreeing to be Taz's, I was more than a little nervous. I'd arrived at Styxx ready to work, but Nitro had just grinned at me and told me to get my ass over to the clubhouse. Apparently, I had the night off. I figured Taz was up to something, but Nitro refused to give me even a hint as to what.

Locking up my car, I strolled over to the front door, which was being guarded by two big men who were watching me with open curiosity. And lust.

"Who you here for, darlin'?"

"Ah, Nitro told me Taz wanted me here, so here I am."

A wide grin spread over his face. "You must be Flick, then. Head on in. He's waiting for you."

Clearly these two knew what was going on. That, or they'd heard about me dumping Taz on his ass last night. I really hated being the last to know anything, especially when it was something that affected me, so hopefully it was the later. On full alert, I stepped through the door, into the clubhouse for the first time. The room I found myself in was rather anti-climactic, all things considered, but I guess it was still pretty early for things to be overly wild. There was a bar along one wall, while the other side of the room was a mix of couches and small tables with chairs. There were a few men hanging around, but not many. I couldn't see Taz anywhere and had no fucking clue where I should go from here to find him. Figuring the guy behind the bar might know something, I headed over there but got stopped before I made it all the way.

"Hey there, darlin'."

Oh, good grief. Did every man here think they were the only ones with a southern accent? It was Bridgewater, Texas. The majority of the fucking population had the same damn drawl, me included.

"Hey, *sugar*, don't suppose you know where Taz is?"

I exaggerated my own accent to throw it back at this guy. But he didn't take the hint. With a smirk, his gaze focused over my shoulder, then he reached to put his hand on my hip.

"I wouldn't—"

The guy manning the bar didn't get to finish his warning before I'd knocked his arm to the side, grabbed it and twisted it up behind his back, so the asshole with the grabby hands was now kneeling in front of me.

"Tried to warn you, Keg. Flick put Taz on his ass over at Styxx last night. You didn't stand a chance, brother."

I glanced up at the man who'd spoken—he'd moved from behind the bar toward me. He was a huge hulk of a man and I wasn't entirely sure I'd be able to win against him. His vest had a patch on it that ironically said "Tiny".

"Flick, honey, you can let my brother go. Trust me, he won't try to touch you again."

"Damn fucking straight he won't. Bastard."

I released Keg, who scrambled to get back to his feet, where he rolled his shoulders with a wince.

"Settle the fuck down, Taz. You flirt with all the old ladies, just thought I'd give you a little payback. Somehow, I missed the story of you getting put on your ass by your own old lady, brother."

Taz had told everyone about me agreeing to be his already? Fuck, he didn't waste time.

Taz's arm wrapped around my middle and pulled me back against him. "That'll teach you for nicking off for the past week. Now you know—don't mess with my woman." He paused to press an open-mouthed kiss on the side of my throat. "Hey, kitty. So glad you decided to drop by tonight."

I scoffed. "Don't talk shit. You told Nitro to send me over here."

"Yeah, but I wasn't one-hundred percent sure you'd follow those instructions."

I shrugged. "Since Nitro gave me the night off, I didn't have anything else to do."

Taz gave me a squeeze as he barked out a laugh. "You don't fool me, my curious little kitty. I know you were dying to know why I wanted you to come here."

"I thought you weren't one-hundred percent sure I'd come?"

"I was ninety-nine point nine percent sure, babe. Now, come on through to the back. Need to introduce you around. The fool you've already met here is Keg, big guy there is Tiny."

They both nodded at me as Taz led me from the room. By the time we made it out the back door, I'd met over a dozen guys and was really grateful their vests had their names on them.

"Cuts, kitty. We call them cuts, or our colors, not vests."

Huh, must have said that out loud. "Okay, well, so long as you boys keep putting your names on them, I don't care what you call them."

Taz chuckled as he led me past a fire pit that was, no doubt, going to get a lot bigger later, over toward a couple of picnic tables. I recognized most of the people sitting at them, either from when I'd gone to Marie's Cafe or from Styxx.

Before Taz could introduce me, Silk smirked over at me. "Hey, Flick, I hear you said yes. It's all over now, you know?"

Zara laughed and came over to give me a quick hug. "We're always open to having new old ladies around the place! The testosterone is liable to get overpowering, otherwise."

She gave me a wink before she returned to sit on Mac's lap. The big, bald, tough-looking man's face instantly softened as he rested his palm over Zara's swollen belly and stroked it. It made something deep inside me ache. Weird. I'd never planned on having kids. Hadn't wanted to. I liked my life, or at least I thought I did. In a matter of days, Taz had upended everything in my world.

"Um, how did you all meet again?"

I grinned at how nervous Taz sounded as Scout stood to pull me in for a fast hug. "Your girl got curious and came down to Marie's the other day. Met us all there." He turned his attention to me. "How you doing, Flick? Guess having club protection as an employee wasn't enough, huh? Had to upgrade to an old lady."

He said it with a wink, so I figured he was trying to be funny, but I felt heat flash in my cheeks. Is that why Taz asked me? In an attempt to keep me safe? Did he not know about Scout already telling me I was under club protection due to my job at Styxx? I glanced at Taz with a raised brow. He leaned in and pressed a kiss to the eyebrow I'd arched at him. "Relax, kitty. I wouldn't have asked if I didn't want you as mine. Protection for you is just one small part of it."

He'd whispered the last part into my ear, but the others obviously heard the first few words.

"Kitty? Seriously? You're calling her a pussy? Taz, get out of the damn gutter once in a while!"

Silk's words set everyone off into fits of laughter. Once Taz recovered enough to talk, he turned to her.

"Control your woman, Eagle. Damn. I call her Kitty because she's so fucking curious about every damn thing." He pointed at Zara who was smirking and trying to not laugh. "You, shut it! *Bunny.*"

Mac rolled his eyes when I looked to him for an explanation. "I started calling Zara bunny because the woman kept running off like a scared rabbit."

"Still tattooed a playboy bunny on her for an extra reason though. Hey, Flick, want a tattoo? A cute little kitty-cat on your ass for Taz to stare at?"

My body shook with my laughter. "I don't think so. I don't have any ink, and I ain't starting by having a pussy inked on my ass."

As I predicted, that set all the men off again. Then Silk got up off Eagle's lap and pulled Zara from Mac's. "C'mon, ladies. We got food to arrange. These boys won't feed themselves!"

Scout got gruff with them for that one. "You know, we can actually. Look after ourselves, that is."

"Shut it, Scout. Marie sent over a couple pies for afterward. Don't piss them off or they won't serve them."

Before I could catch Scout's response to Mac, the two women had me between them, herding me toward the building. With a smile, I let them. I could see why Taz liked it here. This was like a big, messy, slightly crazy family. The whole place felt almost homey, with no tension or stress in the air. And everyone was being really friendly with each other. Hell, this place was easier to be in than my office at the FBI headquarters in Dallas.

I hadn't expected this. I'd figured it would be all serious gruff bikers grumbling and cursing at each other. But I hadn't seen any of that. Surprisingly, there were even a few kids running around the yard.

"So, the clubhouse is family friendly, huh?"

Silk laughed. "For now, it is. These types of parties are for the families. But once it gets dark, most of us old ladies head home. All the kids are definitely out of here. That's when the whores start to wander out of their room and begin to infiltrate the whole place. You should totally stay at least once, just to see how wild these boys can get. But not sure I'd be doing it just yet. Those bitches are gonna be pissed that you've taken their favorite toy away."

I frowned. "Favorite toy?"

"Pretty much from day one, Taz has been their favorite. His stamina is apparently legendary." She'd given me a sly side-eye look with that comment, making me chuckle.

"I'm not one to kiss and tell, but yeah. The man likes to fuck, and he's got the skills to back it up."

"Right, so you're not gonna be real popular with the club whores. I'd recommend waiting till you get your cut. At least then it'll be clear you're an old lady and most of them do understand the pecking order in this place."

"Pecking order?"

"Yeah, old ladies are the queens of this place. The club brothers are the kings, the prospects are like princes, or maybe knights?" She shrugged. "And the club whores are like the hired help. Seen but not heard, type of thing. I mean, don't get me wrong, some of them are quite nice. But some are nasty cows."

Man, maybe I should start taking notes about all these rules and shit?

"And you said when I get my cut?"

I looked at what the two women were wearing, along with the other ladies all bustling around the kitchen.

"Yeah, we get our own cuts too. But we don't wear them all the time like the men do. It takes a little bit of time to get one made up. I'm sure Taz has already ordered yours."

Zara turned and I saw the back of hers had the Charon MC logo in the middle of her back with the words 'Property of' above and 'Mac' below. Damn, but they really took the whole property thing all the way around here. I wasn't sure how I felt about being property at all, let alone *belonging* to a man. Guess since I'd already said yes, I'd better hurry up and get used to it.

Silk snickered. "You could always come down and see me at Silky Ink and I'll ink a Charon patch on you?"

"Oh, leave her alone. I'm sure you'll get her in your chair soon enough."

I focused on Silk's arm. She was inked from the wrist up to under her shirt sleeve. Large red roses with black and gray swirls and shit behind and around them. It looked pretty damn awesome to be honest. Maybe I could try a little ink...

"Thinking it would be best to start small. And that winged skull thing is not small."

Zara groaned. "Don't tell her that! Damn it. You'll have a full sleeve or something by the time she pops that baby out."

Silk nodded. "That gives us three months. Totally doable."

I felt the blood drain from my face. What the fuck just happened?

Taz

Several hours later, we'd all finished eating and it was just Scout and me sitting at the table.

"Your girl is settling in nicely."

Flick totally had. She'd slid right in with the old ladies, helping with the food. She was now inside helping clean up with the other women. It probably helped she'd met Silk and Zara before. How had I not known about that?

"Why didn't you tell me she'd come into Marie's?"

Scout laughed. "Settle down, Taz. There hasn't been time to tell you, it was only two fucking days ago."

Since I couldn't really argue with that, I took a drink of my beer instead of even trying. Things really were going way too fucking fast with me and Flick, but it felt right. Especially now she'd admitted to me she didn't see me as just part of her assignment.

"What's the word on Gus? He gonna pull through, or what?"

I tilted my head and glanced at my president. "What? Your contact at the hospital stop informing you?"

"Quit trying to rile me up, boy. The doctor down at the hospital only informs me when someone gets brought in that he thinks I should know about. Nothing more. Now, fill me in while we've got a minute alone."

"Well, like I mentioned on the phone, Flick is Gus's niece. Well, half niece. Looks like Gus was the product of an affair. Flick had no idea he was living in town before she got the call from the hospital."

Scout adjusted the ever-present bandana on his head as he spoke.

"Seems odd that she's listed as his emergency contact then, doesn't it?"

I shrugged. "Not really. Gus has no one in town. Their family doesn't seem real big, or that close."

"Okay, well, is she gonna sign things over to you, then?"

"Not without talking to him first. We're hoping he'll come off sedation tomorrow enough that he'll be able to at least understand us and give the go ahead for me to keep things open for him. I think that's about all we can expect until he's back on his feet. And honestly, this is more of a favor to a friend kinda thing. I can't see him agreeing to sell the place. Not even now he's got his health to worry about. That place is his life. Hopefully he'll sign the agreement to let me work there. If he won't even sign that, I guess we just risk the authorities coming to ask questions if they discover it's not Gus sitting out there every day. Hooking up with his niece will hopefully help. I'm not just some random, but family now."

Scout shook his head. "Cowboys won't be happy with that long-term. Fuck. I'm not sure what they're gonna pull to get the ball rolling here."

"Can't we move the shit for them some other way? Why the hard-on for the gun shop?"

"Who fucking knows? They ain't told me what's so special about the place. Maybe they just want a shop front to sell guns through for smaller orders. We're not so far from the border that Mexicans won't come up here to get what they need. And we all know Gus won't sell shit to anyone he thinks is gonna use it against Americans. Can't fault the old bastard on his patriotism to Uncle Sam."

Unease ripped down my spine. "What do you think they're gonna do next? Any chance they'll wait for him to get over his heart surgery?"

Scout huffed and took a swig of his own beer. "No idea, brother. I'll call Viper, maybe Maverick as well, tomorrow, see what I can swing. But they're not the type of MC that'll just sit back and wait. Shit will fly over this. It's a good thing you've claimed Flick. Give her some extra protection. At least, hopefully they'll honor her status as your old lady." He adjusted his bandana again. "What a fucking mess."

"Yo! Taz! Come handle your woman!"

"What's she doing?"

"Her and Tiff are getting into it in the hallway."

I had to smirk at Keg. "What? You too chicken to get between two women?"

"It's not being a chicken to know to steer clear of a woman you know can put you on your ass. You're the crazy fucker that's claimed her ass, so you can go deal with it."

Scout was chuckling as he rose beside me. "Got a good feeling about your girl, brother. She's made of the same stuff as the rest of us here. Don't take no shit from no one, including her old man. Tell me, Taz, you done with the whores now you've claimed her?"

We walked over toward the back door. "Yeah, got no interest in any pussy other than what's mine."

"Well, fuck. Guess we should encourage a few of the bitches to move on, then. Gonna have too many floating around bored without you to pound them all for us."

With a shake of my head, I flipped off my president, tossed my empty bottle in the bin, then headed in the back door with him by my side. There was a small crowd gathered about halfway up.

"What the fuck is going on here?"

Scout's voice was loud and serious. All signs of the man who'd joked with me a moment ago were instantly gone. People parted and I followed Scout through, not sure what the fuck we were about to find. I groaned when I saw my girl. Tiff was face-first against the wall, puffing like she'd just run a marathon. Flick had Tiff's arm up behind her back, while one of her own arms was braced across Tiff's shoulders. My cock jerked in my jeans. Flick's feet were in a fighter's stance and she didn't appear to be straining at all. More like she was casually dealing with an annoyance, while poor Tiff looked like she'd been fighting for her life for hours.

"Flick, wanna tell me what's going on here?"

I stayed to the side of Scout, letting the president handle shit for the moment. Once this was publicly sorted, I'd take care of my woman. How would her ass look all red from a spanking? Would she submit to it? Or would she kick my ass for even suggesting it.

Could be interesting.

Chapter 14

Flick

After what Silk and Zara had told me about the pecking order, I didn't think I was going to get into trouble for what I'd done with this little bitch. But Scout sounded seriously pissed off and I was way outnumbered by the club members who'd all come to watch the girl-fight.

Wasn't much of a fight, really. The woman I currently had pinned to the wall had come at me with all anger and no skill.

"Hey, Scout. Um, I was just heading outside when this little bitch tried to jump me. She said something about me taking what was hers. After that, I just defended myself. She's really not an effective fighter, no training. Maybe she should go down to the gym for Mac's classes?"

Scout's eyes sparked with humor, but he shook his head and frowned. "Let her go, Flick. She won't try anything else." I dropped my hold and stepped back but kept my stance light and my hands ready to come back up. "Tiff, you attacked an old lady on club property?"

The other woman shrunk against the wall, away from Scout.

"Sorry, Scout, I wasn't thinking. And…and, I didn't know she was his old lady! Please don't send me away."

With his arms crossed over his chest, Scout glared at the woman for a few moments.

"That's bullshit. Everyone here tonight knows who Flick is to Taz. It's the whole fucking reason for the party. And you know the rules, Tiff. You don't mess with the old ladies, and you sure as fuck don't start fights with them. Sorry, but you're out. Go grab your shit and head off, you're done here."

The girl's eyes went wide in shock, then narrowed and she turned on me again.

"This is all your fault, bitch!"

She flew toward me and since none of the men seemed to know what to do with her, I blocked her attack and threw her back against the wall, rougher than last time. Her face may have hit the wall—you know—just maybe.

I moved to speak straight into her ear, making sure I had a good grip in her hair so she couldn't fucking head butt me. "Don't come at me like that, bitch, unless you got the fucking skills to back your mouth up. I will put you on your ass. Every. Damn. Time. We clear?" Then I pulled back and spoke louder. "Yo, Scout? You want me to take this outside, or what?"

"Fuck me. Old ladies aren't supposed to do the fucking dirty work around here. Keys! Take Tiff and get her out of here, make sure she knows to not fucking come back. Or try any shit out in public."

"Sure, prez. Let her go, Flick. I got her."

I released her slowly, giving Keys a chance to get a grip on her before she could try anything else. Once the screaming woman was out of ear shot, I glanced up at Scout.

"Am I in shit for any of that?"

Scout readjusted his bandana, which seemed to be a subconscious habit for the man. He did it often, especially if he was thinking about something.

"I don't stand for fighting in the clubhouse, but seeing as Tiff attacked you and you were just defending yourself, you're good." He ran his gaze around the room as I took a deep breath and moved over toward Taz. "Right, back to having fun, boys and girls! Keg, can you round the whores up and give them a little reminder of the rules and make it clear that just because Flick ain't wearing a patch yet, it doesn't change the fact she's an old lady?"

"Sure thing, prez."

Taz wrapped an arm around my waist and pulled me in tight against him.

"Fuck, I love watching you in action, babe."

Before I could respond, his mouth was on mine and my thoughts turned to mush. Especially when he ground his thick erection against me.

"C'mon, kitty, come out and sit by the fire with me."

I let him guide me outside. Now that night had descended, there were no more kids running around however a few of the old ladies were still here. As we passed them, they high-fived me with a whoop or two for putting the whores in their place.

"Do those women step out of line often?"

"Not normally, and never that obviously. They all know if they break the rules, they're out, as you just saw. But they are known to glare and make the old ladies feel uncomfortable if they think they can get away with it. It's why they're not to leave that room until later, when a lot of the old ladies have gone home. They definitely aren't allowed to roam around while there's still kids here."

I nodded as Taz led me over to the fence, back from the fire. Once in the shadows, he sat, leaning against the weathered timber and indicated I sit in his lap with a wriggle of his eyebrows.

"How about you come sit on my lap, and we'll talk about the first thing that pops up?"

With a laugh I moved to straddle his lap. My skirt cut into my thighs and limited how close I could get.

"Well, we can't talk about your dick then, because that popped up some time ago."

He laughed with me, before cupping my face and pulling my mouth toward his. I braced my hands on his shoulders as he kissed the fuck out of me. Catnip. He really was my own special brand of catnip that I couldn't fucking resist.

Within moments, my body heated and I started to squirm in his lap. His hands left my face, and his rough palms glided up my thighs, pushing the material of my skirt up with them. When he had his hands on my ass cheeks, he gave each one a squeeze and pulled me in tight against him.

"I was kinda hoping Scout was gonna tell me I needed to punish you for that stunt with Tiff. Got fucking hard thinking about spanking this fine ass of yours."

I ground my rapidly dampening panties against his jean-clad dick, trying to get more friction where I needed it.

"Didn't realize you were kinky."

"I don't mind mixing things up some, keepin' it interesting."

"Explains the cuffs."

"So it does. Undo my belt, babe. Let me take you here."

I froze a moment before glancing over my shoulder. Several couples were sitting around the yard in the shadows and I could make out enough in the dim light to know they were getting busy, too. One of the picnic tables was getting put to good use. One of the club whores was naked and spread out over it face up. Scout was thrusting his cock down her throat while another man I couldn't remember the name of, was giving her pussy a pounding. Taz, stretching my tank down, and popping a boob out of my bra, had me gasping and turning back to him just in time to see him wrap his mouth around my nipple to suckle me. Arousal coursed through me and I suddenly didn't give a shit that people might see us fucking, so long as I got him inside me ASAP.

I reached for him, unbuckling his belt and unzipping his jeans. His cock broke free to greet me because Taz clearly didn't believe in underwear. I gripped him and gave him a couple strokes, playing with the piercing on each pass over the head. His hands went back to my ass, his fingers digging in to pull me closer. He released my breast so he could watch his cock as I shoved my panties aside and guided him into my core.

"Fuck, that's a sight I ain't ever gonna get tired of."

I threw my head back as I rode him. He felt so fucking good inside me, that piercing of his sliding over nerves and sensitive flesh. He released my ass to pull the other side of my tank and bra down. As I rode him, he tugged and tormented my nipples, all the while he held my gaze with his heated one.

I swiveled my hips, grinding down, so my clit got the stimulation it needed and with a whimper I hung right on the edge of climax. I could barely believe I was about to come for my man in the middle of the fucking Charon clubhouse yard. When I tightened down on his dick, he sat up with a growl. Then he leaned in to take my mouth, swallowing my screams of pleasure as he gripped my hips and slammed me down on his cock hard, again and again, until I felt his length kick within me and he filled me with his seed.

As I slumped forward against his chest, wincing when my nipples scrapped over the patches on his cut, I swore I heard him say he loved me. But I couldn't be sure, and my mind shut down, forcing me to sleep before I could ask him to repeat what he'd said.

Flick
The following morning, after finally getting away from Taz, I made my way to the hospital. I could easily see how he was a favorite with the MC's club whores. His appetite for sex was huge and I was seriously going to have to start having afternoon naps to make up for the lack of sleep every night. Adding the stress of my uncle and my assignment on top of the lack of sleep, and I was one tired woman as I entered the hospital and made my way to Uncle Gus's room. He was now out of ICU and the doctor had been hopeful yesterday that today he'd be lucid enough to be able to speak coherently. I hoped he was right. I was going to have to make a call on his shop and range soon if he didn't wake up enough to give his opinion. With how little I knew the man, I wasn't comfortable making any huge decisions for him. Not with his business. With his health, it was easy. I basically just agreed with whatever his doctor suggested.

Rubbing the back of my neck, I walked into my uncle's room, focusing on the bed. I should have known better. With all my training, I should have scanned the room first for any threats. It didn't matter how safe it should have been. The barrel of a handgun pressing against my ribs as I stepped toward the bed reminded me of that fact.

"Don't try anything, darlin'. And not a word outta that pretty mouth of yours. I'd hate to have to shoot you here in front of your uncle, but I will if I have to."

Damn it all to hell. I tried to think of a way to get away from the gun, and the hand that gripped my forearm on the opposite side. But with the barrel digging into my side, I couldn't think of how without him having time to pull the trigger. Licking my suddenly dry lips, I glanced around. Three big bikers stood around the room, their cuts looked similar to Taz's but not the same. As the one holding me guided me toward the back of the room, another man stepped forward, showing me the large patch on his back along with the words 'Satan's Cowboys'. Dammit. He crowded in beside my uncle's bed, clearly trying to be as scary as possible. For the first time, I noticed my uncle was awake, his skin was pale and he clearly wasn't well, but he was awake and lucid.

"So, Gus, as I was saying before little Felicity arrived, we need you to sign over your property. However, you told me to go get fucked. That doesn't sound like a man who's motivated to do the right thing now, does it? So maybe, we'll take your niece with us and have some fun while you think about things. I'll come back in a day or two with the paperwork for you to sign, if you're a good boy and sign like I ask you too, we'll set her free. Understand?"

"Fine, I'll sign it over, just leave her be. She's got nothing to do with any of this shit."

Tears pricked my eyes that he'd throw down for me like that. We barely knew each other, yet he was going to sign over his shop and range—which from what I'd heard, he loved—to keep me safe. Fuck, I wish this bastard holding me would lower his weapon. A few seconds. That was all I needed.

"Then she'll be free and clear soon enough. For now, she's with us."

Clearing my throat, I spoke up. "Can I at least say goodbye to him?"

The big guy who'd spoken to my uncle rolled his eyes but nodded. "Fine, but don't try anything. You've got two guns trained on you and these boys are looking for an excuse to shoot."

Glancing to my right I saw the second gun, held steady on me by a younger man who smiled like he was the devil. Yeah, that one would enjoy putting bullet holes in a person. I quickly slid to my uncle's side, leaning in to kiss his cheek and whisper to him. "Call Taz. Please." Then louder I said. "Love you."

The look in his eyes cut me down to my soul. Such pain. "You hang on, I'll find a way to get you outta there."

"Right, enough. Let's get outta here before a nurse decides to call the fucking cops or something."

Blinking back tears of both frustration and fear, I let those bastards lead me out of the hospital to a car. Guess they'd planned to snatch me all along. From what I'd seen, bikers didn't like to be shoved in a car. I glanced around the parking lot, hoping Taz would ride in and save me, but there was no sound of a Harley roaring, just a couple of cars that I knew wouldn't get involved with bikers.

Fuck. Today was gonna suck.

"Time for you to have a nap, darlin'"

"What? No!"

I went to twist free but before I could, pain exploded through my skull.

Chapter 15

Taz

I was in the office at the gym with Mac when my phone rang. Seeing the hospital number, I answered with a frown. Normally Flick rang from her mobile.

"Flick? That you?"

"Ah, no, this is a nurse. I'd, ah, I'd rather not give my name. Gus Shell asked me to call you with a message. Three Cowboys came and took Flick. Lead man's name patch said Animal."

Instantly I was on my feet and on full alert. "When? When did they grab her?"

"About an hour ago—"

Fury burst through me. "And you're just calling now? Have you any idea what those fucking bastards will do to her?"

"I'm sorry, but we had to stabilize Mr. Shell first before we could call you. His health is our first priority."

"Tell him I'm on it."

I hung up and dialed Scout straight away. Mac was on his phone calling in Eagle. We might be with the

Charons now, but the three of us would always have each other's backs no matter what, and Mac knew from the little he'd heard of my conversation that shit had gone down.

"Scout, here."

"Cowboys made their fucking move. Snatched Flick from the hospital an hour ago."

"Fuck! Get a name? Who told you?"

"Gus got a nurse to call me, said Animal was lead. You know him?"

I didn't know many of the Cowboys, just the few that had come down last year when we were dealing with the shitstorm the Iron Hammers had brought our way. Animal hadn't been in that group.

"Fuck! Dammit to hell. I haven't had a chance to speak with Viper or Maverick yet, they don't know she's yours. Listen, I'll get Keys on pulling video from the hospital parking lot, see if we can work out what vehicle they're in. I'll get Bulldog to start calling all the brothers in while I call Viper. You and Mac get your asses here to the clubhouse. I'm guessing you've already pulled Eagle in?"

"Yeah, Mac's talking to him now."

"Right. See you soon."

The line went dead and as I lowered my arm, I noticed my hand shook. I never fucking shook. Next thing I knew Mac was in my face, a palm on each of my shoulders.

"We'll get her back, brother. Remember who she is. That woman of yours will kick their asses the first chance she gets."

I stared into my friend, my brother's, eyes. "So how the fuck did they get her in the first place, then?"

"At a guess, it was either at gunpoint or they knocked her out."

I growled and Mac gave me a shake. "Calm the fuck down, so we can get moving. We will get her back. Should you be telling the feds about this?"

I shook my head. "Not yet. They come barging in, her cover will be blown to hell and the Cowboys are more likely to kill her."

Mac nodded. "Good point. Okay, let me get changed real fast, then we'll head over to the clubhouse. Fucking wait for me, understand? Let me guard your back with this shit."

The whole time it took Mac to change I paced the front of the gym. My mind was flashing all sorts of nasty images at me, some memories of what Gordon had done to my mother, others from what I'd seen over in the Middle East. If anyone had hurt my woman like that, I'd take them all out. I'd been the best sniper the USMC had, and I'd use my skills to take out each and every Cowboy who'd fucking dared to touch what was mine. I was pretty sure Gus would supply me with whatever ammo and weapons I needed for the task.

"C'mon, brother. Chip's gonna keep the gym covered. Let's ride."

Eagle was on his bike waiting out the front for us, and with a nod, we saddled up and followed him over to the clubhouse.

The parking lot was rapidly filling up with bikes and cars as everyone came running from whatever they were doing. I ignored them all and went straight for Scout's office. No tech was allowed in the meeting room where we held church, so I was fairly certain he wouldn't be in there yet. Sure enough, I found Keys and Scout staring at a laptop.

"What've you got for me?"

Keys flicked his gaze up over the screen to me. "They took your girl out at gunpoint, knocked her out before putting her in a black Escalade. Original, I know. I'm now trying to track its movements from the hospital while I'm waiting for the results on the plates."

I shook my head. "Plates won't make a lick of difference. The Cowboys have her, that's who'll own the damn car. Scout, you get hold of Viper?"

Scout looked every inch the MC president in this moment. Fury had his gaze hard and cold and his body tense, ready for a fight.

"No, bastards aren't answering my calls. We need to call church to agree on what to do, but I say we go for a ride. A show of force to get back what's ours."

I moved toward Keys and with a jerk, he slammed the lid on his laptop shut and stood, which was beyond fucking strange. What was he hiding from me? I flicked my gaze between the two men, frowning. "What's going on?"

"Later, brother. Let's get your girl back first, this other shit can wait till after."

I followed them back to the meeting room, not feeling at all comfortable at whatever they knew and were keeping from me. It had my instincts flaring. And not in a good way.

Flick

Blinding pain pounding inside my head woke me up. I raised my hand to examine my skull for injury before risking trying to open my eyes. I wasn't surprised when I found a patch of my hair on the back of my head was matted with blood. Not a lot, and thankfully it seemed to be no longer bleeding.

"Don't you fucking dare try to keep me from her!"

I knew that voice. It was rougher than it used to be, but it wasn't so different I didn't recognize it. Abandoning my assessment of my head injury, I blinked open my eyes and squinted until they adjusted to the sunlight filling the room. A quick scan of my surroundings assured me I was alone, so I swung my legs off the bed and tested my balance. I was a little shaky, but considering that prick had probably given me a fucking concussion by cold-cocking me with the butt of his gun, that was to be expected. I weaved my way over to the barred door on the otherwise normal-looking hotel room.

"Andrew?"

"Tank, get out of my fucking way *right* now."

"Sorry, brother. No can do. You need to take it up with Viper if you want in that room with her. For now he doesn't want her messed with."

There was a growl followed by the sound of a gun cocking. "You fucking pervert, she's my *sister*. No one better lay one fucking finger on her, or I'll rain all sorts of hell down on them."

I let the tears roll down my face as I gripped the bars and tried to see my brother. I hadn't seen him since before he left for his last and final deployment, nearly four years ago.

"Andrew!"

The sounds of a scuffle sounded and then my brother was in front of me, shoving his hands through the bars to hold my face.

"Fuck, sis. Turn your head, let me see that wound."

I did as he instructed, all the while doing my best to keep my gaze on him. He'd gotten bigger, broader with more muscle. He still had his hair cropped short. At a guess he did it himself with a buzz razor, as though he didn't care about it enough to do anything else.

"Damn, they got you good. How you feeling? Seeing double?"

"It knocked me out, and I only just woke up. I can't believe it's really you."

I turned back to face him and reached through the bars to touch him. The stubble on his cheek was rough against my palm.

"I'll get Doc to come check you over. Then I'm going to Viper, the president, to see about getting you out of here. This is bullshit. Why the fuck are you here? What did you do?"

"Uncle Gus had a heart attack a couple days back, and he had me listed as his emergency contact."

"This is about Gus? How old is he now? Should be too old to be causing this kinda shit."

I shook my head, wincing at the pain that set off at the movement. "It's not Gus's fault. He owns a gun shop and range in Bridgewater, and your club wants it. They've told him to sign over the business or he won't see me again."

He shook his head. "Fuckin' hell. And last I heard your employer wasn't someone our club is too fond of. You, sister dearest, have the worst fucking luck."

"My old man will be coming for me."

He jerked back, out of my reach. "You're involved in club life? What the fuck? How?"

"I'm with Taz, from the Charon MC."

The color faded from his face. "Pretty sure it ain't no accident you've hooked up with one of the men who hauled me in. How the fuck do you even know about that?"

"Get us somewhere private, and I'll tell you whatever you want to know. But until then, go tell Viper that Taz will have the entire Charon MC on their way here by now. That will include Taz, Mac and Eagle. You know what their skills are and what they'll do to get me out of here."

"It'll be a bloodbath."

"Yep, and no one will win a fucking thing."

He started pacing the hallway for a moment. "Right. I'm gonna go see if I can talk with Viper about getting this shit sorted out. I'll be back as soon as I can, and then I'll find us somewhere we can talk."

He stomped away, cursing the entire time. Still a little in shock at seeing my long lost brother, and my headache not improving, I stumbled back over to the bed to lie down and close my eyes.

"Sure don't look like much for all the trouble you're causing."

The deep rumble jolted me out of sleep, tense and ready to fight. I opened my eyes to see another large man leaning over my body. Did bikers only come in one size? His voice was familiar—this was the man Andrew had been talking to earlier—Tank he'd called him.

Slowly, I moved to sit up on the bed. He stepped away two steps, before folding his arms over his chest.

"What do you want?"

"All sorts of things, but nothing you can give me. None of us even knew Stone had a sister."

"Stone?"

"Yeah, Stone. As in stone cold killer. It's what he's been for the past three years. Never seen him show any emotion, until he saw your face as Animal dragged your ass in here. Then he went fucking nuts trying to get to you."

My heart ached for my big brother. What the fuck had happened on his last deployment that had damaged him so badly? He never used to be cold.

"So help me, if you've laid a hand on her, Tank."

The big man rolled his eyes. "Keep yer panties on, Stone. Like I'm that fucking stupid?"

I switched my focus onto Andrew, drinking in the sight of him. Our folks were going to be over the moon that I'd finally found him. They'd moved up north after Dad took a job in New York, so it would take them a while to get down here. Forgetting that we weren't alone, I blurted out a question I'm sure he didn't want to answer.

"Why didn't you come home?"

Andrew's eyes hardened and he lifted his chin. "Got nothing to say about it. Come with me, you're gonna be staying in my room until we can get this shit sorted out."

"Viper okay that?"

Did Tank have a fucking death wish? My brother didn't look like he was in the kind of mood to negotiate anything at the moment.

"Where the fuck do you think I've just been?"

That wasn't a straight answer. Did he have permission to take me out of this room? Before I could ask out loud, Andrew grabbed my hand and pulled me up off the bed and toward the door. I followed down the hallway, then a flight of stairs, confirming my earlier observation that this building must have been a hotel before the MC got hold of it. We'd just come out into a large game room on the next level down when a loud voice stopped Andrew in his tracks.

"Stone! What the *fuck* do you think you're doing?"

He dropped my hand and turned to face off against the man who'd threatened my uncle. His name patch read Animal. Seemed appropriate.

"She's my sister, you really want to push me on this? After you fucking bashed her skull in?"

"Had to knock her out, brother. Unfortunately, I didn't have any chloroform on me at the time so I used what I had available. Guess I could have shot her instead."

The growl that vibrated around the room had several younger men looking to each other nervously, but not Animal. He just stood there smirking.

When a hand wrapped around my bicep and pulled me back, my instincts took over and I twisted with his movement, swinging my hand in a palm-heel position as I turned to crack him in the jaw. With a curse, he stumbled, before fire lit his eyes and he came at me again. Fuck, I was pretty sure I knew why they called him Tank. Other than pissing him off, my blow didn't do much. Kicking out, I took out his knee and sent him crashing to the ground before he could reach me. Another set of arms wrapped around my middle. I lifted my legs up, dropping my weight. Whoever held me cursed and loosened his hold. I drove my elbow back into his torso, before spinning to deliver a palm-heel strike to his nose. The crack was satisfying, as was the blood spraying free. Especially when I realized this was the bastard who'd held a gun to my ribs. With a sneer I grabbed his shoulders and kneed him hard in the groin. He hit the floor, unconscious, as I spun to take in the rest of the room. A hard jab to my ribs had me cursing and turning on my next attacker. He got a second shot into my ribs before I could focus through my fucking pounding head to disable him. I'd just spun with my leg out to swipe out his legs when pain flared in the back of my head again. I dropped to all fours panting through the pain, and black spots floating through my vision.

A foot slammed up into my gut, flipping me over and making me grunt out in pain. Fuck, I hurt all over.

"Stupid bitch."

I tried to blink through the spots to see what was coming at me but all I saw were several blurry faces. I looked for Andrew. Where was he?

"Don't fucking touch her! Let me the fuck go!"

I tried to lift my arm to reach for him, but my body wouldn't move. The black spots grew until I couldn't see anything, then I couldn't feel anything, either.

Chapter 16

Taz

Church had been over quickly, but important decisions had been made. Naturally, no one argued the suggestion of riding out to get Flick. She was my old lady, therefore club property. No one fucked with what was ours and got away with it. The suggestion of taking John's book with us took me by surprise. Silk's dad, John, had left her several books detailing the dirty deeds of various organizations. Satan's Cowboys MC being one of them. It was a good idea to have the thing with us to help with the negotiations. If we could get Flick out of there peacefully, it would be great. Being on the Cowboys' bad side wasn't a place any MC in Texas wanted to be, but we weren't leaving one of our own behind, either.

It was a two hundred mile ride to get to Cutler, which was located east of Dallas. That was where the Cowboys' lead chapter was located. It was also the direction Keys had tracked their car heading. Leaving enough brothers behind to keep Bridgewater protected, a group of over a dozen of us had headed out to ride up there. Scout led the pack and when, about two hours into the four hour trip, he turned off into a truck stop, we all followed, cutting our engines when he did.

Scout hopped off his ride and with his phone to his ear, walked straight toward me as he started speaking into it.

"Been trying to call you for a while now, Viper. I believe you've got something that belongs to one of ours."

I stayed quiet, trying to work out what the other half of the conversation was.

"Yeah, I get you didn't know who she was to us when you fucking took her. But maybe if you'd answered your fucking phone this morning, all of this could have been avoided, yeah? Bridgewater is our town, not yours. We had the situation in hand." Pause. "Yeah, his heart attack fucked things up time-wise but in the end it helped us out, because none of knew he was Flick's uncle until then. With Taz claiming her, that makes him family."

Scout chuckled, and it wasn't a happy sound but rather a dark, nasty one. "Yeah, she's got teeth. Just ask Taz, he knows all about how it feels to be put on his ass by his old lady." Pause again. "She took down how many? Including Tank? Fuck. See? All you had to do was answer your fucking phone and this never would have happened. Where is she now?" He winced and my body went on alert. It had been a good, long while since I'd gone into the type of fury that had earned me my nickname. In my younger years, I'd fly into a rage and destroy anything—or anyone—around me. The USMC soon tamed that beast into something more focused, but the name stuck. And right now, with my girl in danger, I was on the edge of losing my focus. "Taz ain't gonna be happy about that little fact. She alright to ride? Because we didn't bring a cage." Another pause, which drove me further up the fucking wall, because obviously Flick was injured. "Yeah, we're about two hours away from you, so we'll be there soon. See you then."

He hung up and stared at me for a minute.

"Flick's one hell of a complicated chick, isn't she?"

I frowned. "What the fuck is that supposed to mean?"

"You know who Stone is, right?"

Mac and Eagle were on either side of me and both of them sat up straighter on their bikes at the mention of that name.

Scout scoffed. "Yeah, figured you'd know the name. You know? Since he is the Marine you lot got dishonorably discharged—"

A growl escaped my throat, cutting Scout off. "That's not what happened. The shit with Stone was a big part of the reason behind us retiring when we did. None of us liked how that shit was handled. We were sent after a small group of rogue Marines. Stone wasn't one of the rogues, he'd gone after them to stop them. But not on orders, so at the end of the day the brass threw him in with the others."

"Yeah, figured there was more to it than what Keys managed to find when you boys first joined us. Well, because your girl isn't fucking complicated enough, turns out she's Stone's sister. Did you know that?"

I actually felt the blood drain from my face as I processed what Scout said. "Fuck me."

Her real name was Vaughn...Stone had been Andrew Vaughn. That's why the name had sounded familiar when I'd heard it back at the hospital. What a fuckin' mess.

"Guess not. And yeah, it's a fucked up situation. Anyhow, Stone tried to get her out of the clubhouse and met some resistance. Your girl took down a few Cowboys. On her own. Stone was being held back while Flick took out Tank, then a couple prospects trying to show off. Animal ended it. They've got her and Stone both locked down. Viper's pissed as hell and I dare say shit is gonna still be flying when we get up there. On the upside, I'm pretty sure they're gonna want your girl out of their hair sooner, rather than later. However, I've got no fucking clue where they're standing on the shit with Gus now. We still need to have a sit-down with them when we get up there. So, no going fucking crazy when you see her, okay?"

"I'll do my best. Don't like the idea she's been hurt, and from what you said on the phone, it sounded like that was the case. She good to ride?"

"Oh, she got hurt good by the sound of it. Of course, she dealt out more than she got. And don't worry, we'll get her on the back of your bike even if we have to fucking tie her there. But that girl of yours is tough, she'll hang on fine all by herself, I'm sure."

Again, I got the impression there was something more Scout wasn't telling me. Especially when he held Keys' gaze for a moment before he moved to get back on his bike. Did they know about her being a fed? With a shake of my head, I started my bike. Surely, they wouldn't be going to all this effort to get her back if they did.

Flick

This time when I woke it wasn't just my head that fucking hurt. Fucking hell, everything hurt. Dammit. With a groan I rolled over onto my side, so I could bring my knees up. It helped the pain in my stomach slightly.

"Here, take these."

I groaned and forced my eyes open to look at my brother.

"What are they?"

"Nothing illegal, just a couple Advils."

I probably shouldn't trust him, but I was in enough pain, I was willing to risk it. And it wasn't like Advil was strong enough to knock me back out or anything. It would, however, hopefully take the edge off enough for me to think straight.

After a painful struggle to sit up, I took the bottle of water and pills from Andrew's hand and swallowed them down. He moved to sit beside me on the mattress, moving carefully like I might spring up and slit his throat at any moment.

"I'm not going to hurt you."

"Yeah, well, after seeing you in action earlier, I think I'm entitled to be a little cautious."

I shrugged one shoulder, then winced when pain flared in my ribs. "I've trained hard and have good instincts. Well, most of the time." Those instincts had let me down big time this morning when I'd been grabbed at the hospital. I hoped Gus hadn't hurt himself with worrying about me. What if he had another heart attack? Was that even possible after bypass surgery?

"Yeah, I didn't realize you could fight like that. Not many people have ever taken down Tank. Taz know about your skills?"

That thought had me smiling. "Oh, yeah. He learned to not come up behind me pretty quickly. He snuck up and wrapped his arm around me. I was on edge at the time so I flipped him over onto his back before I realized it was him. Unfortunately for him, it was at the club bar. Not sure he's ever gonna live that one down."

"And yet he still claimed you. He really must be as crazy as they say."

"Taz isn't crazy. Who says that?"

"It's the reason he got his name."

"I thought it was because he's Australian."

Andrew shook his head. "That's what most assume, but it's because when he loses his shit, he goes crazy.

Like that cartoon character, the Tasmanian Devil. Remember him?"

"Yeah, little guy that spun really fast and destroyed everything in his path."

"That's the one. That's the reason your old man is called Taz."

"And the reason you're called Stone is...?"

He winced and took a deep breath in, before blowing it out slowly.

"The Middle East—it's a different fucking world. Brutal, bloody. You can't experience it and come back the same. At least, I couldn't. The only way I could survive was to shut off my emotions completely. It's why I couldn't come home. I wasn't the same man who'd left. I couldn't face you, Mom and Dad with who'd I'd become and keep all that shit shut off. Then I stumbled on the Satan's Cowboys and I found somewhere I fit. They call me Stone because they think I'm stone cold. Before you came crashing in here, the club believed I had no family. A man with no family can be dangerous, because we've got nothing left to lose. The club has used that, honed me into something useful."

I'd done enough research into MCs to know what he meant. "You're an enforcer?"

He chuckled, darkly. "Something like that."

"While you seem to be in a mood to chat, what happened to get you kicked out of the USMC? I thought it was something to do with whatever happened that made you not come home. It's why I started working for my employer."

I was also curious as to how he knew about that, too.

"I'm not able to talk about it, sis. You know that." He shook his head. "But I'm guessing you'll hound Taz until he tells you. Kinda surprised you haven't already."

He gave me a questioning look, and I glanced around the room, looking for cameras.

"The room isn't bugged, sis. Keep your voice low, no one that's out in the hall will hear you, either."

I didn't like it, and I didn't want to admit anything.

"I was told to wait with my questions until after my assignment is over. Taz doesn't realize I'm your sister."

"He will now. Viper will tell them as soon as he manages to make contact."

I sighed. "I figured as much. Now quit stalling, and tell me what happened."

"One night, a couple of my fellow teammates decided to go for a late night stroll. I'd heard them planning it earlier." He paused and glanced at me. "You sure you want to know this?"

"Yeah, I do. I need to know why I lost my brother."

He squeezed his eyes shut, and I wondered if I shouldn't let it go. I'd found the man, did I really need the reasons anymore?

"Fine. These men, they were the kind that got off on hurting others. We'd passed an orphanage on our way to where we made camp that night and these guys planned on hiking back to it for some late night fun. After they left, I armed up and followed them. I got held up getting out of the camp." He paused again, and my heart ached for my poor brother. "They paid for my delay. Those poor girls were just fucking kids. When Taz and his crew came in, I'd killed one and was about to take out a second. They had orders to bring us all in, which they did. And at the end of the day, I wasn't acting on orders, so got thrown to the wolves. I should have reported to our CO what I'd heard them say earlier.

"I'd been the new guy on the team. I knew it would come down to my word against theirs, and they'd been in the USMC for years longer than me. I wasn't so stupid I didn't realize how that would have gone. So, I figured, I'd just go handle it. And because of that, I have to shut off all my emotions, my humanity, or I wake up at night screaming as I see all the bodies those bastards left in their wake."

Tears were pouring down my cheeks. My poor brother. No wonder he'd run off. I reached for him, wanting to hug him. Comfort him. But he jerked back with a growl and stood from the bed.

"So, now you know. You can get back to your life and leave me the fuck alone."

I slowly shook my head.

"I won't abandon you. We're family. Mom and Dad are going to be so excited we've found you."

He spun on me glaring. "You can't tell them. I can't be your brother, their son. I can't do it."

"Why not? All we want to do is love you. You can't accept your family's love and care?"

He shook his head. "Not without waking beasts I'd prefer not poke. I like my life. I eat, sleep and breathe for the Satan's Cowboys. They understand me, know why I need to keep to myself and not get too involved whenever they do anything with all the old ladies and kids of the club."

Wiping my eyes, I huffed out a breath. "You know, you and Taz are a lot alike?"

"Yeah, well, I'm not happy you've hooked up with him, either. I'd prefer you off married to some accountant and popping out grandbabies to keep Mom and Dad happy."

"That'll never be me. I'm not built that way. I tried it, but I hated it. I need some action in my life. I didn't expect to like the club life so much, but I do. I'm working in the Charon's bar, and went to the clubhouse last night. I know what you mean about finding where you fit. I fit there. The other old ladies, they're like me. They want more outta life than to be some Stepford wife."

A roar filled the air, and it sounded like a whole heap of Harleys were coming toward us.

"Sounds like the cavalry's coming for you, sis."

I frowned at him as he didn't make any move to leave. "Shouldn't you be out there?"

"I'm locked in here with you for the moment. Can't go anywhere."

I winced. "Shit. I'm sorry. I didn't mean to go nuts out there. I don't like being grabbed from behind, my reflexes take over."

He laughed. "Now who's a good match for Taz?"

Guess he had a point. I glanced down at myself. "He's not gonna be happy to see me like this."

"If he knows you, he'll be expecting you to look like you do. If you hadn't attacked, all you'd have is that lump on your head from this morning."

"Yeah, I know."

Taking as deep a breath as my sore ribs allowed, I leaned back against the wall. All I could do was wait and see what was about to happen. I hated being forced into a corner. But it seemed to be happening a lot lately, so I probably should get used to it.

Chapter 17

Taz

The poor prospect manning the door to the Cowboy's clubhouse just about passed out when we all came roaring into the yard. I didn't blame the kid. Over a dozen bikes rocking up with no prior warning was enough to put fear into anyone with half a brain. As we lined up our rides, others came out onto the porch. Maverick slapped the prospect on the shoulder and said something that had the younger man relaxing his stance.

Scout came over to me. "No grandstanding, Taz. Understand me? Let me deal with this and get your girl out."

"I'll do my best, prez. But no guarantees on what I'll do when I see her injured."

He turned to Mac and Eagle. "You two are in charge of keeping him contained if he loses his shit. Understand me?"

"Yes, sir."

With a shake of his head he turned and started toward the clubhouse. We all fell in behind him.

"Maverick, nice seeing you again. Wish it were under better circumstances."

"Same here, Scout. Got Viper waiting on us in church, but we don't want your crew causing trouble while we talk."

"They'll behave themselves, won't you boys?"

Everyone grunted in agreement, except for me. I didn't like to make promises I couldn't keep. Maverick didn't miss my silence. "What about the girl's old man there?"

"He'll be with me, so not a problem."

With a nod Maverick turned, and after opening the door, ushered us all in.

"Well, in you all come, then. No girls around, but the bar's open."

Ten minutes later I stood behind Scout, who was sitting opposite Viper at their meeting table. Thing was fucking huge, with their insignia carved out of the center of it.

"Prefer to keep this between you and me, Scout."

"Well, give the man his old lady back, and it can be."

Viper sat back with a huff before turning his full focus on me. I didn't flinch, but it was a close call. Hard not to crack under a stare like Viper's.

"You don't get to tear through my men because she's hurt. She attacked us."

My hands curled into fists. "I saw the footage from the parking lot outside the hospital. She didn't do one damn thing when one of your men knocked her out by slamming the butt of a gun down on her head."

"Well, when she went on her little rampage earlier she broke his nose and knocked him out cold. I think justice was served on that one. The rest of her injuries were from my men defending themselves."

"You're not making me feel real good about her condition, Viper. What the fuck happened?"

As Scout spoke, Viper trained his gaze back on the Charon president.

"Stone took her out of the lockdown room, Animal was telling him to put her back. Tank came up behind her—" I groaned and rubbed a hand over my face. I knew what had happened. Fuck it all to hell. "Gather you've tried to do that at some point?"

Scout barked out a laugh. "Yeah, Taz grabbed her from behind at Styxx. Girl put him on his ass in front of half the club. Gonna be a while before he lives that one down."

Viper chuckled. "I bet. Well, you can't be surprised she got hurt when my men tried to stop her, then. She took out three of them before Animal stepped in."

"What was Stone doing while all this went down?"

"Stone got his name because he's stone fucking cold. It's made him one of my best enforcers. Never before have I seen that man show any emotion, but when he first caught a glimpse of Felicity's face, he showed plenty. Man's deadly on a good day. With his calm shattered? I'm not risking that shit. I took his guns after he pulled one on Tank earlier. Animal held him back initially, then handed over his containment to two others when he stepped in to deal with her. I've got them both in the lockdown room now. Hoping he'll cool the fuck down by the time we're finished here."

"If you're not gonna let Taz go get her until we're done, then he's not going anywhere and we best get this shit done. Long ride home ahead of us."

Viper's gaze hardened, as though he didn't like me being here. But like Scout said, I wasn't going anywhere that wasn't closer to Flick, so he could just fucking get over it.

"Fine. You know what we want, and you haven't delivered."

I opened my mouth but Scout held up his hand to stop me. I stood back and stayed silent, letting Scout handle things. For now. I respected the hell out of my president, but I wouldn't let him sell out Flick.

"Gus don't like MCs much. It's been a slow process to get him to trust Taz. We were getting there, and had plans in place to speed things along once he had his heart attack. You jumping in and snatching his niece hasn't helped. He'll probably flat-out refuse to deal with any of us now."

"I don't know, you returning his niece to him should go a long way."

"Maybe. For us. He'll never consider doing business with the Cowboys, though. Why'd you want the shop, anyway? Maybe if we know why you want the damn place, we can sort something else out."

Viper stayed silent for a minute.

"You're halfway between us and the border. Perfect location. We keep losing shipments on route, we need to break up the runs."

"You don't have to use a gun shop for that. Hell, we can find a warehouse or something you can use."

Viper shook his head. "Nope. That range is sitting on a bunker that no one knows about."

I frowned. I'd never seen any signs of a bunker being out there.

"And how do you know about it, then?"

"Gus didn't always own that land. We recently got some information from a previous owner. Enough information that we want control of that place."

Scout shook his head. "You can't have it. With Taz claiming Flick, Gus is family. We'll still push for Taz taking ownership, and we'll do what we can to help you out with the runs. But the title will not be in Cowboy's hands. Not that you'd want it to be. What do you think will happen when the feds find out you've bought the place? They'll be all over it, and you won't be able to move anything through it. In fact, it'll probably end with the feds shutting the whole place down."

"Fuck. I hate the FBI. They've been sniffing closer lately. Dammit it. Okay, if Taz can get ownership of the place and you let us use that bunker as we want, I'll accept that. But it needs to happen soon. We can't keep losing shipments like we are."

"We won't move drugs. Weapons are fine, but no fucking drugs."

"You don't get to demand that. We need to move both through that place."

Scout's shoulders bunched up. I didn't know why, but he was hardcore anti-drugs. I cleared my throat before leaning down to whisper in Scout's ear. Viper letting me stay in the room didn't mean I had permission to actually be a part of the conversation.

"Use the ledger."

Scout nodded to me before turning his focus back to Viper.

"We got something else you might be interested in. You ever had anything to do with a man by the name of John Bennett?"

Viper clenched his jaw and a tick formed above his left eye.

"I'll take that as a yes. John was Bulldog, my VP's, brother. After he and his wife died in the 9/11 attacks, his daughter came to live with Bulldog and his old lady. Then, last year the L.A. mob came after her. Turned out John left some ledgers behind in a bag that missed the flight that he died on."

"Are you shitting me? Airports don't keep shit that long."

Scout shrugged. "They don't normally. But things were a mess after those planes took down the towers.

Somehow, the cart of baggage that missed the flight got pushed aside and forgotten about. Someone did some cleaning up at LAX and found them. Contacted a reporter about it since the fifteenth anniversary was coming up. Long story, short—we got a ledger with your name on it."

"Is that so? And what? You've just been sitting on it all this time? Is this why we're having more issues with the feds lately?"

The tension in the room was off the fucking charts and I knew it wouldn't take much to have things explode.

"Don't be a fucking idiot, Viper. There were several of them and we stashed them all in our safe. Only reason we still have it is because with all the shit that's gone down since then, we kinda forgot about them. So, if we hand it over, will you not bring drugs into my fucking town?"

Viper shook his head. "Need to keep running powder, Scout. No way around that. I can promise we won't push it in your town. None of our drugs will hit your streets. But we need to use that bunker to store shipments. I'll also put the word on my men that no one is to go after Felicity for what happened today."

"And Gus?"

"He's safe from us."

Scout turned to me. "Go out and grab that ledger for me, let's get this shit done. Then we'll grab your girl and get back on the road."

With a nod, I headed out to find Keys to grab it. I couldn't wait to have Flick back in my arms. I was still unsure of what condition she was in. Although, at least with her being locked up with her brother, nothing more was being done to her.

Taz

Once Viper took possession of the ledger, he stood and led us out of the meeting room. I still had the digital copy we'd made back when we first found the books, so if any of the Cowboys went back on the agreement, the feds would be getting a present. But no one needed to know about that.

"Let's go get your girl. I'll warn you, Stone doesn't want her going with you."

"He can fucking get over it. She's my old lady. He hasn't even seen in years, he has no claim on her."

Viper gave a small nod and moved up a flight of stairs. The Satan's Cowboy's clubhouse was an old hotel. Three floors of various rooms. Wasn't a bad setup, especially for a club as big as theirs. Up on the third floor Viper slowed down.

"Our lock-up rooms are up the end here."

He pulled out a set of keys as he stopped in front of a prospect. "You can head off now. Job's done."

"Yes, prez."

The big guy lumbered away and Viper led us further down to a room with a barred door on it.

"Stone, you calmed the fuck down yet, brother?"

"Yeah, prez. You can let me out."

"Not until you promise me you won't go after Animal."

A growl filled the air. "You know he was rougher than he needed to be with her."

"Yeah, well, we don't call him Animal for the fucking fun of it. I'll let you get in the ring with him later, but you are not to go after him outside of that. We clear?"

"Yes, prez. Crystal, fucking clear."

"Good."

With that, Viper unlocked the door and took a step back. It was like looking at a ghost of my past when Stone walked out. Closely cropped hair, messy beard, and hard fucking eyes. He was bigger than he'd been back in the Middle East. Guess he'd spent his time since then bulking up.

"Stone."

"Taz." He came to stand right in front of me. "Don't like my sister being an old lady. She's a fucking accountant, and should be off somewhere married to a desk jockey and pumping out some grandkids for our folks."

"That just proves how little you know her. That life would drive her insane in a fucking heartbeat."

His glare intensified but I didn't back down. I'd taken him down once before, I could do it again. He was bigger now, but then so was I. And when it came to Flick, I wasn't gonna let anything get in my way.

"Hurt her, I'll come after you."

Then before I could say a word in response, he shoved past me and left.

"Okay, then. That was nice and dramatic. Now, come get your girl and get out of here before something else fucking happens. I'm over the drama today."

I didn't need to be told twice. A second later I was rushing into the room. A lump formed in my throat at the sight of my Flick sitting there beaten to hell, but smiling up at me.

"Hear you had an interesting morning."

"Yeah, you could say that. How about you?"

I strode over to her and pulled her up off the bed and against me. Wrapping my arms around her, I palmed the back of her head to cradle it against my shoulder. Having her warm body pressed against mine finally allowed me to let go of my fear for her.

"Fuck, Flick. You've taken ten years off my life today."

She shuddered against me when I pressed a kiss to the top of her head, avoiding the wound on the back.

"Let's get home. You right to ride? Because Scout offered to tie you to me if you can't hang on."

That got a chuckle out of her. "I'm sure he did, but I can hang on. How far away are we?"

"We're up in Cutler, about a four hour ride home."

"Damn. That's one hell of a ride."

"We'll stop a few times. You'll be fine, but Scout wants to get back home tonight. We brought most of the club with us to come get you."

She rubbed her face against my shirt. "Really? Why?"

Cupping her face, I tilted it up so I could hold her gaze. "You're my old lady, my property. That makes you club property, we protect what's ours."

Her eyes filled with moisture but she blinked it away. "Is that why you asked me? To give me protection?"

I shook my head. "I asked you because I like fucking you on the regular."

Then, I kissed her before she could say something else. I didn't want her thinking so much about my reasons for making her mine. So long as she still wanted to be my old lady after everything that had happened today, things were good.

"C'mon, you two. We don't have time for you to have your reunion fuck here and now."

"Damn, Scout, you're such a giver."

"Yeah, well, with Taz you gotta be, or we'd be watching our very own live porn show for the next hour or so. Damn man has stamina, that's for sure."

Listening to Scout and Viper talk about me like I wasn't standing right there was pissing me off. "You two done?"

Scout grinned. "If you are."

With a shake of my head, I turned back to Flick. "You all right to walk or do you want me to carry you down?"

"I want to walk."

"No attacking anyone on your way out, you hear me?"

With a smirk, she nodded to Viper, then I took her hand and led her out of the room and down the hallway. If I wasn't so on edge over her injuries, I'd laugh at the way all the men tried their best to get out of our way while watching Flick with caution. In short order we were all back on our bikes, and with Flick's arms wrapped around me, we took off. For some reason, I was still on edge but I couldn't put my finger on why. The fact Scout had been fucking strange around Flick didn't help ease my thoughts.

No matter how late it was when we got home, I knew it wouldn't be the end of the day for us.

Chapter 18

Flick

Nothing felt quite like how being wrapped around Taz on the back of his bike did. Especially with jeans on. So much better than a short skirt. Every few minutes, he'd put his palm on my thigh and give it a squeeze, like he needed to be sure I was still here. I was still damn sore from all the hits I'd taken, but I wasn't going to let go and fall off any time soon.

Even with a helmet on, the sound of so many Harleys for four hours was enough to have my ears ringing by the time we pulled into the Charon's clubhouse lot. I'd kinda hoped Taz would have taken me straight home, but I guess we needed to do some kind of debrief.

Taz took my hand and we followed the others into the front room. Once we were all in there, Scout called everyone's attention.

"Thank you all for your help today. The Cowboys took one of ours, and I appreciate the way you all stepped up to help get her back. I know it's late, so y'all head on home or upstairs and I'll see everyone in church in the morning." He then caught Taz's gaze. "Not you, brother. We need to see you and Flick in church, now."

It was a testament to how tired and sore I was that I didn't pick up on anything being wrong until after I'd entered the room. Taz had dumped my bag that Viper had returned to me as we were leaving, along with his own phone in a locker outside the room. I'd tensed, but he'd told me it was normal and that no technology was allowed in church. Since he said it was normal, and the others were doing the same thing. I went with it without protest. I started to realize I was in trouble when it wasn't just Scout that came in with us, but several of the older club members. But not Eagle or Mac. I knew Scout, Bulldog, Keys and of course Nitro, but the other man I didn't know, and he didn't look friendly.

The door was closed and Nitro stood in front of it with his arms crossed, a clear statement that particular exit was now closed.

"What the fuck is going on here, Scout? Starting to feel like an ambush."

Nitro spoke up. "Not on you, brother, but her. Got something you want to tell us, darlin'?"

I slowly glanced at each of the men in the room. They knew. They fucking knew! Dammit.

"Why don't you tell me what you think you know?"

The guy I didn't know stepped forward. "Quit fucking around. You're a fucking fed. An FBI spy sent in to do who knows what. And now we know, we need to fucking deal with you. Which is gonna be so much fucking fun considering it's gonna involve ripping out my brother's heart to do it."

"You don't touch her, Arrow. No one does."

Scout pointed directly at Taz. "You don't look surprised. You fucking knew who she was. Don't think I won't be asking you more about that in a minute, but first, I need you to shut the fuck up while we deal with Ms. Felicity Vaughn here." He paused and turned his full attention on me. "It's time to come clean and tell us why the fuck you were sent here. You can come clean now, or we can take you downstairs and you can tell us after we persuade you a little. Your choice."

Taz growled, but didn't say a word. I could feel the fury radiating out from him. My own heartbeat was pounding in my ears and I glanced around once more to check for exits. Nothing had magically appeared to save my ass. I clenched and released my fists a couple times. Not that I really had a choice. Going down to their basement would mean painful, bad things that I might not survive, no matter how much Taz tried to save me.

"Fine. Yes, I'm an undercover FBI agent. I was sent down here to gather intel on the Cowboys. Not the Charons. The feds had gotten word that the Cowboys had been focusing in on your club lately, and they want to know why. I believe they chose to send me because of my ties with Taz, through what happened to my brother. I haven't made it a secret that I've been searching for the truth behind why my brother was booted from the USMC. My boss told me once the assignment was over, I could ask Taz, Mac and Eagle about my brother, if I found myself in a position to do so."

"Were you aware your brother was with the Satan's Cowboys before today?"

I shook my head. "No. Andrew vanished after he returned from his last deployment. Neither our parents nor I have heard from him since then. We've been extremely worried about him."

"What have you reported back to your boss so far?"

"Not much. I reported that I had successfully become Taz's girlfriend, but they don't know about me being his old lady yet. I also had to tell them about Gus, since the hospital had me listed as my real name, not my cover. Is that how you found out?"

"Fuck, yeah. Their little hack on the hospital's system was easy to spot." Scout glared at Keys for speaking. "Sorry, prez."

"Anything else?"

I was going to try to keep Taz, Mac and Eagle out of this shit storm, but I wasn't sure it would be possible if Scout kept asking questions. Especially when the man had already worked out that Taz knew I was a fed before today. But that meant I couldn't give him anything that I'd learned from Taz, only what I'd seen myself around the clubhouse. Which was fuck all.

"I don't know anything else to tell them. Well, I do after today, but I haven't had a chance to check in with my boss since you all so kindly came to my rescue."

"And if we let you walk out of here, what do you intend on reporting?"

I didn't have to fake my anger. "Well, first up, will be why they fucking ignored my distress call."

That had Keys looking at me with interest again. "What call?"

"It's a button on my phone. I pressed it at the hospital when I leaned down to give Uncle Gus a kiss goodbye. Has anyone called him and let him know I'm okay?"

"Not yet, because it's still to be decided if you will be."

That had me backing up and swallowing past a sudden lump in my throat. Hands gripped my shoulders and I tensed.

"Don't you dare fucking throw me again, woman."

Taz's rough voice had me moving back further, until my body was pressed against his. He was the only one here that was safe.

"Answer the fucking question already. What are you planning on telling them about today?"

"I— I don't know. My head's kind of a mess right now. I need to think it all through before I can report on any of it."

"Well, we need to lock you down until you decide what you're gonna do. Because if you decide wrong, this isn't going to end well for you."

I licked my lips. "What do you want me to report?"

"That depends on what you want at the end of all this. Is this just a fucking job to you? Are you going to be on your way as soon as you're done here, without a care to the mess you leave behind?"

I went to speak and Scout cut me off. "And don't fucking lie to me."

"Originally that was the plan, but I didn't expect to actually fall for Taz. To like the club. Even before today I'd already started having regrets about coming in like I had. Wishing I was just a normal woman who could hook up with whoever caught her eye."

Scout fiddled with his bandana before re-crossing his arms over his chest.

"You'll spend the rest of the night downstairs while we decide what we're gonna fucking do with you. You'll not come to any harm down there, but no Taz, no creature comforts."

Shaking my head, I reached my palms back to grip his thighs. No Taz?

"Not negotiating here. Taz has his own issues we need to deal with. Now, you gonna be a good girl and go willingly or do I have to knock you out first? I'm not gonna tolerate you fighting your way through my men tonight."

"If you promise I'm not going to come to any harm, then I'll go willingly."

"You won't tonight. Tomorrow might be a different story, though."

Taz pressed a kiss to the side of my head. An unspoken vow, he had my back. And considering I'd really rather stay conscious, I gave in.

"I'll go willingly."

Taz

Would this fucking day never end?

Watching Nitro and Arrow lead my girl out to take her downstairs was like having my guts ripped open with a rusty blade. Fuck.

When they returned, Mac and Eagle were following them. Fuck, shit was about to hit the fan in a big way. They both gave me a raised brow as they passed, but I just shook my head. We were all in deep shit no matter what I said at this point.

"Right, boys. Something tells me all three of you are involved with this shit. I'm also guessing you three have been keeping one hell of a fucking secret from us. It's now time to tell us every-fucking-thing. Understand?"

I turned to face my Marine brothers. "Flick's cover is blown."

Mac nodded. "And ours, by the looks of it. We'll tell you everything, but you need to hear us out before you act. Can you give us that at the least? And if worse comes to worse, you promise to take care of our women. Silk and Zara have nothing to do with any of this shit."

Scout nodded. "Done. Now speak."

"This is gonna take some time. Mind if we all sit down?"

Scout nodded but didn't say a word, or move to sit. I followed Mac's lead, taking a seat with him and Eagle. Mac had been our Gunnery Sergeant in the USMC, and it still felt natural to defer to him in things like this interrogation.

"Guess I'll start at the beginning. We weren't at that poker run by accident. Our CO had contacted us the week before and asked us if we'd consider going undercover. Apparently, the Charons were getting big enough to make the feds nervous and they wanted some eyes on the inside. We'd been riding around the country aimlessly for a while at that point and figured we might as well check you out and see if we could do a little more service to Uncle Sam.

"It didn't take long for us to rethink our take on things, though. We were still prospects when we'd all felt like we'd found our place in the world with the Charons. We could clearly see you weren't doing anything that the feds needed to be worrying about. When the shit went down with Silk and the L.A. mob, they got pushy. Started making threats, so we gave them a copy of John's ledger on the mob. Figured it was fifteen years old and wouldn't be much use anyhow. And it had no ties to the Charon MC.

"That was one harsh lesson on who we could trust. The bastards leaked it to them within days, the fuckers. Lucky for us, Runt was also doing the dirty on the club so he took the brunt of that when it came out. After that little fuck up, Eagle told them to piss off, that after they'd risked his girl like they had, he was out."

Bulldog looked like he was ready to rip into Eagle. Silk was his niece and Eagle had already copped one beat down for falling for her. I really hoped this shit wasn't gonna end with another round of beat downs. Although, that was a better outcome than a round of bullets.

"We all went silent on them after that, but we knew it wouldn't last. And when Zara came to town with the shitstorm that followed her, they put the pressure on us again. We gave them the least we could, and never anything on the Charons. Our handler got really fucking pissed when he discovered I'd hooked up with Zara while I'd been telling him we hadn't seen her. Not sure what he was playing at, but after everything shook out with the Iron Hammers, he vanished. Flick told Taz that he was dirty and no one has seen or heard from him since then. Guess he's over the border, but I don't really give a fuck. We'd hoped they'd forgotten about us, but we were shit-out-of-luck on that one because along came Flick."

Scout cut him off with a question. "What was her real reason for coming in to town?"

Mac nodded my way. Great. My turn to try to save our asses.

"The FBI realized they'd lost Eagle and Mac as assets but they wanted to try to save me. They knew I wouldn't turn on my club, so sent Flick in to charm me into helping her focus on taking down the Cowboys."

"So, your relationship with her is all a lie?"

"Hell, no. It's real. Trust me, all this shit would have been so much simpler if it was a lie. Flick made sure she had me hooked good before she admitted her real reason for being here." I paused to blow out a breath. "If I didn't give a shit about her, I would have just sent her on her way."

"No, you wouldn't have. She threatened to out us to Scout, to tell him we'd reported in on the Charons. Which is bullshit, by the way. We've never said a thing about the Charons to the feds."

Mac was right. I would have. To keep us safe, and to stay with the club, I would have gone along with her plan.

"How does she feel about you? She just playing along?"

I took a moment to think over my answer. "She's told me I'm not just an assignment. That she wants to be with me. That was when I asked her to be my old lady. I made it clear that was a permanent arrangement and if she intended to fuck off once her work was done, then she should say no. She said yes."

Scout nodded. "Okay. Finally, what do you three want to happen at the end of this shit? Eagle?"

"I want to stay. I love being a Charon, love my life here. But I want my brothers by my side. It wouldn't be the same without Mac or Taz with me. And I'm not giving up Silk. No fucking way. Only way I leave her is if I'm in the ground. However, I would prefer to stay breathing, to be here for the birth of our baby and to raise 'em here in Bridgewater, in the safety of the club."

Scout nodded again. "Mac?"

"Same as Eagle. I found where I belong here with the Charons, I don't want to leave it. But I won't leave my brothers either. Same as Eagle, I want to be above ground to see the birth of Zara's and my child and to raise kids here in town with my Charon family."

Another nod. "Taz?"

"Ditto to what they said. Didn't think I'd find somewhere I fit after leaving USMC, but I did. Here with the Charons. I'm sorry we didn't come to you before now about how we came to be here, but we didn't want to risk what we had. I'd appreciate being able to keep Flick with me. Honestly, I didn't expect to fall for anyone. Ever. But she's a hell of a woman and I'm pretty sure she's it for me. You take her out, I'm alone forever. Assuming you don't put me in the same hole as she goes in."

Fuck, I hated talking like this. This was my fucking family and here I was talking about them potentially putting me and my girl in the fucking ground. It was bullshit.

"Right. Well, we need to figure out what the fuck to do with you all. So, that means you three get locked down while we discuss it. Don't need you running off on us, or trying to bust out your girl. You gonna be good and go down willingly?"

"If it means we're more likely to be able to stay in the club, then yeah, we'll go willingly."

With an ache in my chest, I trailed behind Mac and Eagle as Nitro led us downstairs. What would we do if we all got kicked to the curb? I was sick of being told I wasn't welcome. Sucks to be me, apparently.

After that fucking fire that took my mum and sister, and ripped my world apart, the only family I had left was my dad's older sister here in the States. Child services shipped me over to her and left me there without so much as a second glance. Fairly certain, I would have done better with a foster home in Australia than with Aunt Pam.

She was ten years older than my dad had been, and was a bitter, nasty old woman. Having buried her brother and parents, she'd buried herself in her grief. Had let it eat at her. She'd never married and put all her time into running her ranch. Damn, but the fact she had all that land and cattle and horses had been a God-send to me. It had given me an escape from the house. Worked my ass off the entire time I lived there. When I hit eighteen, she made it clear she'd done her duty. I didn't argue. It was hard to try and live somewhere you knew you weren't wanted. Apparently the fact I looked just like my father was a major crime in Aunt Pam's book.

I thought the USMC was going to be my new family for the rest of my life. But after that shit with Stone and those asshole Marines, things changed. I guess it made me take a good look at myself. At all the lives I'd taken and I didn't really like the man I'd become anymore.

Leaving the Marines hadn't been that hard to do really, not with Eagle and Mac with me. But being kicked to the curb by the Charons was gonna fucking hurt. Here with them, the three of us really had a chance at a life in a family that would always have our backs.

Fuck, we never should have agreed to go undercover. Should have said no way, then come down to that poker run to check the club out anyhow.

Too fucking late now, though. Because, like always, the past was what it was. Set in stone and unchangeable.

And wasn't that a bitch?

Chapter 19

Taz

We were left in the cells for fucking hours. At least they put the three of us together, and when no one came to deliver a beat down we considered it a win. I remembered the shape Eagle had been in after the one he copped last year. Also remembered the fit Silk threw afterward. I was pretty sure if the club touched Eagle again, Silk would keep to her word and walk away from the club for good, taking her man with her. Hopefully Bulldog remembered that fact when they were discussing punishment.

The clank of the door being unlocked had all of us tensing. Nitro swung the door open.

"C'mon, you three. Time for church."

"What about Flick?"

Nitro shook his head. "Not yet, brother. Soon, though."

Knowing arguing was pointless, I turned and pounded my way up the stairs and followed the others into the meeting room. Hopefully, not for the last time.

Like earlier, it was just the club officers. The president, vice president, secretary, treasurer and sergeant in arms, all standing beside each other made one hell of an imposing sight.

"You three should have come forward with this shit earlier, you know that, right? The fact we had to stumble over it isn't helping your cases."

Mac spoke for us all, as per usual. "How? We discussed it several times but none of us could think of a way to say it that wouldn't have ended with us dead or at least left bloody and booted out. Especially after what y'all did to Eagle."

Scout huffed, adjusted his bandana then re-crossed his arms over his chest. "We like you boys. You've been a good addition to the club. Hate to see you y'all go. But you need to pay a price to the club to make this shit right."

I groaned. I couldn't help it. A beat down was coming our way and it was gonna suck.

Bulldog chuckled. "It ain't what you're thinking, Taz. Can't risk giving you three beat downs for a couple reasons. There's the fact that Silk will pack up Eagle here and leave us, but mainly, we'd have to tell the entire club what's gone on here. And we don't think that'll help the club as a whole."

I blew out a breath in relief as Scout took back control of the conversation.

"First up, you all need to cut all ties with the FBI. If they threaten you in an attempt to get you to stay with them, let me know and we'll deal with whatever it is. We can't have undercovers in the club. Next thing, you're all on fucking probation. I'm not taking your top rockers, but it'll feel like I have. You'll get cage duty, and shitty jobs for the next year. The club will probably notice and start asking questions, but you'll all just fucking shrug that shit off. I don't want the truth getting out and killing the morale of our club. And we'll be watching you three closely for anything that looks like you're reporting anything to someone outside the club. Again, if the feds contact you at all for anything, you come straight to me with it. Understand?"

We all spoke at the same time. "Yes, prez."

Fuck, we were getting off light, really. The next year would suck, but it would pass soon enough.

Scout then turned his full attention onto me. "We're gonna cut Flick loose. She's paid her dues at the hands of the Cowboys. You can keep fucking her, but so long as she's FBI, she ain't welcome in the clubhouse, or any other club property. Got me?"

"Yeah, I got you."

Fuck. Flick wouldn't be happy with that. She'd enjoyed her time here at the clubhouse, and she seemed to love working at Styxx. This was basically going to come down to Flick picking either me or her job with the FBI. I honestly wasn't sure which she'd choose.

"Nitro, go get her up here. We need to deal with this shit before everyone comes in for church in a couple hours."

"Can I take her upstairs for a bit before she gets shoved out the door?"

They all chuckled at me, but I didn't care. "Yeah, you can go help her clean up and say what you need to. Then I need you to go with her to see Gus. Without her present for the conversation, I need you to get the keys to his property off him. Gonna need to find this fucking bunker Viper's got a hard-on for."

A few minutes later, I winced as she walked in. She was walking stiffly but held her chin up. My girl was made of strong stuff. But she was fucking hurting, and the night in the cold basement wouldn't have helped anything, I'm sure. I reached for her and pulled her in against me. Wrapping my arms around her, I kissed the top of her head.

"I said *after*, brother. Let her alone long enough for us to get this shit done."

Turning her around in my arms so she faced everyone, I kept my hands on her hips. She folded her arms over her chest and leaned back against me. Despite, trying to appear casual, I could feel the wariness coming off her, along with a good dose of fear.

"As far as we're concerned, Flick, so long as you vow to not report anything you've found out about us or the Cowboys to your superiors, you've been punished enough with what the Cowboys did to you. But we can't knowingly allow a fed in the clubhouse. So, you have a choice—you're either loyal to the Charons or the FBI. You can't be both. If you pick the FBI, we're not gonna stop you from seeing Taz, but you won't be welcome at anything club related."

Her shoulders rose and fell as she took a breath then exhaled it.

"How much time do I have to make my decision?"

"None. You're out unless you leave the FBI. You get in contact with me if you choose to be loyal to the Charons, and we'll discuss how we can let you in. You'll be watched closely for the next year, regardless."

She nodded. "Okay. I'll let you know. Am I free to go?"

"Not just yet. Taz is gonna take you upstairs so you can get cleaned up, then I need you to take Taz with you to go see your uncle and let him see you're safe."

She gave Scout a nod, and in turn, he gave me one. "Get out of here, all of you. We got church in two hours. Taz, I doubt you'll make it since you got shit to do this morning, but if you get back and we're still in here, come and report, yeah?"

"Sure thing, prez."

Taking her hand, I led her out, gathered our shit from the locker and headed upstairs. When I found my old room was vacant I guided her in there, booted the door shut and locked it. Then I was fucking on her. Moving her up against the wall, I pressed myself against her as I took her mouth. With a moan she melted for me, parting her lips and letting me in. Her palms slid under my cut and down my sides until she could slip them up under my shirt and against my bare skin.

I pulled back and stripped out of my cut and shirt, tossing them on the chair beside us. I toed off my boots and was going for my fly when she pulled her own shirt off. I hissed at the bruising she revealed.

"Fuck, babe. What'd they do to you?"

"Boot to the ribs. Pretty sure they're bruised." She shrugged, like it was no big deal she'd been hurt. "They'll heal up soon enough."

She unclipped her bra, and shoved down her pants, kicking them off, along with her shoes. Even with the dirt and bruising, she was fucking beautiful. And I was gonna fucking lose her, I knew it. It was how my life went. I was lucky that Scout and the others had decided I could keep my MC family, but it would come at the cost of my love. Sucks to be me, because fuck it all, I wanted to keep both.

Flick

Tears stung my eyes at the look Taz was giving me. He'd stalled out stripping with his pants half undone. The moment I was fully naked, he'd stopped and just stood there staring with all the longing in the world on his face. This was him saying goodbye. He was assuming I wouldn't pick him. That he was too fucking broken or some shit for me to want him. That was the biggest load of shit, but I couldn't tell him that. Not yet. First, I had to head north to Dallas and report in. I had no idea what the

FBI was going to do with me. So, until that was handled, I couldn't get Taz's hopes up, just to break his heart even worse in the end.

With a swing of my hips, I swayed up to him, pressing a kiss over his heart as I slid my hands inside his pants to push them down.

"C'mon, babe. Let's get cleaned up."

He didn't say a word, but allowed me to take his hand and pull him into the bathroom once he'd stepped out of his jeans. I turned my back to him as I sorted out the water. Apparently, the sight of my bare ass was enough to snap him out of his funk. I felt his heat a moment before his body pressed against mine. His dick was hard and nestled between my butt cheeks as he surrounded me. I shuddered against him as he wrapped his arms around me, stroking his palms over my skin. Fuck, I hoped I would be able to come back to this man. I knew full well I was leaving my damn heart with him, whether I made it back or not.

Once the water was warm, I moved under the spray, Taz following me, kissing my shoulder as he cupped my breasts once we were under the spray. Lifting my arm, I ran my palm over his face, over his stubble, then around so my fingers ran through the short hair on the back of his head. He kissed his way up my neck and along my jaw, before he cupped my cheek and turned my head so he could kiss me again. With each lick and nip, he undid me even more.

Tears formed and flowed, getting lost in the spray of the water as he began to gently clean me. I didn't fight him, but let him move me as he wished, while he ran the soap over every inch of me. By the time I took the soap from him to return the favor, I was nearly panting with arousal. He stood still for me, following my every move with his hot, hard gaze as I ran the bar of soap over his every muscle. Fuck, I was going to miss him. Why couldn't I be a normal girl who fell for a bad boy, instead of a complete failure of an undercover agent who fell for a bad boy? I washed him head to foot, leaving his dick and balls till last. Lathering up my hands, I slipped the soap back into the dish before I gripped him.

As I ran one hand over his balls, and the other around his hard length, he hissed and threw his head back. I sighed at the sight that was oh, so very masculine. Shifting to the side to let the spray wash the suds away, I lowered myself down to my knees, wrapping my lips over the head of his dick before he could say a word to stop me. I flicked my tongue over the metal he had pierced through him and he shuddered. One hand shot out to brace himself against the tiles while the other he wrapped in my hair, guiding my movements.

The water pouring over me began to cool and he pulled me away from his dick, before he leaned over to flip off the taps. I rose slowly, sliding against his wet skin on my way to stand.

"Fuck, kitty. You slay me."

He lifted me up and pressed my back against the tile. I barely felt the hardness of them, as I wrapped my legs around his hips and his dick slid home inside me. My fingers dug into his slick shoulders as he rested his forehead against mine and began to slowly thrust in and out. On each stroke in, he ground his hips so he teased my clit. This slow and sweet thing was new for us. Every other time we'd come together, it had been fast and furious. I closed my eyes against the rising emotions. It was on the tip of my tongue to tell him I loved him, but I still had to go to Dallas, still had to leave. There was no point in telling him things that wouldn't change anything, except hurt him more.

Taz nuzzled his face in against my throat, sucking on the skin there, branding me. Whispering his name, I allowed the sensations of him loving me gently to push me over the edge to an orgasm like I'd never experienced.

When I floated down, I found myself lying on the bed, Taz pressing kisses over my face and jaw. I ran my palms up his hard arms, following the lines of the muscles up to his shoulders. With a growl, he moved to kiss his way over my breasts and torso. My hands dropped from his skin as he shifted between my thighs and covered my core with his mouth.

Still sensitive from my climax, I arched up against him as he thrust his tongue deep inside me. Then he slid his palms under my ass, holding me to him so he could thoroughly devour me. And he did. Fuck, he had a talented mouth. One more thing I was going to miss.

Taz didn't ease off until I'd come twice more for him. By the time he crawled up over my body, I could barely move. My mind pleasantly buzzed with all the endorphins, I grinned up at him as he covered me.

Chapter 20

Taz

Flick was fucking killing me. What looked suspiciously like love shone bright in her gaze as she stared up at me, but she hadn't said the words. And I knew she wouldn't. I had to keep my own fucking mouth shut, so I wouldn't start begging her to fucking choose me and stay here.

Only way to shut myself up was to keep my mouth busy, so I kissed her again. Absorbing as much of her taste and scent as I could, I slid my cock deep within her again. Her channel was tight from her orgasms and rippled around me. I loved that I could take her without a condom. Before her, I'd never gone bareback, but now that I'd had Flick with no barrier, I couldn't imagine having to put one between us. Couldn't imagine fucking anyone else, either.

I was in so much fucking trouble, but right now I didn't want to think about it. I had her wet and willing beneath me and I intended to take full advantage. For as long as I could.

I kept my strokes slow and steady, enjoying every fucking second of the feel of her flesh against mine. I kissed her mouth, suckled on her perfect fucking tits. And shuddered when she arched up beneath me and dug her fingernails into my shoulders.

Making love to Flick had my arousal building slowly, and I didn't expect my climax to hit when it did. It was a sudden explosion that had me jerking inside her, and sweat dripping down my spine.

"Fuck me."

My arms gave out, and my weight dropped on her.

"Hmmm."

Rolling to the side, I kept her with me, holding her close in against me. Her lips were soft against my chest as she feathered kisses over my skulls and web tattoos. Over my stupid fucking heart that she now owned.

"Flick, kitty—"

"Don't say it. You know I don't really have a choice here. Don't make this harder than it already is."

My stupid fucking eyes started stinging and I held her tighter so she wouldn't see I was struggling. After a few minutes, I pressed a kiss to the top of her head, then rolled out of bed. Heading back to the bathroom, I quickly cleaned up before getting dressed. My clothes from yesterday weren't too bad, thankfully. Flick, on the other hand, definitely needed to find a change of clothes before we visited her uncle.

"Wanna go via your place first? Then over to see Gus."

She gave me a sad little smile as she pulled her dirty shirt back over her head. "That'd be great. You know where it is?"

"Of course."

Hadn't been inside it, though. Seemed strange that the first time I'd be seeing where she'd lived while she'd been in Bridgewater was on the last day we had together.

"C'mon, let's get moving before everyone starts arriving for church."

We managed to get out of the clubhouse without too much trouble and it was a fucking bittersweet feeling having her wrapped around me on the back of my bike. It wasn't until I pulled up to the front of her building that it hit me, and I chuckled.

"What's so funny?"

"Just realized you're in the same fucking hotel that Zara stayed in when she first came to town."

"Huh. Guess there's not much around here that's this cheap. Bet Mac liked her staying here."

I scoffed. "First time he came and saw the inside, he packed her up and shifted her down to the clubhouse. Of course, she did have trouble on her heels."

The conversation stalled out as she slid off from behind me.

"You wanna come in while I get changed?"

I shook my head with a wince as my cock hardened at the thought. "Better not. Or I'll have you up against the wall and we'll never get to the hospital."

Her eyes dilated and she licked her lips, making me groan. "Woman, quit that shit right now and go get changed. I only got so much control around you."

With a completely adorable little gasp, she spun and fled up the stairs to her apartment, or was it a hotel room? Not that it mattered, she wasn't staying. Which left me alone to adjust my erection—riding with a hard-on was a bitch and a half. I tried to think unsexy thoughts as I waited but my brain wasn't playing fair. It seems stuck on a loop of images of Flick and wouldn't fucking quit.

Ten long minutes later, she came back out and slid on behind me without a word. I took off toward the hospital, half wanting to get this day over with, and half wanting to drag it out. This shit was why I'd never done relationships. This feeling rejected shit at the end of it fucking sucked. Big time.

Flick

This prolonged goodbye shit sucked ass. Sorrow radiated from Taz like a fog that surrounded him. It was gutting me to watch him suffer, but I couldn't fix it. I didn't have that power, at least, not at the moment. My uncle however, I could cheer up. We entered the hospital and I ignored all the stares from the staff. I was sure by now everyone knew I'd been led out at gunpoint yesterday. With my chin held high I walked to Uncle Gus's room, where I found him looking almost as miserable as Taz did. They were a pair.

"Hey, Uncle Gus."

His face brightened as I entered the room with Taz beside me.

"Damn, it's good to see you, girl. Come here."

I went over to him and gave him a hug and a kiss on the cheek.

"You're a good man, Taz. Thank you for bringing her back. What did it end up costing?"

"It was the club that saved her, Gus. Most of the Charons rode up to get her back late yesterday. We got back early this morning."

The older man winced. "Never thought I'd see the day I'd owe a fucking MC."

I cocked my head at my uncle. "Why do you hate them so much? MCs, that is."

"Because they cost me my life." He paused and with a sigh gave my hand a squeeze. "I had a girl once. Suzi. She was the love of my life. But her parents wouldn't let us be together. Not with me being who I was. Single mother, no father. We'd both just turned eighteen. So fucking young." He gave a sad chuckle. "Young and dumb. Anyhow, Suzi threw a fit at her father for stopping her from seeing me. Told him if he thought I was bad, just wait for who she brought home next. Crazy girl went out to the local MC, wanting to find a biker to bring home to daddy." With a shudder, Gus rubbed his face. "She was so sweet and innocent. Feisty as hell, but no match for those bastards. By morning she was dead. They'd drugged her up, used her well, then drugged her up some more till she OD'ed."

I couldn't speak. That was horrific, and I could feel his heartache, it was that strong. I wrapped my arms around him and rested my head on his shoulder.

Taz's voice was rough. "I'm sorry for your loss, Gus. The Charons would never allow that to happen. We're drug-free. You have to have seen that we keep that shit off the streets here. We sure as fuck don't allow it in our clubhouse. Hell, if we heard of that happening to a girl now, we'd ride out to fuck up whoever was responsible, no matter who they were."

Gus's large hand patted my back a few times before he spoke again.

"Of course I've heard the rumors. But a lifetime of hate is a hard thing to let go of, son. You saving my niece goes a long way toward it, though, depending on what the fuck it's gonna cost me. Tell me, do I still have a business?"

"I'll leave you alone with Flick for a few, then we'll chat about what needs to happen going forward. But rest easy, you and Flick are safe."

"Not overly reassuring there, Taz."

Taz shrugged and ducked out of the room.

"Girlie, what the hell is going on here? Don't think I missed the doctor and nurses suddenly calling you Abbott instead of Vaughn."

I huffed out a breath, wincing as my ribs protested. Turning, I dragged a chair closer to sit beside the bed.

"It's a long story. Basically, when Andrew vanished after he returned stateside, I wanted to find him. That led me from accounting in private practice, to becoming a forensic accountant for the FBI. Then, my supervisor sent me down here undercover for an assignment. It's all blown to hell now. So, I have to go up to Dallas today to report in to my supervisor. No clue if, or when, I'll be back in Bridgewater."

"You don't sound too happy about that. You fall for that man, Taz?"

Damn, but he didn't miss much.

"Yeah. I didn't mean to, but I totally did. Not that it matters. My life isn't my own at the moment."

"Some advice? Make it your own, sweetheart. Plenty of jobs out there. You don't have to stick with the same one as though there are no options. If the FBI is controlling your life to the point you can't live it, maybe it's time to leave, yeah? Assuming I still have a damn business after all of this, you're always welcome to come work for me. I'd be more than willing to hand over all the bookwork."

I gave him what I knew must look like a weak grin. "I'd kind of been thinking the same thing about my current employer, but I need to hear what they have to say. And I'm sure you'll still have your business. Taz won't allow you to be hurt like that."

"So you say. Now, off to Dallas, to do what you have to, then if you want to make Bridgewater your home, you come back here and do it."

I gave him another kiss on the cheek as I stood to leave.

"I'll see what I can do, and I'll see you later."

I paused at the doorway when my gaze caught on Taz, pacing the hallway like a caged lion. When he caught sight of me he stormed up to stand in front of me.

"I need to go back to Dallas. Report in."

He nodded, and his Adam's apple bobbed as he swallowed. Then with that growl he did that made me melt, he snatched me to him and covered my mouth with his. Thrusting his tongue between my lips, he invaded me all the way down to my soul. I gripped his arms as he held me close and continued to kiss me stupid. Someone clearing their throat, loudly, had us pulling apart. Then with a shake of his head, he was gone, slipping into my uncle's room and shutting the door.

I have no idea how long I stood there, just blinking and trying to catch my breath and get my brain firing again.

"Darlin', if I found me a man who kissed me like that, I'd have him in front of the nearest preacher so he could never get away."

I shook myself free to see an older nurse fanning herself over at the nurses' station. I gave her a tight smile before I turned and rushed out to my car, which was thankfully where I'd left it yesterday. Had to love a small town.

I wanted to go home, have a long shower and curl up in bed for a day or two and feel sorry for myself as I caught up on sleep, but I couldn't. My day was far from over and I had a feeling none of what I had to do once I got to Dallas would be enjoyable.

Chapter 21

Taz

By the time I made it back to the clubhouse, I was so fucking over this day. Eagle was behind the bar, stocking and cleaning. Great. Our punishment had begun.

"Hey, mate."

"Hey, yourself. How'd it go?"

I shook my head. "She's gone. We all knew she wouldn't choose me."

Not wanting to discuss it, or hear Eagle's opinion or sympathy, I kept moving before he could respond. I needed to find Scout, get this shit over with so I could get on with whatever shit job he'd found for me to do. Figuring he'd be in his office, I headed in that direction.

"Hey, prez."

"Hey, Taz. How'd things go with Gus?"

"As predicted, he was pretty happy to see Flick alive and well. Before she left, Flick asked him about his hatred for all things MC. He has good reason." I filled him in about Gus's lost love.

"Well, damn. It explains a lot, though. You set him straight that we'd never let that shit happen?"

"Yeah, told him we're completely drug-free and if we'd ever heard of something like that happening we'd take care of it. Anyway, as it stands Gus is happy for me to work out there. He signed the paperwork to make me his manager, so we shouldn't attract too much attention from the authorities with me running the place while he recovers. He still doesn't want to sell it yet. Says he's got nothing else to do with himself, so he doesn't want to let it go."

"Ask him about the bunker?"

I nodded. "He didn't know anything about it, but he did admit that he's never really bothered to deal with the land outside the range. He figured early on that he'd let nature take care of it. He's happy for us to go search and use whatever we find, so long as we don't let any of it ever fall back on him."

Scout nodded. "That's good. When are you opening up the shop for him?"

"Up to you. I could go this afternoon, or leave it till the morning. It's only been shut a couple days and Flick's already put a note on the door saying Gus was in hospital."

"Okay. Leave it till morning, and I'll send out a group to start looking for this bunker while you're running the place. I'm guessing the fucking thing will be below ground and built by some doomsayers. Damn, I hope there's no fucking traps set on the thing."

I shrugged. "We'll deal with it if there are. Gus told me about some of the toys he's got out there that'll help us look for it. The boys will have a field day."

Scout scoffed. "Yeah. I'm sure they will. So, Flick's left for Dallas?"

I blanked my expression, not wanting to get into it. "We all knew what she was going to fucking do. It wasn't really a choice."

Scout sat there staring at me for so long I wanted to squirm, but I held strong. I was a fucking Marine, not some pansy who'd cave at being stared down.

"Fuck me, get out of here. I want to mess with you over this shit, but I feel like I'm kicking a fucking puppy. Go, drown your sorrows tonight, and be ready to work tomorrow."

With a nod, I took the out and left. On my way to the door, I passed the whore room. I could go in there and bury myself with all the fucking I could handle, but considering my cock was limp in my pants, that wasn't an option. I shook my head. Even if I was hard, I knew I wouldn't be going back in that room. Only one woman flipped my switch these days. With a sigh, I headed out to my bike. Maybe I should go see if Silk could fit me in for a new piece. With a chuckle, I scrapped that idea. Knowing Silk, she'd ink a fucking cat on me someplace I couldn't see what she was doing till it was too late.

I could go fire off a few rounds at the range, but knowing I'd be out there alone had me scrapping that idea too. That left drinking or working out. Since it was still early afternoon, I figured a work out first, then I'd go get shit-faced.

Starting up my bike, I made my way over to the gym, grateful I kept my gear there so I didn't have to go home first. I started questioning my decision when I strolled out of the locker room and Mac took one look at me and winced. What the fuck? I pointed at him.

"Not a fucking word. I don't need anyone's pity or fucking opinion right now."

His expression cleared into a mask of indifference.

"If you don't want to talk, how about we head out the back and beat the shit outta each other for a while then?"

That made me smile. "Sounds fucking perfect."

I followed him toward the rear of the building, through the adjoining door and into the back room. This room hadn't been touched in the renovation. Where everything out front was smooth, clean lines and modern technology, back here was the opposite. I was pretty sure the ring had been installed by some of the Charon brothers who'd come back from World War II and the bags hanging around the outside of the room looked nearly as old. This room was everything you thought of when you thought about an old-school fight club.

Mac tossed me a pair of gloves and head gear. "Don't give me shit, insurance demands it."

I scoffed at him. "Bullshit it's about insurance. You don't want to explain to Zara why you're beat to shit because you got in the ring with me."

He smirked as he geared up. "Well, yeah, there is that."

Flick

After heading back to the apartment to pack up the few things I'd brought with me, I drove out of Bridgewater. I'd barely cleared the township when my phone began ringing. Hitting the answer button, I identified myself.

"Vaughn."

Greg's voice flowed from my car's speakers. "What have you got for me?"

Yep, that was my boss. No "how are you," or "glad to hear you're in one piece," just "what have you got for me."

"I'm coming up to Dallas now to report in person. It'll be late by the time I get there. So, I can come straight in, or can you wait till morning?"

"Is it safe to wait until morning?"

Oh, now he fucking cared whether I was safe? Typical.

"It's safe. I want a night in my own damn bed, after a long fucking shower. Then I'll see you first thing in the morning."

I ended the call and focused back on the road. I hoped between the four hour drive, and the night in my own bed, I could calm down enough to not simply tell Greg to go fuck himself and walk right back out again. I doubted that would end well for me.

Flipping the radio on, I settled in for the long drive. Maybe I'd figure out what the hell to do with my life by morning too. Because right now, I wasn't sure what the fuck to do. I'd joined the FBI for two reasons—first, to find my brother, or at least find out what had happened to cause him to disappear from our lives. The second was to help make America a better, safer, place to live. But was that what I was really doing? I wasn't sure. Most of the time, I was safely tucked away in my office pouring through accounting records of various corporations and individuals. It wasn't just that I thought I'd find answers about Andrew on this case that had me excited—I was getting out of the office and into the field finally. The real field, where I got to interact with other people, not just sit alone in some high-rise office where I stared at computer screens and ledgers until I discovered whatever crime had been hidden.

Solving corporate crime wasn't thrilling in any way, shape or form. And who did it help? More often than not, the only one who profited from my work was the IRS. But what else could I do? I guess I could go back to being an accountant in a private firm somewhere.

Or I could do what I actually wanted to do. Go back to Bridgewater and help Uncle Gus run his shop. I certainly had the training to do it. I sighed and changed the radio station, trying to find a station with music, not just a DJ who loved the sound of his own voice way too much. Once I found one, I went back to pondering my life.

When I finally pulled into the parking lot of my apartment building in Dallas, I was so tired I could barely keep my eyes open. Deciding against cleaning up first, I headed straight to my bedroom, dumped my bags in the corner, then fell on my bed.

Bright light across my face woke me. I blinked awake to see I hadn't shut my curtains before crashing. Turned out to be a good thing, because I hadn't set my alarm either. I probably would have slept half the day away if the sun hadn't been so kind as to wake me up. Checking the clock, I groaned and forced myself to move. It was already nearly eight am, so I only had about half an hour to get my ass down to headquarters.

After the world's fastest shower, I pulled on some clean clothes and rushed out the door. Figuring I would make better time on foot, I bypassed the parking lot and headed straight for the busy Dallas streets. I only lived a couple blocks away from the office, so it didn't take me long to get there, and up to my office. I'd just put away my handbag when the phone on my desk began ringing.

"Vaughn."

"Great, you're in. I need to see you right away."

"Be there in a sec."

Hanging up, I stopped to take a few deep breaths. I hadn't had time to plan out what exactly I was going to tell my boss. I glanced around my office. Assuming I wasn't about to get fired, was I really ready to walk away from this for a man I'd met less than two weeks ago? I shook my head when I added it up. Ten days. It had been ten days since I'd first been given this assignment, and only seven since I'd first met Taz. Talk about explosive, instant chemistry. With a sigh, I headed through the door and over to Greg's office. Might as well get this shit over with.

Whatever the outcome, I'd deal with it, and get on with my life.

Taz

"Is anyone else getting a sense of déjà vu?"

Eagle chuckled at my comment as he, Mac and I left our bikes and headed into a cafe in Houston.

"I wasn't surprised when he called. Not after everything that went down. But it should be interesting to hear what he has to say."

Indeed. Their former CO, Sergeant Major Johnson had called Mac yesterday to request they meet again. It had been the Sergeant Major who'd originally asked them to sign on for the assignment with the FBI, so like Mac, I hadn't been surprised when he'd called us to meet with him the day after Flick told her boss the three of us had chosen our side, and it wasn't with the feds.

Straightening my cut, I followed Mac and Eagle through to door to find the Sergeant Major once again standing to greet us.

"Men. Good to see you. Take a seat."

We followed orders and sat down at the table with him. He'd picked a table toward the back, and I noticed that all the tables around ours were empty. A waitress came and took our orders, then once she was gone, the Sergeant Major's expression turned serious as he cleared his throat.

"I hear you three have been busy since you got to Bridgewater. Care to fill me in?"

"I think you know already. Flick's boss called you, didn't he?"

He nodded slowly. "Yes, I received a call. But I want you three to tell me what's happened. And you know I have clearance to hear all of it."

Eagle started it off, recapping how we prospected in and how he fell for Silk. How in protecting her we handed over some information to our FBI handler, only for it fall into the L.A. mob's hands.

Mac took over next, explaining what went down with the Iron Hammers and Zara. He also pointed out the involvement our FBI handler had in that fucking mess, before he vanished when it was all over. Then it was my turn.

"After all that, and the fact we'd all found our place within the club, we didn't want to work for the FBI anymore. But we had no fucking clue how to successfully end our arrangement."

"You call me. That's how you end this, you call your CO and I handle it. Did any of you think of that?"

Heat crept over my cheeks. I hadn't. Not once. But we totally should have.

"Sorry, sir."

He scoffed, shaking his head. "So, instead they sent sweet little Felicity Vaughn down to entice you to stay with them."

The ache in my chest lit up like the Fourth of July. Fuck, it had only been what? Forty-eight hours since I'd last seen her, but damn I missed that woman.

"I wouldn't call Flick sweet, but yeah, they sent her down to work with me." I gave him a quick rundown of how the past couple of weeks had rolled out. "In the end, it blew all our covers out of the water. Scout, the Charon's president, told us if we wanted to stay, then we needed to cut all involvement with the FBI. We told him we would. He told Flick to report that to her boss."

"So, all three of you are sure you wish to remain with the Charon MC?"

"Yes, sir."

"Do you believe Andrew Vaughn will be an issue now he knows where you are?"

Mac shook his head. "He would have heard that we were with the Charons when everything went down with the Iron Hammers. If he didn't come after us then, he won't now."

I spoke to back up Mac's point. "When we rode up to rescue Flick, Vaughn was with her. He had more than one chance to come at me and he didn't. Well, other than to warn me to not hurt his sister, that is."

Sergeant Major frowned as our food was delivered, waiting for the waitress to leave before speaking again.

"I'll let them know that you three are out, then. If they try to draw you back in, you contact me. Understand? I won't have them giving my men shit."

"Yes, sir."

All three of us spoke at once and I could see the Sergeant Major fighting not to grin at us.

"Old habits die hard, sir."

"That they do, Lee. That they do."

Which he was proving, because even though we'd left the USMC, our CO still had our backs and was willing to fight for us. Had to admit, it felt good to have someone not simply toss me away when I'd become a little difficult.

Chapter 22

One week later
Flick

I'd never been so nervous in my life. I probably should have called Taz before now. That would have been the smart thing to do, but this whole crazy fucking plan had been on impulse from the beginning. Including me rocking up on his doorstep late at night.

It hadn't taken long for me to come to the conclusion that I'd truly fallen in love with Taz. Now, I was betting everything on the fact he felt the same way. Or at least felt like he could love me one day.

Maybe I was making a mistake.

I stood frozen for a moment. This could end so very badly. What was I doing? I was still standing next to my car, staring at the front of Taz's house, when Eagle emerged from the shadows beside the building. I watched him approach, but still I couldn't move.

"Hey, Flick. Whatcha doing?"

"Hey, Eagle. To be honest, I've got no fucking clue."

He ran his gaze over my car, zeroing in on all the boxes and bags inside. It wasn't by accident this man got the nickname Eagle. Although even a moron couldn't miss the fact I basically had my entire life inside my car.

"Silk told me you went to see her today."

I nodded. "She tell you why?"

He nodded and zeroed his gaze in on my feet. "She did."

"She's really good."

His lips quirked, like he knew I was stalling. "That she is. Wanna show me?"

I tugged up the bottom of my jeans, as I turned to show Eagle the small Tasmanian Devil that now resided a little above my ankle.

"He'll love that." There was a spark of humor in his voice before he grew serious again. "Tell me, Flick. You pick today to come here on purpose?"

I winced. Of course his friends would know the significance of the eighth of April to their friend.

"Yeah, it's on purpose. But I'm late because I've spent hours driving around, trying to build up the courage to actually come here. Maybe I should go to a hotel tonight and come back in the morning..."

"No, you shouldn't do that. He needs you."

I wasn't entirely certain of that, I mean, he hadn't exactly called me over these past seven days. Did he really miss me?

"I can see you have questions. I'd suggest you select what you ask him tonight with care."

I turned to stare at Eagle's dark eyes. "Why? What's happened?"

"He's a good way through a bottle of Jack."

I swallowed past a lump in my throat as tears pricked my eyes. My poor Taz. Finally, my feet unfroze from the ground and I took a step toward the front door.

"No, he's not inside. Follow me, I'll take you to him, then I'll leave you be. I've been hanging back in the shadows watching, making sure he doesn't do anything too stupid in his drunkenness, but now you're here, I'll leave him to you. If you need me, just call out. I won't be too far away."

I couldn't speak. Too many emotions bubbled and roiled inside me as I followed him down past the side of the house and around to the back. Eagle stopped while we were still in the shadows and I stepped up to stand beside him. Following his gaze, the sight I found broke my heart in two. Taz sat on his porch, drinking straight from a rapidly emptying bottle of Jack as he ran his palm over something leather that sat across his lap.

"What's he holding?"

I whispered low, so my voice wouldn't travel. Eagle shook his head. "You'll need to see that for yourself. Go on now, go fix my brother. We'll see you around tomorrow, no doubt."

With that, Eagle melted into the shadows once again and I took my first step out of them, toward my man. My poor, broken, suffering man. I was halfway to him when he looked up and caught sight of me. The bottle was halfway to his mouth and he froze for a moment before he brought it the rest of the way and took a large swallow. I climbed the back stairs, and still he remained silent.

"Hey."

He took another drink as he watched me, and I started fidgeting as I began to feel like a science experiment.

"Pretty sure you're just my imagination, but you know what? I really don't give a fuck."

Considering how far through the bottle he was, I was impressed he could talk straight. Especially if he thought he was hallucinating.

"I'm real, babe. Can I sit down?"

He slowly nodded. He was sitting on an old-school porch swing, in the middle, but he didn't shift over. Nope, he just patted his knee. That was when I saw what he had in his lap, what he'd been stroking. He had a vest, no a *cut*. It had "Property of Taz" written on the back, around a Charon patch. Shit. He was sitting out here on the twentieth anniversary of the death of his mother and sister, getting shitfaced drunk, while stroking the leather he'd wanted me to wear. My heart seized up with hope, and pain.

With a gentle smile, I walked to stand directly in front of him, nodding at the leather. "That for me?"

"Was meant to be. No fucking clue whether you want it anymore, though. Fuck, I wish this was really you. That you'd really wear my patch."

Slowly, I reached forward and picked up the cut. Relief washed over me as he released the leather and let me take it. I slipped it behind me and threaded my arms through it, pulling the front halves in over my chest. I wanted to look down, to see what the patches said, but instead my gaze stayed glued to his. His blue irises flared with heat as he took another drink from his bottle. Moving forward, I slipped a knee up next to his thigh on one side, then the other, lowering my body until I straddled his lap.

"Tell me you're real. That I'm not imagining this."

"I'm real, Taz. I'm real and I'm here to stay. If you'll have me."

He shuddered beneath me and unable to hold back any longer, I leaned in and pressed my lips to his. He tasted like the whiskey he was drinking, and he didn't have the same finesse he normally had when he kissed me. But that was understandable, considering how much he'd had to drink tonight. I kept the kiss short, then leaned back to sit against his legs, but kept my palms on him, stroking over his shoulders, chest and torso. Now that I was touching him again, I couldn't make myself stop.

"Dream fucking come true. I think it's a first."

"What's a first?"

"Something fucking good with a female, my curious little kitty. And a first that I had a dream that was fucking good, because, babe, my dreams? They're normally fucking nightmares. Especially this time of year. But the few nights I had you beside me, I fucking slept. First time in a bloody long time, I had dreamless sleep."

"I'm glad I could give that to you, Taz. And I plan to give you so many more nights like it. For the rest of our lives, if you'll have me."

"See? You keep saying shit like that? Like what I'm desperate to hear, and I'll never believe you're real."

I smiled. "Well, I guess when you start tripping over all my stuff I've left around your house, you'll start to believe it. I'm kinda messy."

He was still staring at his property patch over my heart. "That's okay, babe. The USMC made sure I keep shit neat as a pin. We'll be fine." He took another mouthful of Jack. "You gotta promise to never leave. I can't handle another woman leaving me. Understand?"

"Your mother didn't leave you on purpose, Taz. She didn't abandon you, she was ripped away. And I promise I won't ever leave you. I've only taken this long because I had to get shit sorted out in Dallas before I could move down here permanently."

He leaned forward and pressed his nose against my throat, inhaling deeply before pressing a wet, open-mouthed kiss there that left me shuddering on a moan.

"You smell real, taste as fucking good as I remember. And I know Mum didn't leave me by choice. Well, she could have kicked that fucker Gordon out before he ever got the idea in his fool head to strangle her, then light that fucking fire. But no, she didn't leave me. Doesn't matter, though. First my dad died, fighting some fucking enemy in some far off country no one's meant to know anything about. Then Mum and Gracie were gone. Then even Aunt Pam, the old bitch, threw me out as soon as she could. Stupid fucking cow. You'd think she'd make the most of the free fucking labor I was providing and be willing to keep feeding me. But nope, as soon as I turned eighteen, she told me she couldn't look at my bloody face anymore. Apparently looking like my old man is a crime in her book. But somehow, you leaving, you choosing your work, the fucking F - B - I over me, that hurt worse. How'd you make me love you so fucking much in such a short amount of time, babe? I can't work that shit out. In a week, you got me wrapped completely around your little finger."

Clearly, he still didn't believe I was real. That or the alcohol was starting to affect his deeper thought processes. When he went to lift the bottle again, I pried it from his hand.

"I think you've had enough of that, babe. How about we get you up to bed? We can talk everything through in the morning."

He narrowed his eyes on me as I set the bottle down on the ground, away from his easy reach.

"I don't wanna go to bed. That means sleep. Means you disappear, and the nightmares come back."

My chest ached for him. I cupped his face between my hands, his stubble scraping against my palms as I stared directly into his eyes.

"How can I prove to you that I'm not a figment of your imagination? Wanna come out the front and see my car? How it's filled with everything I own? Will that do it? Maybe we could call Eagle back over here to tell you I'm real."

He frowned. "Eagle was here?"

I rolled my eyes. "Of course your friend was here. He knew you were hurting and didn't want you to do something stupid because you got drunk off your ass to cope with it. He said he'd leave me to handle you once I got here, but I bet he won't go to bed until he sees the lights are off over here."

He scoffed. "Interfering bastard. And he calls himself my mate."

I gave him a little shake. "You know he's your best mate, him and Mac both. Now, how about we go inside, you can drink a big glass of water, then we'll head upstairs and get you into bed? I just need to run out to my car to grab a couple bags for the morning, then I'll be right beside you all night. Okay? That sound good?"

He nodded, then winced. Yeah, all that Jack was starting to really kick in now. Fuck, I hoped he didn't pass out. He might not be much taller than me, but the man was solid fucking muscle and I was certain I wouldn't be able to carry his ass if he passed out.

I slid from his lap and taking his hand, led him into the house. Leaving him leaning against the kitchen bench, I poured him a glass of water and waited for him to drink it before I refilled the glass to take upstairs with us. His head was gonna hurt like a bitch in the morning, after this little drinking binge of his.

The closer we got to his room, the more sleepy he got. By the time I had him standing next to the bed, his eyes were half closed and he wore the stupid grin drunk people got. It had me chuckling as I stripped off his clothes. No matter how much Taz joked around, he always had a serious, hard edge to him. Like, at a glance you could tell he was a Marine. Right now, he was all teddy bear, soft and cuddly. I couldn't wait to be wrapped in his arms to sleep the night away.

Once I had him stripped and tucked in. I leaned down to kiss his temple. He hadn't said a word since we came inside and it was a little freaky, really. And what he said next didn't make it better. Nope. Kinda wished he'd stayed quiet as soon as he started speaking.

"That fire isn't my only nightmare, you know? Nope. That fucking orphanage is one of the worst I have. All the bodies. You wanna know what happened? Why your brother couldn't fucking come home? It was because he's a good fucking man, who got stuck in a shitty, shitty situation. He did the best he could, but still got burned for it. Those men he was trying to stop? Now they were animals. The worst fucking kind. Of course, they weren't the first bunch of military men to turn evil in a war. But to rape and murder your way through a fucking orphanage? That takes a special kind of evil, that does. Fuck, Flick. By the time we got sent in, it was nearly too late to save any of them. Kids...they were just fucking kids. Their bodies torn up. The few adults that were there? They'd clearly tried to fight. Naturally, against fucking Marines they'd had no fucking chance. But your brother, Vaughn—he snuck in behind them. We got there after he'd killed the first and was going after the second. On. His. Own. We went in with a team to contain those pricks, but your stupidly brave brother ran in on his own. Probably saved more than a few lives that day. And his thanks? Dishonorable fucking discharge, because no one cared enough to separate out the good from the bad before they swept it all under the fucking rug to never be seen again."

By the end his voice had slurred out to the point he was hard to understand, then he was asleep before I could form a response. Not that I could. Tears ran down my cheeks—for Taz, for Andrew—for everyone in that orphanage. After I stood there for probably half an hour, crying silent tears and watching Taz sleep, I shook myself free and headed down to grab my bags, lock up and turn off the lights so I could curl up with him.

Although I was pretty sure it was me that was going to be having the nightmares tonight.

Taz

There were little men with fucking sledge hammers inside my skull. And the bastards wouldn't stop pounding on me. Fuckers. With a groan, I rolled over and stumbled to the bathroom. After relieving myself, I opened the cabinet to search for some Advil. When I saw the packet sitting next to a glass of water beside the sink, I frowned. What the fuck? Since thinking hurt, I stopped trying to remember how it got there, and just took two of the bloody things, washing them down with a long drink of the cold water before I brushed my teeth to get rid of the funky taste I had in my mouth. When I went to return to bed, I stopped in my tracks.

My bed wasn't empty. Nope, not at all. Like my dreams come true, Flick lay before me, with her black hair spilling over my pillows like silk. My cock grew hard in an instant. She was facing away from me, but all that black hair could only be my kitty. I scrubbed a hand over my face as I tried to get my poor, abused brain to function. What had happened last night? I remembered going out on my back porch with a bottle of Jack. I'd intended to drink myself into oblivion so I wouldn't fucking think about, or dream about them. Or her. When had Flick turned up? And why the hell had she stayed?

I slipped back beneath the covers and didn't complain when, jostled by the movement, Flick rolled toward me, gifting me with a glimpse of her tits as she moved to drape herself over me. Her eyes were still closed and she clearly wasn't fully awake, but I couldn't not touch her. I ran my fingers down her cheek, before rubbing my thumb over her lower lip. Fuck, she was beautiful, and so soft. Her lashes flickered a few times before she opened her eyes and stared up at me, looking wary.

"Morning."

"That it is. Whatcha' doing in my bed, babe?"

She went to push away from me but I quickly wrapped my arm around her back, holding her against me.

"I ain't complaining, not at all. Just curious as to how you got here. I, ah, I don't remember much from last night."

"Well, the fact you believe I'm actually here is an improvement from last night."

That had me frowning. "What on earth is that supposed to mean?"

"Last night, when I got here, you were convinced I was a figment of your imagination."

I cringed. Although, I wasn't surprised. "Yeah, you probably shouldn't have come over last night. It wasn't a good time."

She reached up and cupped my cheek in her palm as her gaze softened. "Where else would I be on the eighth of April?"

Pain pierced my chest and I squeezed my eyes shut against the onslaught.

"You shouldn't know what the date means."

Fuck, my voice sounded like I'd swallowed gravel.

"You know the FBI gave me a file on you before I ever met you. It was only facts and figures, nothing but dates and stats. It didn't speak of the real you, didn't tell me how the fuck a thirteen-year-old boy coped with not only losing his mother and sister, but also being shipped halfway across the world. And until last night, I had no idea you were left with a cruel and mean aunt."

That had me wincing again. "Clearly I got way too chatty last night. I don't remember, dammit."

She smiled softly at me, easing some of my pain.

"Not too chatty. Although, you not believing I was real got a little frustrating." She shifted and ran her palm over my chest. Over their names. "Tell me about them? The good. I don't want to know about the end, but how they lived."

That ache set up in my chest again. I did my best to not ever think about them. But maybe that was my problem. Just maybe, if I told Flick about them, just a little, it might help. Hell, I knew bottling it all up hadn't ever helped one fucking bit. I closed my eyes and brought up their faces.

"Mum was the best. She kind of lost herself after my dad died, but before that, she was everything a kid could want in a mum. She was pretty, too. Blue eyes like mine. Aunt Pam always said I was a spitting image of my dad, but I remember my mum had the same color eyes as me. And dark brown, curly hair. When I was little, she had it long, hanging down to her butt. I think my dad must have liked it long. She cut it short a week after he died.

"You know my dad was a Marine?" She nodded. "I don't remember much about him. He was off on deployment more often than not, but whether he was home or not, we'd go this little park down at the end of our street a few times a week. We'd take a picnic lunch down there if it wasn't a school day.

"We lived in Newcastle, that's on the east coast of Australia. Similar weather to here, actually. No snow in winter, but one year, we all went down to the ski fields for a holiday. Even though I was only seven, I still remember that trip. It was the last family trip we did before Dad died.

"After he was gone, Mum moved us down south. Not sure why she did that, but that was where she met that fucker Gordon. Only good thing about him was that I got Grace. She was this little bundle of energy. She got the blue eyes too, and had this reddish-blonde hair that was all tight curls and frizz. Used to drive Mum nuts when she'd try to brush it out. Not that my Gracie cared. Nope, that girl could have had dreadlocks and not cared one bit. I loved her so much, Flick."

Fuck me, but my eyes were stinging. "She'd crash tackle me every fucking day when I got home from school. On the weekends she'd come jump on my bed until I got up to make her pancakes for breakfast. She was only three fucking years old when she died."

I ran my palm up Flick's back, before I stroked her face again. Her cheeks were wet with her tears, and I brushed them away. "She'd be twenty-three now, if she'd lived." I stalled out, unable to speak. My heart ached from the memories, and from seeing Flick cry for me like she was.

"Only two years younger than me. I'm sure we would have been friends, that she would have helped me gang up on you."

A short laugh left me. I hadn't ever thought of what Grace would have been like as an adult before now. "Hell yeah, she would have. Damn, the two of you together would have had me running fucking scared, babe."

I leaned down to press a kiss to her forehead as I held her tightly against me.

"So, my curious kitty, you gonna tell me why you came over last night? After leaving me hanging for a fucking week?"

She pressed a kiss to my chest, making my heart skip a fucking beat.

"I missed you. Before I even made it back to Dallas, I missed you and wanted to turn the fuck around and come back here. But I had to deal with my job first. I didn't go in until the next day, and even before I walked into my boss's office, I knew my heart wasn't in it anymore. Between falling for you, seeing how good life is within the club, and finding my brother and getting the answers I'd been searching for when I'd joined the FBI—not to mention, they didn't respond to me hitting my panic button—I was more than ready to leave."

"You ask your boss about that one?"

"Yeah, apparently they were tracking my GPS, and would have come for me eventually. But they didn't want to blow my cover so were letting the Charons handle it."

I could hear the anger in her voice. I didn't blame her, I'd be furious over being abandoned like that.

"You know, the Charons would never do that. No matter how much trouble you're in, we'll always fucking come for one of our own."

"Yeah, I get that. I haven't spoken to Scout yet. I was hoping you could take me to him today? You know, if you still want me. You gave me the cut last night, but since you can't remember doing it, and you were giving it to what you thought was an imaginary person, I'm not sure it counts."

I'd gotten her in her cut and had forgotten it? Fuck me. That was a sight I never wanted to forget.

"It counts, kitty. You're the only one who'll ever wear my property patch. Fuck, I'm pissed I can't remember that."

She lifted a shoulder slightly. "Maybe you'll remember later. You're probably still half drunk at this point."

"I'm sober enough to be hung over."

She chuckled and the sound had me smiling. "That I believe. Anyhow, so I have all my worldly possessions sitting out in my car, I have no job, no place to live—"

"Bullshit. You'll fucking live here. Forever. And your uncle will take you on. He's been telling me all week how he hopes you'll wake up and move down here. That, or you could go back to working at Styxx. You did good there, Nitro and everyone else down there likes having you around."

Hope had flared bright when I'd seen her in my bed earlier. Now, with her saying she wanted to stay with me? I could see why I hadn't believed she was real last night. Fuck, I was beginning to wonder if she was real this morning...or if maybe I was asleep.

Chapter 23

Flick

I could see Taz was struggling to process what I was saying. Probably didn't help he was hung over as hell. I shifted and slid further up against his side, so I could reach to kiss his mouth. I pressed my lips to his before pulling back to stare into his baby blue irises.

"I'm here because I choose you. Over everything and everyone else. I. Choose. You."

A ghost of a frown passed over his face, before a smirk of male pride took its place. Then with a growl, he rolled us over and took my mouth in a hard kiss, thrusting his tongue between my lips to dance with mine. He tasted like mint, so I guessed he must have gotten up before coming back to bed and waking me up. Pushing himself up off me with a hand against the mattress beside each of my shoulders, he held my gaze.

"I love you, Flick. I haven't said those three words to anyone other than you in twenty years."

Taz was still my own personal brand of catnip. He melted me with both his words and actions. His eyes shimmered with moisture, but my big, tough Marine didn't let them fall. He lowered again and kissed me some more. I wriggled around until I could shift my legs out from under his body. As his dick came into contact with my pussy, he groaned and broke our kiss. He moved to bury his face against my throat as he pulled his hips back, and as soon as his cock-head lined up with my opening, he slowly slid into me. I wrapped my hands around his shoulders, digging my nails in as he hit all the nerves within me, lighting me up.

"Hmmmm."

"You feel so fucking good, babe. Ain't ever gonna get tired of fucking you."

"This ain't fucking, Taz. We're making love here."

He turned his face and nipped my jaw, before licking away the sting. "I'm always gonna call it fucking, babe. But with you, it'll always be more than that. You're just gonna have to translate. Now, shush. I need to focus."

I chuckled, until he started moving. Then, all I could think about was how fucking good it felt to have him moving inside me, over me. Putting my feet flat on the bed, I met his every thrust. He kept his strokes slow, yet oh, so powerful. That piercing of his did its job and found all the nerves I hadn't been aware of before meeting Taz. I'd missed him—this—so much this past week.

Wanting more, I clenched around him. With a growl he stopped thrusting, and moved to kneel between my legs, then he gripped each leg behind my knees and lifted them up so my legs rested up against his torso and chest.

Then, with a smirk, he leaned forward, pulled his hips back and thrust back in fast. With a gasp, my back arched and my eyes rolled back. Holy fuck, he went in so deep like this. He increased his speed, pounding into me as he rubbed his thumb over my clit. I didn't stand a chance trying to hold off and make it last, and I blew apart beneath him. Stars exploded behind my eyelids and I was vaguely aware of Taz grunting and his dick twitching within me as he came with me.

I came back to myself to feel Taz pressing kisses against my closed eyelids. With a smile, I sighed contentedly.

"So, believe I'm real yet?"

"I'm starting to. And I see you got some ink."

That had me opening my eyes, wanting to see his reaction.

"I may have gone and caught up with Silk yesterday. She fit me in, even though it was getting late."

He sat kneeling on the end of the bed, his dick semi-hard and glossy from the sex we'd had. It had my womb tightening with want. However, for once, his gaze wasn't on what lay between my thighs. Nope, it was focused on my lower leg that he was now cradling in his palm.

"I bet she did. I guess someone told you why I got my nickname."

"Andrew."

He scoffed. "I can just imagine what *he* told you. Why the fuck are you even here, after hearing his version of why?"

I shrugged as I looked down at the small Tasmanian Devil that now resided on my lower leg. I got him doing his spinny thing, so you could only see about half of the little brown animal through the little tornado he was in the middle of. "So what? You have a temper, and you lost it once or twice. That's not gonna make me run from you, babe."

Taz opened his mouth, but closed it with a shake of his head before he uttered another word. Then he climbed off the end of the mattress and headed into the bathroom. With a frown, I pulled the covers over my body, unsure of what the fuck was going on. Did he not like the fact I didn't care he had a temper? Tears pricked my eyes at the thought that maybe I'd fucked up and now he wanted me gone. I blinked rapidly, not wanting them to fall.

When he came striding out a moment later holding a tube of something and a wet washcloth, he stopped short as he looked at my face.

"What the fuck? Why are you crying? What happened? Did I hurt you?"

He was sitting on the mattress by my side in seconds, gathering me up in his arms. Cradled against his chest, embarrassment rode me hard.

"I, ah, I thought maybe I'd pissed you off and you didn't want me anymore."

"Fool woman. That ain't ever gonna happen. You've not had ink before, and you've let it dry out. You gotta keep cream on it, or it won't heal right. And it will get itchy as hell."

With that, he set me back on the mattress. First, he wiped the washcloth over my pussy and inner thighs, cleaning me up. Then he tossed the cloth on the floor, and moved to hold my leg again, picking up the tube from where'd he'd tossed it on the bed and carefully soothed some of the ointment over my new artwork. We were both silent as he took care of me, and as soon as he had the tube shut and on the bedside table, he looked at me with heat in his eyes.

"Where's your cut, babe?"

I rolled my eyes with a grin. "Wondered how long it would take till you wanted me back in it."

I crawled off the bed, and grabbed the leather up from the chair I'd laid it across last night. On top of his. Keeping my back to him, I slid the vest on, making sure I didn't pull my hair out from under it until he'd had a few moments to admire his name on my back. Dropping my hair down over the back, I turned and grinned. Taz sat in the center of the bed, leaning against the headboard. He had his thick, hard dick in his hand and was stroking it as he watched me with a very heated stare.

"Get back up here, babe."

Feeling flirty, I moved to stand at the end of the bed for a few moments before I put a knee on the mattress and crawled over to him. When I got to his feet, I gave his ankle a nudge and he got the hint and spread his legs. I slowly moved up closer, loving how the leather rubbed over my nipples with each movement I made. When I got up to his groin, he was still stroking his dick. On his next down stroke, I wrapped my lips around the head and gave him a hard suck.

"Fuck, babe!"

He released his erection to wrap his hands in my hair. Heat pooled between my thighs as he controlled my movements while I licked and sucked his cock. I could taste a hint of myself on him and it was a little dirty, and made this whole thing even hotter. The next time I sucked hard on the head of his dick, he growled and pulled me off him, lifting me up so he could take my mouth in a hard kiss that left my lips stinging and my heart racing.

Then, before I could catch my breath, Taz easily manhandled me so I was facing away from him. I gripped his thighs as he lifted my ass up, then lined his cock up with my pussy opening. After moving both his hands to my hips, he pulled me back, impaling me on his dick.

"I think I'm gonna be taking you from behind a lot from now on, babe. Fucking love seeing my property patch on you while you ride my cock."

I shuddered at his words, and even though I was on top, with his tight grip on my hips, he controlled every move. Every stroke in hit a sensitive spot inside me that had me crying out. Within minutes, he had me coming hard for him. Before I could fully come down, Taz had me on all fours, with him standing next to the bed behind me. He slid back inside me and with a whimper, I dropped my head down as my arms gave out.

"Love this, love you. Gonna go shopping today. Buy what I need to get this ass ready for me too. I'm gonna own every fucking inch of you, babe. You're mine. All. Fucking. Mine."

"And you're mine. Goes both ways."

"Damn straight it does, kitty."

My heart just about burst out of my chest at his possessive tone and his hard thrusts.

The risks had been worth it. This man, my man, was worth everything.

Taz

After a long shower where I managed to get my cock back inside my woman again, we made fast work of breakfast. Half of me still didn't believe she was really here to stay. Without letting her out of my sight, I followed her out to her car to see that, true to her word, it was filled with boxes and bags.

"How about we head over and see Scout on my bike, then I'll grab Eagle or Mac later to help unload all this?"

She tilted her head as she watched me, before she came and pressed herself up against my front, her arms slipping under my cut and around to my back.

"Sure, babe. I kinda figured, what with your lack of trust that I'm actually real, you'd want to bring all my crap in now. You know—as further proof."

I pressed a kiss to the top of her head. "You should be grateful I haven't left you chained to the bed. You know—to make sure you stay."

With a chuckle, she pushed away and taking my hand, led me back toward the house.

"C'mon, caveman. Let's go see Scout."

I couldn't seem to shake the shock that Flick had chosen me. That she'd given up her job, her life in Dallas, for me. I'm sure my hangover wasn't helping me process. Within minutes, I had her sitting behind me on my bike, her arms wrapped around my waist and her curvy body pressed up against my back. My cock throbbed for her and with a wince, I did my best to adjust things so I wouldn't damage myself on the ride. Flick chuckled, obviously picking up on my issue.

"Quit laughing, woman. It's all your fault. It's been a long fucking week. I missed you."

"So, no visits to your fan club at the clubhouse after I left?"

She was trying to sound like she was joking, but I could hear the fear in her voice. I twisted around so I could look her in the eye.

"Flick, you're it for me. I doubt I could even get hard for another woman anymore. I sure as fuck had no desire to go fuck some club whore while you were gone."

Not when I was too fucking busy pining after her like some lovesick fool. But I kept that thought to myself.

With a gentle smile, she leaned up and kissed my cheek.

"Good to hear. Now, let's get moving. I'm nervous what'll happen at the clubhouse. Are you sure it's a good idea to meet Scout there? I really don't want to get locked up again."

I gave her thigh a squeeze before I slid my key in, ready to start my bike.

"That won't happen, babe. He told you to pick where your loyalty lies, you have. With us, so everything will work out fine. Not telling him you're back, now that will probably get us both locked up."

With that, I revved the engine and took off toward the clubhouse. I wasn't sure what Scout would say either, but if he tried to lock my woman up again, it wouldn't end well. I'd fight for her. Hopefully it would help that she was wearing her cut. That thought had me smiling as I pulled into the clubhouse lot. My old lady was wearing my patch and sitting right behind me on my bike. Life didn't get much better than that.

Being a Sunday morning, there were quite a few bikes in the lot. Guess the party last night had been a big one. Thankfully, Scout's was one of them. I'd rung him this morning while Flick got dressed. I'd needed the distraction, or I'd never have let her cover up. He told me to bring her over as soon as we were ready. So, here we were.

I took her hand in mine as we walked over to the entrance, which was being manned by one of the newer prospects. I gave him a nod before pushing my way inside. I winced at what Flick must think of the sight that greeted us. Damn, clearly it had, indeed, been a big night last night. A few of my brothers were sleeping on couches with naked, or nearly naked, chicks draped over them. Not all were asleep, either. Nope, Keg was awake and getting a morning fuck. The naked club whore was kneeling on the couch, Keg behind her, pounding her ass good. Her mouth was busy taking Tiny's cock. The big man had his hands wrapped in her bleached blonde hair, forcing her to take his full length on each stroke.

Funny, a month ago, it would have been me waking up like that after a big night. Now, I couldn't imagine anything worse. For the first time in my entire life, I was a one-woman man, and perfectly happy about it. I pulled Flick in close and took her lips, kissing her deep and dominating her mouth. I wanted to fuck her again. Running my palm down, I gripped her ass through her jeans.

"You should have worn a skirt, babe."

With a chuckle she pulled away, shaking her head. "No way. Not today. Whenever I wear a skirt, you fuck me all day long and today we have some serious shit to do before we can get back to that." She paused, running her gaze around the room. "So, this shit is normal, huh?"

I shrugged and took her hand back in mine as I started walking toward Scout's office.

"Pretty much, for a Sunday morning, anyhow. Saturday nights can get pretty wild."

"Yet, you chose to stay home and drink rather than come party..."

I squeezed her hand but didn't say a word. I wasn't going there with her right now. No way. After a quick knock, I pushed the door open and with a smirk, pulled Flick behind me. She didn't need to see this.

"Sorry, prez, I thought I gave you enough warning with the phone call."

Scout had a pretty little naked thing on her knees giving him a morning blow job. He pulled her off his dick, helped her stand, then teased her tits for a moment before he turned her away from him and with a slap to her ass, told her to get going. Without an ounce of shame, she strolled past, running a heated gaze over me and a glare at Flick, who naturally hadn't stayed behind me.

Scout simply grinned at us as he tucked himself back into his pants. "What can I say? Now you're off the market, we all gotta step up to fill the void you left, brother."

I flipped him the bird before I pulled up a seat in front of his desk, and tugged Flick to sit in my lap. She came willingly and something deep inside me settled when she wrapped an arm behind my neck and made herself comfortable on my lap.

Scout was still smirking at me—bastard—before he shook his head and sighed.

"Okay, so, Flick? I gather because you're here and wearing Taz's patch, you've left your previous employment?"

"Yes, sir."

Scout cut her off with a wave of his hand. "You can cut that shit out. Call me Scout."

I tried not to smile when her cheeks reddened. My tough chick didn't get flustered often, but Scout had managed to do it.

"Ah, okay. Yes, Scout. I've quit and left the FBI for good."

"And what reason did you give them for leaving? Are they going to attempt to come *rescue* you from us?"

She shook her head. "They didn't respond to my distress call when the Cowboys took me. I was very articulate in my displeasure over that one. They are also aware that I found my brother at the Satan's Cowboys clubhouse while being held there, and that I'd never do anything to risk him. I told them I was moving to Bridgewater, so it's safe to assume they know I'm here with Taz and with the Charons. I can't see them bothering to rescue me now when they didn't bother to do so when I actually needed it."

I stroked my palm up and down her thigh as she'd spoken, wishing she'd worn a bloody skirt. Her skin felt so much better than denim.

"Okay, and what do you plan to do now you're here? I realize Taz will do his best to keep you locked up so he can fuck you all day and night, but in case you're actually looking for some work to do, what are your plans?"

"Fuck off, Scout."

He raised his eyebrow at me. "What? Don't think I can't see what you're thinking right now. And it ain't got nothing to do with her gaining paid fucking employment."

I frowned when Flick stood and took a seat in the chair next to me.

"What the fuck, babe?"

"Maybe if I'm over here, you can stop thinking about sex for a minute. Maybe."

She said it with the sweetest smile that made sure I was definitely thinking about fucking her now. Dammit.

Chapter 24

Flick

Before Taz could respond, I turned my attention back to Scout. "I was planning on going to see my uncle once we finish here. He told me when I last saw him, that if I wanted to make my life here in Bridgewater, he'd take me on at the shop."

Scout nodded, but I could see he had other things in mind.

"If you wanted to keep doing a night or two per week at Styxx, I'm sure Nitro would appreciate it. And I believe Mac would love your help with his self-defense for women classes. But, that's up to you. Just let me know if you want either one."

At the mention of the classes, I sat up straighter. I'd really liked what Mac was doing with those classes.

"I'd love to help out Mac with the classes, but I would just be assisting him. He's doing a great job and I have no intention of trying to take over. I'm not sure about the bar. It was fun, but let me talk to Uncle Gus first. This heart attack is going to slow him down for quite a while, and I think he's going to need me more than he realizes it at the moment."

Scout nodded. "Mac will soon tell you if you piss him off. Well, he'll probably bitch to Taz about it, then you'll hear about it from your man. Either way, you'll know. Do either of you know how long before Gus will be back in the shop?"

"Initially the doctor told me it would be two to four weeks for him to return to work. But since he runs his own business, I'm guessing he's already trying to get back into the shop."

I glanced to Taz.

"Yeah, he's tried to come in to work and I keep sending his ass home. Crazy bastard won't ever get better if he pushes himself too hard this early on."

I nodded, not surprised. "Hopefully with me in town helping to look after everything, he can relax and focus on getting better."

Scout nodded. "Sounds like a plan. Alrighty, you two get going and sort it all out, let me know what the verdict is. Oh, and, Flick, we're hosting some of the Cowboys this weekend. Including your brother—"

Taz jerked in his seat as though he'd been shot, cutting off Scout. "Why the fuck is this the first I'm hearing about this?"

Scout smirked at him. "Because you've been sulking around all fucking week." Then his expression turned serious. "And your boys told me you'd need this weekend off for personal reasons. So, we let you be.

Actually, I need to thank you, Flick. Now you've returned, I can get back to tormenting Taz. Every time I've tried to mess with him lately, I'm left feeling like I've kicked a wounded fucking puppy or some shit. Takes the fun right out of it."

Taz's posture had tensed at the mention of needing the weekend off, so I followed Scout's lead to lighten the mood, and get the conversation away from it.

"Well, considering what, or rather who, my brother is probably doing right now, I think I'd rather leave seeing him until later. Can you tell him to head over to our uncle's place? I want to spend the afternoon with Uncle Gus, and I'm sure he'd love to see Andrew."

"Stone. At least here at the clubhouse, you need to call him Stone. None of us go by our given names in the MC world, darlin'."

I shook my head. "Yeah, of course. Sorry, so used to him being Andrew. That's gonna take some getting used to."

Scout stood and Taz and I followed his lead. At the door to his office, he gave me a hug, leaning in to whisper in my ear.

"Thank you for choosing my brother. He needs you more than you know, Flick."

I smiled and whispered back. "After last night, I think I do know."

Taz frowned at us, but I wasn't going to say anything if Scout wasn't. With a smile, I leaned up and kissed Taz's mouth briefly.

"C'mon, caveman, let's head out. Uncle Gus will be happy to hear I'm moving back for good, don't you think?"

"What were you two whispering about?"

"Nothing for you to worry about, brother. I'll tell Stone to head over when I see him. And talk to Silk or Zara about tonight. Got another club barbecue going on. And don't worry, it's a family one, so the club whores will be back in their box for it."

I cringed at his word choice, but didn't say anything as I followed Taz out toward the front. The chick from the threesome we'd walked in on, was now kneeling in front of a different biker, sucking his cock. Busy girl. The man seemed to like her skills. His head was thrown back as he held her by her hair, and thrust up into her mouth. As Taz dragged me past, a second man came up behind the chick, and after lifting her so she was on all fours, unzipped his pants and slammed his cock in deep. The chick was clearly into all the attention, considering her moans and grunts, and it was strangely arousing to watch.

"Don't even think about it, kitty."

Shaking my attention away from the live porn show, I followed Taz outside.

"Not think what?"

"I'm not ever gonna fucking share you, so no matter how curious you are, it ain't happening."

I laughed. "Just because I was a little mesmerized at the sight, doesn't mean I want to be in her place, Taz. Put your caveman back in his box."

He growled and backed me up against the side of the building. His lips crashed down over mine as he took me over. With a sigh, I wrapped my arms around his neck and let him have his way. I loved how he kissed me, like he couldn't get enough and wanted to inhale me.

By the time he pulled back, I was putty in his hands. He'd melted my brain completely.

"See? This is why you need to be wearing a fucking skirt, babe. I want in you so bad right now."

I leaned up to kiss the corner of his mouth before nuzzling in against his throat.

"And that's why I'm not wearing one. We have things to do, and giving the prospects out front a show, isn't on that particular to-do list."

At that, Taz snapped his head to glance over toward the yard, and confirmed that, sure enough, we'd collected a small audience.

"Fuckers."

Grabbing my hand, he dragged me over to his bike. I tried not to laugh, but he was being adorably possessive. Settling behind his large body felt so natural, like coming home. The vibration of the bike beneath me when he started it was soothing, as was the way he'd pat my hands or thighs as we rode. I rested my cheek against his back with a contented sigh as we rode through town.

All too soon, we stopped outside Uncle Gus's house and reluctantly, I slid off and stretched out my legs as Taz dismounted. He took my hand again before we made our way toward the house.

"You know, I'm not going to disappear if you let go of me, right?"

With a growl, he tightened his grip but didn't comment.

"Caveman."

Uncle Gus was sitting on an old rocking chair on the porch watching us with a smile. Taz pulled me in front of him after we climbed the stairs, allowing me to go to my uncle first. I moved in to give him a peck on the cheek.

"Hey Uncle Gus, how you feeling?"

"Feeling a little better every day. So, you came back, after all."

His gaze took in my clothes with a frown. Taz came to stand behind me and wrapped an arm around my waist.

"Hey, Gus. So, good news for us. Flick's moving to Bridgewater for good."

He nodded in a way that made me think he was deep in thought. "If that's what you really want, I'm happy to have you closer."

I leaned back against Taz. "Of course this is what I really want. Although, I am kinda left without a job with my sudden move and all. If you needed a hand with the shop and range, I'd love to help out."

He laughed, then coughed. "Damn. Don't make me laugh." He paused to take a few breaths before continuing. "Ah, that would be great, sweetheart. Taz has been keeping it running for me, since the damn doc won't clear me to work yet. So you can help him out with it all. I like the idea of making it a family business. I gather you two are together?"

"Damn straight. Never letting her outta my sight again."

Uncle Gus's lips twitched, but he held off the laugh this time.

"Son, I told you not to make me laugh. No way in hell you're gonna be able to lock this one up. Even as a kid, Flick could never be contained, or told what to do.

"Now, that I believe."

I glared over my shoulder at Taz for agreeing, but couldn't stay mad. Not when he was watching me like he wanted to devour me. Again. Suddenly, spending time with Gus didn't seem so important, not when I could be having a lazy Sunday in bed with Taz.

"Right, well, we've got some more errands to run today. I'll come back tomorrow and stay longer. Oh, and Andrew might come to see you later. He's in town visiting. And apparently we have to call him Stone now. Bikers and their nicknames."

I rolled my eyes and my uncle shook his head while Taz growled. With a shrug, I gave my uncle another peck on the cheek before I let Taz take my hand and lead me back toward his bike. Once we were standing near his bike, he handed me my helmet.

"Why the sudden urge to leave, babe? I thought you wanted to spend all afternoon here."

Once I had my helmet on, I moved to press my body up against his, running my palms under his cut, up his torso and over his muscular chest.

"Well, I remembered what I could be doing if we were back at your place."

"Ah, right. Well, what the lady wants, the lady gets. And it's not my place, kitty. It's ours now."

Warmth spread through my chest as he gave me a fast, hard kiss. He pulled his lips from mine way too soon, in my opinion, and I stood staring up at him for a moment.

"Have you any idea how much I love you?"

His grip on me tightened as a wide grin spread over his face.

"That's a good thing, babe. Because I'm fucking crazy in love with you, too."

Then he gave me what I wanted, a nice long, deep kiss that left me squirming for more.

Taz

After spending the entire afternoon naked with Flick, I somehow managed to find the will to put clothes back on me, and her, and take her over to the clubhouse for the barbecue. After returning from Gus' house, I'd grabbed Eagle and Mac to give me a hand bringing in all of Flick's stuff, and they told me that the Satan's Cowboys were heading home in the morning, so tonight was a send-off for them.

After finally locating that damn bunker last week, this weekend the Cowboys had sent a small team down to clean it up and get it ready to be used. I wasn't entirely sure about the hows or whens, but I figured we'd be seeing more of the Cowboys, for a while, at least. Looking over to where Flick stood chatting with Stone, I decided that wouldn't be such a bad thing. I knew what losing a sibling felt like, and I was so fucking happy that Flick had found her brother alive and well. I'd hate for her to have to suffer like I had over the years.

Although, I had to admit that today that pain seemed a little less. As the day had passed, I remembered a few little snippets from last night, and the way Flick had handled my shit was amazing. Thanks to having her curled up next to me all night, I'd had a blissful, dream-free sleep. Now that my hangover was settling down, I was actually feeling pretty fucking good about life.

Because I had an old lady.

Who loved me.

Fuck, I was turning into a sap. Strangely enough, I didn't really care. Not if it meant I had Flick in my life. I grunted when a large hand smacked my shoulder.

"Good to see you could stop screwing your old lady long enough to make it, brother."

"Says the man who had to pull a chick off his cock to meet with me and my old lady this morning."

Scout barked out a laugh and shook his head. "Too true. Like I said, we all gotta step up and fill the void you left, now you're all settled down and shit."

Lifting my beer, I took a swig while Scout did the same.

"Gus is good with Flick working with me at the range and shop. I've been thinking, instead of just having Flick help out Mac, why don't we expand the program? Start running a gun class aimed at women too. Flick's more than capable of teaching it, and I'm sure Gus would give us the go ahead. Might also make his shop more profitable, because I honestly don't know how he fucking affords to eat at the moment."

Scout nodded. "Sounds good to me, why don't you arrange a meeting between Mac, Chip, Flick and yourself. Gus can be involved too, if he wants. If we cross promote between the gym and the gun shop, both will benefit." He nodded toward where Flick was laughing with her brother. "I'm guessing Viper will put Stone in charge of the bunker, since he has reason to visit us now. You okay with that?"

I gave him a chin lift. "We're good. Stone knows it wasn't our fault he got fucked over, we were just following orders when we brought him in that day. It was the brass who decided to ignore the fucking truth and fuck him over. When we realized he was with the Cowboys back when we were dealing with the Iron Hammers bullshit, we were worried he'd come after us.

But Flick told me what he said to her about it, and he doesn't appear to be holding a grudge against us."

"Good to hear. That's the last thing any of us need. So, you, Mac and Eagle really do fucking do everything together, huh? All settling down with an old lady within months of each other. You got your girl knocked up yet?"

Because the bastard had waited until I'd taken a mouthful of beer, I coughed and choked on it.

"Fucker." I paused to cough some more. "She ain't pregnant. Bloody hell. I'm not ready to share her with a kid yet. I've heard what those little poop machines do to a man's sex life. No way. At least, not yet."

Scout laughed and walked away, leaving me to watch my woman and think about how cute a little girl with my blue eyes and a thick mane of black hair like her mother's would look. It lit off an ache inside me that left me wanting to tell her to toss out her pills so we could get to making a baby already. I glanced over toward my best friends. Eagle and Mac both stood with their women, each with a large palm on their unborn child. We really did do all of life's big milestones together.

I needed to talk with Flick.

Dumping my empty bottle into the trash, I strolled over to Flick. Slipping up behind her, I wrapped my arm over her shoulder. When she tensed I cursed and tightened my grip.

"Don't you dare fucking throw me, woman."

Stone started laughing so hard he doubled over, and Flick relaxed back against me with a sigh.

"I really am sorry about that."

"Yeah, well, so long as you don't do it again, I can deal."

"Well, quit sneaking up behind me and grabbing me, then!"

I kissed the side of her head. "I'll try, but after all that careful training the USMC gave me, I can't help but walk around the place silently."

She turned to face me and wrapped her arms around my neck. "And it's all my careful training that means whenever someone is stupid enough to sneak up behind me and grab me, I throw them."

Her falsely syrupy-sweet voice had my cock throbbing to be inside her.

"Well, since you two are gonna start being all sweet and disgusting, I'm gonna go find something I can mess with. Flick, I'll call you when I know when I'll be back in town. I'll drop in again on Uncle Gus before we head off in the morning."

Flick unlatched herself from me and gave her brother a hug, and a peck on the cheek. "I'm sure he'll love that. I'm so glad I found you, An—ah, Stone. Next time you come down, you can stay with us and we can catch up some more."

He winced and I couldn't hold in the chuckle.

"I've heard the rumors, sugar. No way in hell am I gonna be staying where I'm gonna be forced to listen to my sister being screwed all night long. There are some things brothers don't want, or need, to know. Their sibling's sex lives are one of those things."

With a shake of her head, she gave him another peck on the cheek, said goodbye then swayed her way back over to me.

"So, caveman, now you've successfully scared off my brother—"

"I didn't scare him off. He was looking for an excuse to go find something wet and willing inside."

She screwed up her face. "Could you not call them that? I mean, I know they are, but that's a horrible way of describing them."

I shrugged as I lowered my face in against her neck. "Club whores are what they are, babe. But I don't want to talk about them at all. I'd much rather discuss making babies with you."

She laughed. "Well, you can talk all you want. It'll be at least another couple of months before we can do anything about it. I don't take a little pill every morning, Taz. I get the shot every three months."

"And do you intend to keep getting them?"

She pulled back to stare me in the eye. "You're seriously asking me to have your baby, aren't you?"

"Hell, yeah, I am. I never dreamed I'd have a woman of my own, but now that I do, I can't imagine anything better than creating a family with her. I want kids, and I want to watch those kids grow up surrounded by love and protection." I turned her around to take in the rear yard of the Charon's clubhouse. Kids ran around playing, Zara and Silk stood beside Eagle and Mac, with their pregnancies clearly visible. "I want to raise my—our—family here, within the Charon family. Here, none of us will ever be left alone. We'll always be protected and have people who love us at our backs."

Pulling free from my grip she turned back to face me with tears in her eyes. I'd be worried if she wasn't smiling so damn wide.

"Flick, I love you babe, and I can't wait start our family."

"Oh, Taz. You're killing me here. You're too perfect, you know that, right? Fucking catnip."

Shaking my head I pulled her in against my front, cupping her face in my palm.

"Catnip?"

"You're like my personal brand of catnip. I get a taste and instantly, I lose my mind and do crazy shit."

He chuckled, before growing serious. "I'll never be perfect, babe. But I'll always be your rock. I'll always love you and put you first. I'd rather cut out my heart than see you hurt. And I'm glad I make you like that, because you do the same to me, my curious little kitty."

Tears trailed down her cheeks as she pushed up on her toes to hover her mouth near mine. "I love you so much, more than anything else in this world, Donovan 'Taz' Lee."

With my heart in my throat, I kissed her, taking her mouth with mine over and over again. I'd never get enough of her. Of this woman who'd brought my heart and soul back to life, so she could cherish them.

Epilogue

Three years later
Flick

With a sigh, I sat back down beside my two best friends in our backyard. Before I'd met Taz, he had bought the house between Mac and Zara's place, and Eagle and Silk's. They'd soon pulled out the dividing fences so we all shared one big backyard, which I loved. Especially now the kids were all running around. I placed my palm against my growing stomach, as I turned to face Silk. Her belly was as big as mine, which made sense since our due dates were one week apart, which was a little crazy. Zara was leading the charge with this round of kids—her baby was due two months before ours.

"Do you think the boys plan to have everything happen at the same time, or is it just some freaky fucking destiny thing?"

"What do you mean?"

Silk frowned over at me like I was nuts. Hell, I probably was.

"All three of them seem to do big life milestones together. Leaving the Marines was obviously a conscious decision, but meeting and falling in love with us all within months of each other? The first round of kiddos, and now this lot?"

Silk started laughing. "I hadn't thought about it, but yeah, that's some freaky shit. I don't think they discuss and plan any of it though."

Zara began chuckling. "Oh c'mon, I mean, can you just picture it? The three of them standing around discussing knocking us all up at the same time? It's fucking hilarious."

That set us all off. Because Zara was right. It was fucking hilarious. Especially considering the three of them were currently all standing around the barbecue pretending like they were going to cook something. We'd done our jobs, the salads were all inside ready to be served just as soon as the meat was done.

"Oh my, check out our kids. They are so cute."

I turned to see what the three terrors were up to now. Eagle and Silk's little boy, Raven Clint Benally was turning three in two months, while Mac and Zara's daughter, Cleo Beatrice Miller wouldn't turn three until September. My little angel, Lola Grace Lee, or Lolly for short, had just turned two. The three of them sat in the newly completed sandbox happily playing with buckets, rakes and shovels. Well, it was happily until Raven decided he wanted something from the other side of Lolly. Naturally, he wasn't looking where he was going and tripped over Lolly's outstretched leg as he'd moved. The responding scream had me cringing. My little girl had a set of lungs on her, no doubt about that. Poor little Raven froze, clearly panicking over what he'd done. Knowing Lolly wasn't really hurt, I turned to watch for Cleo's reaction. The little redhead was super protective and this was bound to be entertaining.

"Raven's in for it now."

Yeah, Zara knew her daughter, like the rest of us did. I nodded as we took in how Cleo gathered Lolly into a hug while she gave Raven a stare of pure death.

"Yep, she's pulled out her southern-stink-eye-glare. One of the workers down at the daycare called it that the other day. I kinda like it. Fits her to a T. Aww, poor Raven."

Predictably, Raven had raced off toward his dad in tears, as Cleo continued to make a fuss over Lolly, who had already forgotten all about the whole thing. Lolly was trying to get free from her savior as she reached for her bucket, clearly ready to get back to playing already.

Turning my attention to the men, Eagle had gathered his son up and lifted him up against his chest. We were too far away to hear what he told Raven, but whatever it was had the little boy nodding before he wrapped his little arms around his daddy's neck.

"Damn, but I tear up every time I see him with Raven like that. It's like the ultimate in mommy-porn."

I smiled. "Yep, watching your man be a good daddy to your kids is totally swoon-worthy."

Zara snorted a laugh. "You two are nuts. Meanwhile, if Mac or I want to cuddle Cleo, we gotta crash tackle her from behind to keep her still long enough to do it."

With a snort, I nodded toward the sandbox. "Apparently, all you have to do is pretend to be hurt for a few seconds, then you get hugs while your assailant gets a death glare."

That had us all chuckling again. With a smile, I lifted my glass of lemonade and took a deep drink. I really did love this family I'd found myself in. The Charons as a whole were good, but these people right here with me in our backyard? They were the best. The sound of a Harley pulling up had me rising from my chair.

"Who are you expecting?"

"Stone."

Yeah, I did eventually get used to using his new name. And he came around often. Turns out my big brother loved being an uncle. He'd even rung our folks to let them know where he was. No more pretending like he didn't have emotions. He'd called me earlier today, to say he was in town for *club business* so that translated to mean that he would be on his own and couldn't give me an exact time. Not that it mattered, I loved when he dropped around. And Lolly loved her uncle. Raven and Cleo thought he was pretty cool, too.

I walked—not waddled, despite what Taz tells everyone—to the side of the house to greet him. He strolled up with a wide grin before he pulled me into a tight hug.

"Hey, sis."

After he pulled back from the hug, he gave my belly a pat while he kissed the top of my head.

"Where's my favorite trio of trouble?"

"In the sandbox. The guys finished it today, and it's been a real hit."

He chuckled. "I can imagine. Get ready to find sand everywhere now."

I winced. "Yeah, we're already discovering that."

Not that I minded, it gave us another reason to hang out in our joint yard with each other. I couldn't have asked for a better environment to raise my family in. And I couldn't have asked for a better man than Taz. I glanced over at him as Stone and I entered the yard. He was watching for my return. My caveman protector was always keeping an eye on Lolly and me whenever he could, and I couldn't love him more for it.

Taz

At the sound of my daughter's ear-piecing screech, I spun to see what was going on. The fact the women were all sitting there calmly watching the kids stopped me from running over there, but clearly something had happened.

Mac's girl, Cleo was being all momma-bear over Lolly and giving Eagle's boy, Raven a good, long, dark stare. Poor boy still had no clue how to deal with that girl.

Within seconds he was running toward us with tears in his dark brown eyes.

"That boy's gotta figure out Cleo, or she's gonna walk all over him for the rest of his life."

Eagle shook his head. "He's not even three yet, Taz. He's got time. And Cleo's got one hell of a death stare going on."

Mac laughed. "What can I say? My girl's tough, just like her momma."

Eagle scooped up his boy when he got to him. He was a mini version of his father, with straight, dark hair and dark eyes. But his temperament was a mix of him and Silk. I wasn't really worried he'd let Cleo turn him into a doormat. I was sure in a couple of years, he'd take his role as big brother and eldest of the family seriously and keep the girls, and any other kids we all had, safe from all threats, while giving everyone around him hell.

Eagle finished consoling his son, and Raven ran off for the back deck of Eagle's house. Eagle was watching after him, so I turned back to the barbecue, turning the various forms of meat we were cooking for lunch. The girls had finished the salads already and were all lazing around, watching the kids play. Well, until the roar of a Harley filled the air and Flick waddled off toward the side of our place. Fuck, I loved her pregnant. All round and soft. Although she kicked my ass for saying she waddled. But she totally did.

Hopefully our guest was just her brother, but I kept half an eye on where she'd disappeared from view as I flipped another burger.

"Oh, man, I love that kid so much. Taz, you gotta watch this, brother."

Setting the tongs down, I turned toward the sandbox. Cleo was still glaring at the poor boy, but Raven ignored her as he went directly to my Lolly. Leaning down, he gave her a big hug, then when he pulled back, he held out his favorite toy. A Matchbox version of his daddy's bike. I knew he slept with that thing.

"He's giving her his bike? Damn, that is so sweet."

Mac sounded a little in awe. We all knew his Cleo wouldn't share her things with anyone. I turned to Eagle. "I'll make sure I get it back to you before bed time."

"Thanks, as much as the gesture is beautiful, he's gonna be heartbroken come bed time."

A couple minutes later, I relaxed when Stone strolled into the yard with Flick. I still didn't like her out of my sight. Anything could happen. As soon as the kids saw who was here, they dropped all toys and ran for their Uncle Stone. Well, Raven took a moment to pocket his toy bike before he ran over there.

"He's sly. Got it back already."

Eagle chuckled. "Yeah, I caught that too."

I looked around the yard with a grin. This was truly what a family should be. The entire Charon MC was like a big, extended family, and I knew they all would have our backs, but these people here in our backyard were even more than that. I knew no matter what happened to me, or Flick, little Lolly and our unborn baby, would never find themselves alone like I had. They would always be protected and surrounded with love. It was a comforting thought, one that helped me sleep at night.

I loaded the now-cooked food onto the platter and carried it over to the large table on the grass. The girls brought out the salads, and after Mac handed out fresh drinks we all sat down. I stood a little longer, looking over each face here, including my new brother-in-law Stone. He and I were very similar and had a good friendship these days.

I held my bottle up.

"To family."

The others echoed it, and I gathered Lolly up off my seat, and sat down with her on my knee, next to my wife, my old lady, my other fucking half. Unable to resist, I leaned over to kiss her.

"I love you, kitty."

She beamed up at me, glowing with her pregnancy and love.

"Love you too, caveman."

I absently ran the palm not holding Lolly over my chest. Naturally, Flick's gaze followed the movement with a gentle smile. Funny, the names I'd inked on my chest used to be something I avoided looking at, or thinking about, but thanks to my woman suggesting we name our little angel after my mum and sister, the ink held new meaning. It wasn't just about my dead anymore, it was about life, the future. My gorgeous little Lolly.

"I loves you too, Daddy!"

Speaking of which, said little angel planted a big, wet kiss on my cheek before reaching for her mother. Flick didn't have a whole lotta lap left these days, but she managed to take our daughter, and receive her own kiss and declaration of love from Lolly. I had to grin when she wanted back to me the moment she was through.

Yep, I totally got myself a daddy's girl with this one. I pressed a kiss to the top of her head, as I settled her back on my knee. As I'd imagined, Lolly had her mother's black wavy hair, and the Lee baby-blue eyes. She was beautiful, and I knew I was going to have my hands full keeping boys off her when she hit her teen years.

But that was okay. I'd teach her to shoot, while her mother would teach her how to throw blokes that pissed her off over her shoulder, and she'd be fine. Even without me making sure I was cleaning my guns when said blokes came over to take her out.

That had me grinning, too. I could picture it clearly, Lolly rolling her pretty blue eyes and dragging her poor date out of my sight. Mac and Eagle would probably come over and clean their guns with me. Yeah, we'd make it a pact to join forces to scare the shit outta our daughters' dates.

Another glance around the table at all the happy faces eating, chatting and laughing had warmth spreading through my chest. For the first time I could say with confidence, I was completely happy with my life and who was in it.

Other Charon MC Books:

Book 1:
Inking Eagle

*__The sins of her father will be her undoing... unless a
hero rides to her rescue.__*

As the 15th anniversary of the 9/11 attacks nears, Silk
struggles to avoid all reminders of the day she was
orphaned. She's working hard in her tattoo shop, Silky
Ink, and working even harder to keep her eyes and her
hands off her bodyguard, Eagle. She'd love to forget her
sorrows in his strong arms.

But Eagle is a prospect in the Charon MC, and her
uncle is the VP. As a Daughter of the Club, she's off
limits to the former Marine. But not for long. As soon as
he patches in, he intends to claim Silk for his old lady.
He'll wear her ink, and she'll wear his patch.

Too late, they learn that Silk's father had dark secrets,
ones that have lived beyond his grave. When demons
from the past come for Silk, Eagle will need all the skills
he learned in the Marines to get his woman back safe,
and keep her that way.

Book 2:
Fighting Mac

***She's no sleeping beauty, but then he's no prince -
just a biker warrior to the rescue.***

For the past three years Claire 'Zara' Flynn has been at
the mercy of narcolepsy and cataplexy attacks. But after
she witnesses a shooting by the ruthless Iron Hammers
MC, her problems get a whole lot worse. She's now a
marked woman, on the run for her life.

Former Marine Jacob 'Mac' Miller has a good life with
the Charon MC. He works in the club gym and teaches
self-defense classes - in the hopes of saving other women
from the violent death his sister suffered. When the
pretty new waitress at a local cafe catches his attention,
he wants her in his bed. But there's a problem. She's
clearly scared of all bikers. Wanting to help her, he talks
her into coming to his class. Mac soon realizes he wants
to keep her close in more ways than one. But can he,
when his club's worst enemies come after her?

When Zara disappears, Mac and his brothers must go
to war to get her back. Because this time, she wakes up in

a terrible place... surrounded by other desperate women, and guarded by the Iron Hammers MC. Can her leather-clad prince ride to the rescue in time to save her from hell?

CPSIA information can be obtained
at www.ICGtesting.com
Printed in the USA
LVHW082049020421
683211LV00014B/554